THE SEAGULL AND THE SPY

MARCELO ANTINORI

The Seagull and the Spy

Marcelo Antinori

Secant Publishing

Copyright © 2024 by Marcelo Antinori

All rights reserved.

No part of this publication may be reproduced, stored in a retrieval system or transmitted, in any form or by any means — electronic, mechanical, photocopying, recording or otherwise — without prior written permission from the publisher, except for the use of brief quotations for purposes of review.

This book is a work of fiction. Names, characters, businesses, places, events, and incidents are products of the author's imagination or are used in a fictitious manner. Any resemblance to actual persons, living or dead, is purely coincidental.

Secant Publishing LLC
615 North Pinehurst Avenue
Salisbury MD 21801 USA

www.secantpublishing.com

ISBN 9798990356252 (paperback)
ISBN 9798990356269 (ebook)

Part One

THE SEAGULL

1

A seagull landed on Bebéi's balcony. Across the park, Lieutenant Pirilo was playing dominoes on the terrace of the Asturian Tavern, a sign that everything was quiet in Santa Clara. The word "quiet" has a faulty meaning in town — sometimes calm and serene preceded massive storms — but even so, people were enjoying a peaceful afternoon, and the only one complaining was Grená, the lottery ticket seller; with everything so restful, there was no gossip to share.

Pirilo was teaming up with the Asturian, the tavern's owner, to challenge the city's champion duo: Moses and Habib. The two, a Jew and a Lebanese, owned competing clothing stores, one across from the other on Main Street. They fought all day long over clients but were second to none when they joined forces for a dominoes game. They could read each other's thoughts.

According to Pirilo — probably trying to justify his frequent losses — the two did not win by the excellence of their game, but rather by the jokes they told to distract their opponents. For every story Moses told about a Jewish patrician, Habib responded with one about his Arab compatriots. But the truth is that Pirilo had no right to complain, since whenever the two of them were silent, his partner, the Asturian, would quickly come up with a new story, teasing his Galician countrymen.

That afternoon, Pirilo and the Asturian had great luck and managed to win one of the matches. The noise of their laughter, the screams, and the hard strike of the dominoes hitting the table could be heard all over the park, where guayacans were in whole blossoms of yellow flowers.

A few steps away at the hill leading to Our Lady of Mercy Church, Bebéi, the archivist of the French embassy, was ready to hit the streets with his dog Zoubir, and a thousand thoughts echoing in his mind.

He was born in Paris and raised by his uncle as an immigrant, always trying to conceal his Algerian origins and his Muslim religion. He struggled to understand his teachers at school — he was considered naive. His curiosity, however, was endless and he was often a step ahead of the last answer. Thanks to an exceptional memory, he got a job as an archivist at the French Foreign Office where, for years, he dedicated full attention to "keeping safe what cannot be missed and quickly finding what seemed lost."

He was all but forgotten at the very end of the fourth-floor corridor when he heard his boss, Madame Roisson, mention that there was a vacancy for an archivist at the embassy of Santa Clara. His life was dreary, and he decided to risk an adventure before retiring. He applied and landed the job. That was why, on a sad and cold Parisian day, he boarded a plane to cross the ocean and live in the tropics in Santa Clara by the Sea.

Bebéi quickly adopted his new town and felt embraced by his neighbors. The sun was always shining and people were friendly, patient enough to chat on the sidewalks and answer his questions. The work was unwinding at the embassy, and his commitment was highly praised, so he felt comfortable asking to leave the office a little early that afternoon. The reason, he kept to himself — it was personal: during the night, a seagull had landed on the balcony of his apartment. The bird seemed to have a wound on its wing and remained still, keeping its gaze fixed on the sea.

Santa Clara by the Sea is a peninsula surrounded by the sea near Panama City. The city harbors old churches, a few embassies, and ancient colonial manors, such as the one where Bebéi lived. Despite being a few minutes' drive from the country's capital, the city has a small-village atmosphere, where people greet each other with friendliness and chat while sitting on chairs placed on the sidewalks.

Bebéi lived in an amber manor built a century ago by one of the founders of the Republic. The manor was later split into small residential units, and his apartment was on the third floor, with two small balconies: one off his bedroom, where the seagull had landed, and another off the living room. From his balconies he could see the fish market, the pier, the bay full of seagulls, and catch a glimpse of Paris Street, bursting every night with women, nightclubs, and joyful sinners; a privileged view that Bebéi relished, but that had become entirely irrelevant since the seagull settled at his apartment.

Bebéi was shy and dressed every day in the same brown suit, but despite his few words, he quickly became known in Santa Clara for his outdated habit of greeting everyone by tipping his hat.

That afternoon, he closed the large wooden door of the manor behind him and looked across the park to the tavern where his friend, the Pirilo, was playing dominoes. He chose not to bother him; it would be useless to interrupt the lieutenant while he was playing. Bebéi decided to look elsewhere for help. His problem was not the bird's presence — he was happy with the new guest — the question was how to feed it appropriately.

As soon as he began climbing the hill following his dog, Bebéi heard the music of a barrel organ. It was Mimi, the ice cream seller, pedaling a colorful tricycle and carrying a little monkey on his back. Bebéi waited for him; he wanted to enjoy the music filling the street.

Bebéi greeted him with a tip of his hat and the ice cream seller, who was also a magician, stopped pedaling, bowed his head respectfully, and, after murmuring incomprehensible words, pulled a small bouquet from under the monkey and gave it to Bebéi. Bebéi's dog didn't bark; he was used to wizardry. Then, happy as a child, the ice cream seller smiled and pedaled off uphill. On his back, the little monkey stared at Bebéi and his dog with what looked like a laughing expression.

Bebéi followed them, holding the dog's leash in one hand and carrying the small bouquet in the other. For him, the music of the barrel organ was a perfect match for the narrow cobblestone streets walled in by the colonial manors of Santa Clara.

At the top, when he reached the church, Bebéi greeted Grená, passing the flowers to the other hand and tipping his hat respectfully. That corner was his favorite spot in town. Around Our Lady of Mercy Church, locals gathered to chat and share gossip away from the tourist crowds on the boardwalk. Next to the church, Rasta Bong had his barbershop and the Chinaman his small grocery. It was also at the stairs of the church, right in front of the yellow umbrella where Grená gossiped all day selling lottery tickets, that a group of homeless boozers, self-titled the Useless Brethren, liked to drink, curse, and sleep.

Bebéi watched while Robespierre, probably the weirdest member of the Brethren, was yelling at a Finnish tourist that, thank goodness, could not understand a word of what the bum was saying.

Bebéi only stayed there for a few minutes — he didn't want to waste time with distractions — and walked straight toward the barbershop where Jordi, the young waiter who usually served him at Ilona's Café, was having a haircut.

Jordi had just finished the exams to become a high school teacher and wanted to give an excellent impression to the selection committee at the interview scheduled for the next morning. He listened to Bebéi's problem, and offered to go with Bebéi to the Chinese grocery after his haircut was finished to buy a few sardine cans to feed the seagull.

Jordi was excessively talkative that afternoon. He was convinced he had passed the written exams, and not even the interview scared him. What was causing him some anxiety was longing for Cristine, his girlfriend. She had traveled to Boston with a scholarship offered by the Mayor, and as her return approached, Jordi's chest seemed to be tightening.

For him, life without Cristine was bizarre. They lived on the same street, studied in the same school and most of the time in the same classroom. They had only split up at the university, when he decided to study history and Cristine psychology.

When Cristine was at his side, everything seemed so smooth. Jordi always invented new ideas, and Cristine knew how to turn them into reality. He never did anything without first asking her, but how to feed a seagull did not seem to be a transcendental problem, and he volunteered to help Bebéi.

"After all, what could happen when someone feeds a seagull on the balcony of a friend's apartment?"

2

The ring flew over the cobwebs. Bebéi and Jordi barely talked while climbing up the stairs; they were both worried. Neither of them had ever fed a seagull. Surprisingly, feeding the seagull was straightforward; the tricky part was what happened afterward.

When they opened the balcony door, Bebéi's dog stepped outside and cautiously approached the bird. The seagull did not move, probably realizing its defenselessness. The dog was suspicious and waited. Sniffed once, sniffed twice, and only then, feeling safer, laid down next to the seagull as if trying to understand what the seagull was staring at. Bebéi wisely proposed to leave the two animals alone: "Maybe it's easier for animals to understand each other. Zoubir will calm it."

Jordi and Bebéi waited inside the bedroom for a few minutes and then slowly opened the door. They laid the sardines next to the seagull and a dish with food near Zoubir. The dog quickly ate its meal and politely did not touch the sardines of the seagull. The bird remained motionless and took a few minutes before pecking the fish. Although unsure, it slowly ate the sardines and turned its gaze again to the sea. Zoubir silently observed while Jordi and Bebéi smiled behind the glass. Mission accomplished; the seagull was fed.

The dog and the seagull remained unmoving. The calm was so comforting that Jordi stepped outside the balcony. It was the first time he had visited Bebéi's apartment. From there, he could see the whole bay and feel the breeze on his face. Even better, he could think for a moment about Cristine.

The sun was setting, and there were almost no clouds in the sky. Jordi appreciated the yellow sunset light warming the colors of the manors. Lieutenant Pirilo and his friends were still playing dominoes at the tavern, and Jordi recalled the serenades he had made there to Cristine while looking fondly at the ring she had given him.

Jordi knew that the ring was treasured and leaving it with him was Cristine's way of saying that she loved him. Curious, he thought; between them, it was always she who took the initiative. They had talked about almost everything, but they had never talked about themselves. They were best friends, and this was something as natural for them as eating or sleeping. Before leaving, however, she gave him the ring, and that gesture changed everything.

Jordi knew the ring's story. Cristine's mother worked on Paris Street, and her father was one of the sailors who spent a night with her. "But your father was special," Cristine's mother explained, "I realized from the very first moment he kissed me." Before giving him the ring, Cristine even said, "My mother never understood his words. All she knew was that his name was Mikhalis. That he was from the island of Cyprus and that he touched her like no one ever had before."

Jordi watched the seagulls flying, remembering that Cristine's mother never saw the sailor again. Perhaps he never returned, or if he returned, he could not find her. As soon as she became pregnant, Cristine's mother left Paris Street and never worked there again. That is why Jordi took the ring off his finger and gently held it in the palm of his hand — the ring Cristine gave him at the airport as proof of her love — but at that exact moment, the seagull opened its wings as if wanting to fly. Its movement frightened the dog; the dog barked and startled Jordi, who let the ring jump into the air.

Jordi became desperate, looking toward the street. He shouted to a woman on the sidewalk, but she could not understand. The dog was nervously barking, and Jordi tried to scream even louder, telling the woman about the ring that had fallen.

Bebéi heard the commotion, but it took him time to understand what had happened. The dog was of course willing to explain it, but all he could do was bark. Jordi had his two hands on the balustrade and his body nearly in the air, yelling to a group of pedestrians that the ring had fallen. The only one on that balcony who was surprisingly calm was the seagull, oblivious to all the uproar and staring calmly at the sea.

Jordi spoke to Bebéi, but his words were senseless. The only thing that Bebéi could understand was "I cannot lose this ring." Bebéi tried to ease him, and they went together down to the street to look for it.

Jordi was so desperate that he could not control himself. Bebéi and Zoubir, with the help of the next-door store attendant and the cashier of the café on the corner, searched every inch of the cobblestones. Jordi even blocked the traffic, convincing a cab driver to leave his car in the middle of the street while they searched for the ring.

The turmoil they caused was such that people came to help them from the park, the tavern, and the supermarket. They searched for more than an hour and couldn't find the ring.

Jordi was miserable. Bebéi tried to appease him: "If it were in the street, my dog would have found it," and he continued pointing at the building. "We must look on the balcony of the apartment below; it could be there."

Jordi called off the search and unblocked the street. Bebéi was confident and explained to Jordi that the second-floor apartment was vacant. "Let's look there."

It was late evening, and it took a long time for them to reach the janitor at his home. His answer was unhelpful. "I've never had a key," and he added, "Since I started working at the building ten years ago, no one has lived there. The apartment is closed, and the owner doesn't want to rent or sell. All I know is that a law firm pays the bills," and he even acknowledged, "I never went inside it, and from what I know, nobody ever did."

Bebéi wanted to help Jordi, and while climbing up the stairs, he looked at his dog and thought about a last resort. "I know what we can do," he said.

Jordi was surprised, and Bebéi explained: "People who live alone always have a key hidden outside the apartment. Otherwise, how can we get in if we lose our keys?" Bebéi also took the opportunity to clarify: "I have one; if you want, I can show you where I hide it." Jordi was too dazzled to answer, and Bebéi went on explaining. "A long time ago I noticed that my dog stopped to sniff the baseboard on the floor below. Always at the same place, right next to the apartment's door. One day, out of curiosity, I discreetly checked and noticed that the molding was loose and there was a key behind it. I've never tried it, but I believe it can help us open the apartment's door."

Jordi got reenergized, and Bebéi felt that it was his obligation to warn him: "It's important that you know that this is not legal. We do not have permission, and we do not know who the owners are," but seeing Jordi's puzzled expression, he added, "Okay, none of this matters now. Let's do it because we must retrieve Cristine's ring," and after a quick pause, Bebéi continued with a mischievous expression on his face. "It seems to me, however, that we should do it tonight when no one can see us," and, almost whispering, he finished, "and then we will not tell anyone, do you agree?" After a year of living in Santa Clara, Bebéi, despite his rigid and traditional moral values, had already understood that nothing is black and white in the tropics and that there is always an alternative path to follow.

They waited inside Bebéi's apartment and when the streets were silent, they went down carrying a flashlight that Bebéi kept on hand for emergencies. Zoubir remained on the balcony, taking care of the seagull. They checked the loose molding on the floor below and found the key that unlocked the apartment's door.

Jordi carefully opened it, and when they illuminated the interior, they were shocked. The apartment might have been closed for ten years but it was not empty; all the furniture was still there, buried under cobwebs and dust.

Jodi had his mind fixed on the ring and immediately walked with the flashlight to the bedroom balcony. Bebéi stood at the door. A dim light was coming from the corridor, creating a ghostly vision. The piano was the most striking image. Cobwebs hung from a large candelabrum, wrapping it and evoking the setting of a haunted play.

Bebéi stayed at the door. He looked around; a gray veil of dust enveloped chairs, tables, shelves, and even frames on the walls. On the shelves, he saw books and small statuettes. On one of the living room walls was a collection of masks. The layer of dust covered everything. It was a scary but, at the same time, enticing view. Bebéi was paralyzed. He looked to his right at the dining room, where the cobwebs spilling from a chandelier in the ceiling were forming what looked like a shredded circus tent covering the table and the four chairs. Bebéi kept looking speechless from the doorway.

The apartment had the same layout as his. In the living room, in addition to the piano, there were also wind instruments, a guitar, and what appeared to be the box of a violin, all of them leaning against the wall. The piano seemed to have a score on the music rack as if someone had just played. Bebéi was astounded by what he saw. Right at his feet, at the entrance, there was a long-forgotten envelope covered by dust.

Bebéi might have stayed there forever, but he heard Jordi laughing. He had found the ring.

When Jordi returned and spotlighted Bebéi's confused expression, he also realized that everything there looked like someone had suddenly left and never returned.

They walked inside and looked together into the bedroom. The bed was made with sheets and pillows. A lamp, a clock, and some objects were placed on the nightstand. Near the bed, a large pair of slippers awaited its owner — the same way Bebéi usually left his. Inside the bathroom, a towel was hanging next to the shower, a toothbrush and toothpaste were placed on the counter. Everything was entirely covered by thick dust.

"It was a man who lived in this apartment," Jordi said. "Nothing here recalls the presence of a woman."

They returned to the living room, and Jordi slowly illuminated each one of the hanging masks — they were African. Inside the kitchen, they saw that a plate, a glass, a fork, and a knife were still in the sink. No one had been in that apartment for over ten years, but if it had not been for the layer of dust and the veil of gray spiderwebs, it might have looked as if someone still lived there and had just left.

It was a bewildering view, but what Jordi had been looking for was the ring that was again on his finger. They didn't touch anything. The only thing they left behind were the imprints of their feet on the thick dust layer covering the carpet and the floor.

3

The Hungarian was the owner. The discovery of a furnished apartment was irrelevant for Jordi, but for Bebéi, the sight of a residence like his covered by cobwebs prompted discomfort and created a painful doubt: How can someone disappear for ten years without being missed?

Bebéi could not erase what he had seen. The following day, he spoke again to the janitor. He didn't disclose that they had entered the apartment but asked him a few questions. The janitor reaffirmed that he knew nothing and gave the address of the law firm responsible for paying the bills. That was a good start, thought Bebéi.

His next step was to check with Grená; Bebéi knew that nothing happened in Santa Clara that was not discussed under the yellow umbrella of the lottery ticket seller. He approached her cautiously; he knew breaking into someone's apartment was illegal and tried to conceal his interest. He casually asked her if she knew who had lived before in the place he was renting. She answered, and Bebéi listened with an attentive expression. Then, keeping the same casual expression, he asked if she knew who had lived in the apartment below his.

Grená, who was handling the change of one of the nurses from the health center, halted for a second and looked at Bebéi suspiciously. But she went on, answering his question: "It was a foreigner, I think a German, who taught music at the municipal school. He was timid and lived in Santa Clara for a long time. He never bought a single lottery ticket from me, and I never understood it. How is it possible that a man who lived off the ridiculous salary of a schoolteacher never wanted to risk the lottery? It doesn't make sense! Carmela, the school's principal at that time, explained to me that most foreigners don't play the lottery. I don't understand, but I didn't question her. She is the one that had studied, not me." Grená paused to recall what else she knew and added, "Carmela also told me that, one day, he disappeared."

The information was meager, but Bebéi was pleased. He knew Carmela, and she would surely tell him everything he wanted to know. After she retired as a teacher, Carmela got a part-time job at the French embassy handwriting the ambassador's reception invitations, and her desk was next to Bebéi's.

Bebéi didn't reveal to Grená why he was asking these questions, and in the absence of an explanation, the lottery ticket seller deduced the reason: "I suspect Bebéi is looking for an apartment to buy." Like much of the information she spread, it was not necessarily correct, but it helped to spark a conversation with the first person who passed by.

That same morning, after filing papers and locating documents required by the embassy officials — an activity Bebéi carried out with zeal and perfection — he chatted with Carmela. The office was calm and they both had plenty of time to spare.

"Arpad Corvinus was his name," Carmela said while drinking a coffee in the embassy's break room "He was not German, but Hungarian." Bebéi nodded, demonstrating interest, and she continued, "Arpad was very polite and a considerate man but seemed to be a lonely person. He taught music at the public school and was respected by students. I'm sure your young friend Jordi would remember him. However, one day, when the school year was almost over, he stepped into my office, saying he would no longer teach. He just informed me and left. I never heard from him again."

It was not much, but at least Bebéi knew his name.

That same afternoon, when he met Jordi after his interview with the selection committee, he repeated what Carmela told him.

"Of course I knew him. He was our music teacher," replied Jordi, who was proud of his performance at the interview. "I didn't know that he lived in the same building as you. Cristine liked him very much, and she played with an orchestra that he set up for the girls. They even performed at City Hall." Jordi continued while they walked, following Bebéi's dog: "That's why he had all those instruments we saw inside the apartment."

Zoubir stopped for a quick relief on the hydrant near the barbershop, and Jordi, ignoring the Hungarian, began to talk about his girlfriend. Bebéi listened for a few minutes and then politely reminded Jordi that his interest was the music teacher, not Cristine.

"I also remember," Jordi continued, frustrated, "that he knew how to play several instruments but couldn't play any of them well since he had two fingers missing on his left hand." After a few steps in silence, he continued, "Sometimes, when giving classes, he seemed to forget what he was saying and stood there, speechless, staring at us. Weird. But I remember him well. He was a nice guy."

Bebéi was intrigued. How can anyone abandon an apartment fully furnished? And it was not just that; how could a teacher disappear without anyone noticing? He didn't share his concerns with Jordi, who had to go to Ilona's Café to work. Bebéi continued to walk alone with Zoubir. His doubt grew even more dramatic: What if the Hungarian had died?

The Hungarian's apartment was the same as his and, like Bebéi, he didn't have a family. Did that mean that if he died, nobody would notice? Unacceptable. Perhaps he should tell Lieutenant Pirilo everything he had seen. The lieutenant was his friend and a master in solving mysteries, but he hesitated; he had broken into the apartment without authorization. He walked a little more and finally decided to go; Pirilo would understand that breaking into the Hungarian's apartment was necessary to recover the ring.

Pirilo was the second son of Grená and worked, but not much, as the head of the Mayor's security. He was an excellent professional, keeping Santa Clara safe, but had a reputation for laziness that, according to Bebéi, was not fair: "His passions are dominoes and soccer, and that is what he mostly does."

Bebéi's description was partially accurate. He could have mentioned the third and perhaps the most important of Pirilo's passions: women. Pirilo was a tall and handsome man in his late thirties who had inspired wedding dreams among many women in Santa Clara. He preferred, however, to maintain a strict loyalty to the women of Paris Street: "Beauty and pleasure, without further responsibilities," as he liked to point out.

Bebéi met him at the tavern; Pirilo always lunched there. Bebéi told him everything he knew and proposed visiting the Hungarian's apartment. Pirilo was unconvinced; the apartment had been abandoned for more than ten years, and he barely remembered who the Hungarian was. But Bebéi insisted, and Pirilo realized it would be easier to accompany him on a quick visit. It was just a short walk crossing the park, and it would help his digestion before the dominoes game. But the task ended up being quite intriguing.

They got inside with the same key hidden in the baseboard. The daylight made the Hungarian's apartment seem even more mysterious. Little sculptures were scattered around the room, and they found clothes still hanging inside the closets. The drawers, both in the bedroom and in the living room, were filled with linen and paper. Even the kitchen was fully equipped. In the refrigerator and the cupboard, there were still food boxes, the contents long consumed by ants. Pirilo noticed that the general power switch was disconnected and commented that the place would be ready to be rented if not for the dust. The bed was made, and the towels were in the bathroom. The medicines were in the cabinet, the toothbrush, the comb, and the nail clipper. All of them were covered by ten years of abandonment, dust, and cobwebs.

The masks — thirty-two, according to Bebéi — were hanging on the wall. They were all Africans. They looked less scary in daylight, exhibiting their colors and vivid details. The musical instruments seemed to be ready to play. On the wall at the entrance to the kitchen, some hanging dolls appeared to be Indonesian puppets. In the living room, a collection of golden daggers reminded Bebéi of the one he had in his apartment, which was the only remembrance he kept from his Algerian uncle.

Pirilo was intrigued, going from one room to another while Bebéi looked intensely at everything and fed his memory with the images.

Bebéi was impressed with the photos on the wall behind the dining table — certainly more than a hundred. Some were from a city that looked similar, but not equal, to Paris. Others were from African places with lakes and mountains; the Hungarian appeared with a few friends in African garb. There was also a picture of what looked like the Casbah of Algiers and photos of the desert. Bebéi followed Pirilo out of the apartment, expressing his perplexity: "How could no one notice he was gone!"

Pirilo went back to the tavern, puzzled. Was it just a case of a missing person, or was there something else? He played two domino games and lost both. He was not focused. His mind was on the Hungarian's apartment, and he decided to visit the law firm. He went by himself and didn't invite Bebéi — better be careful.

The law firm office was tiny, and the lone young lawyer didn't seem to be a seasoned professional. He explained that they were the local representatives of a larger Miami law firm, and he only knew that the apartment belonged to a Hungarian. To Pirilo's surprise, he didn't know the Hungarian had disappeared.

The lawyer explained that they followed instructions handed down years ago. They paid all expenses and taxes using the resources of the Hungarian savings account that they also managed. "We strictly followed his instructions," he explained, "and as the interest on the savings account is higher than the expenses, we have continued to do the same for many years, and we never received a complaint." Who would complain if they were making money out of it? reckoned Pirilo, but he kept the thought to himself.

"The apartment is not his only property," said the lawyer. Pirilo only jotted it down without questioning. He was curious to know who the Hungarian was, not what he had.

The lawyer confirmed that the Hungarian's name was Arpad Corvinus and that he was born in Budapest in 1926. He also confirmed that Arpad was a musician by profession and worked as a teacher at the municipal school, but the lieutenant left as intrigued as he entered.

Two days later, Lieutenant Pirilo received a visit that puzzled him even more. It was a lawyer from the Miami office — an older one and a well-dressed man — who apparently had traveled to Santa Clara on short notice to meet him. The lawyer didn't have answers, only questions. He asked about the Hungarian and his eventual heirs: "Now that we know that Mr. Arpad has disappeared for such a long time, we need to find the other family members."

The lawyer's questions seemed reasonable, but Pirilo was suspicious. Why would a lawyer fly from Miami just to talk with him? Something in the lawyer's expression — or perhaps his tie, which seemed extremely expensive — bothered Pirilo. It might be true that he was lazy, but he was not stupid, and amid those questions, he realized that the lawyer was hiding something.

"Better keep our eyes open," was his comment when he met Bebéi again.

4

Nobody cares about the Hungarian. Life was so calm those days in Santa Clara that, for lack of better news, the wounded seagull on Bebéi's terrace became the talk of the town. Almost no one mentioned the Hungarian, but everyone knew the seagull. Bebéi insisted on keeping her safe on his balcony until she was fully healed. On the sidewalk in front of the amber manor, people stopped to photograph the bird, quite visible behind the balustrade.

The Portuguese supermarket owner, who always took a chance to promote his business, posted an advertisement that the seagull was vigilant to ensure his prices were the best in town. He also positioned a telescope at the store entrance so everyone could see Bebéi's seagull on the balcony.

Every day, someone invented a new story. For some, the seagull was a solitary bird mourning a beloved partner who died at sea. Others, more playful, suggested that it was the soul of a deceased wife waiting for the widower to approach one of the women at Paris Street to fly and peck him in between his legs.

So many people were talking about the animal that even Grená abandoned her lottery tickets under the yellow umbrella to visit Bebéi's apartment and see it up close. The real problem started when an image of the seagull appeared in the local news, triggering a pilgrimage of young kids anxious to see it eating sardines and being guarded by Zoubir. Bebéi could not refuse a child's request and spent the whole weekend receiving kids in his apartment. The pilgrimage only ended when the doctor from the Public Health

Center warned that the bird could transmit contagious diseases, and Pirilo saved Bebéi from his torment, attaching a poster on the manor door: *Visits to the seagull are prohibited by order of City Hall.* After that, the only exception was the Mayor, who took his assistants for a photo published in local newspapers, where he appeared kneeling on the balcony, handing a sardine out to the bird.

The Mayor of Santa Clara never missed an opportunity to promote his image, whether it be taking photos with a now-famous seagull, distributing toys to children after Sunday's mass, watching the city baseball team's game in uniform, sponsoring concerts of rock bands in the park, and even delivering bottles of wine to the tramps of the Useless Brethren, far from the sight of his wife, who was president of the Traditional Catholic Women's League. But there was something else that most people knew: he was a highly corrupted politician and a permanent womanizer.

Some people in Santa Clara disregarded the latter part of that sentence, but not Cristine, Jordi's girlfriend. She did an internship in the City Hall and started to investigate accusations of sexual abuse by other interns. That's why the Mayor had "distracted" her by offering a scholarship for a master's degree in Boston. With Cristine gone and his wife focused on social work, the list of the Mayor's lovers became endless. Every new woman who arrived to work at Paris Street was reminded to pay a special visit to him. The gossip about his sexual adventures was so extensive that people didn't have enough time to talk about corruption in the government. Many people didn't even know that City Hall contracts, with no exception, were handed over to the Mayor's friends. They were also closely monitored and carefully administered by his brother, responsible for collecting the Mayor's cut.

Everything within City Hall was strategically and professionally structured by the Mayor's Serbian assistant, a mysterious mature woman, a combination of a masseuse, psychologist, and private trainer who, according to some foreign ambassadors, had occupied a similar position next to an Italian Prime Minister. Public resources were scarce, and they limited what the Mayor could do. The Serbian was the one who came up with the idea of a large long-term loan from a pool of foreign banks to finance an ambitious tourism project on which repayments would only be due after the Mayor's tenure was long over. The loan resources almost tripled Santa Clara's public investment, making the city prettier and increasing the secret bank accounts that the Mayor had in Grand Cayman.

The boardwalk, the pier, the theater, the fish market, the parks, and even some churches were fully rehabilitated, and all street cobblestones were renewed as part of a contract signed with a Romanian friend of the Mayor's. The garbage collection contract was renegotiated at an outrageous price with an Italian partner, another close friend of the Mayor. "A perfect alliance between the public and the private sector," as the Mayor liked to brag to his closest friends.

Thanks to the tourism project, Santa Clara was living a glorious period; more tourists were coming, and everybody was profiting. The new Portuguese supermarket, which, according to Grená, looked like something out of an American movie, was always crowded and, with more tourists, new hotels were built, accommodating more guests. A group of Spanish investors — also friends of the Mayor — refurbished previously abandoned manors to transform them into luxury inns. In the whole city, only one house remained in ruins: a wrecked mansion entangled in a conflicting inheritance, or — according to Grená —protected by a spell cast by an older woman who lived there. But that old manor was the only one; every other building was restored, painted, and shining. All small businesses owned by locals, such as the barbershop, the bakery, the little Chinese grocery, and Ilona's Café, were also booming. Even Bobo Ashanti, the Rastafarian cooperative created by Rasta Bong to take tourists sailing through the bay, purchased five schooners and hired all Rastafarians who lived around town.

From the boardwalk full of foreign tourists to Our Lady of Mercy Hill, where locals daily visited the yellow umbrella of Grená to hear the latest news, everybody was pleased. Santa Clara had that unique combination of historic architecture with a small-town atmosphere. It was not just a bunch of colonial houses refurbished to impress visitors; it was a real town, as happy as its people. But despite the serenity, Bebéi was still confused, and the seagull was not his greatest problem.

"How can someone disappear, and no one can tell where he went?" he asked Pirilo insistently while dining at Ilona's Café, a favorite meeting point for tourists and locals in town. The dinner was per Bebéi's invitation; he wanted to convince Pirilo that knowing more about the Hungarian was essential.

Ilona, the café owner, had reserved them a table at the end of the terrace. An explanation is necessary here since Ilona was one of the most admired and respected people in Santa Clara by the Sea. She arrived there a long time ago, running away from an obsessive and abusive brother. She was and continued to be a ravishing and captivating woman. For many years, Ilona worked on Paris Street and was a pioneer who started "the Castle," the most famous women's house on the street. Later, she found love, left work on the street and opened her restaurant with a spectacular view of the bay. Ilona's love passed away, but the café remained, and with the money she made, Ilona helped virtually all people who lived in the city.

She brought a *pastis* to Bebéi; she knew he was unsettled. Ilona had a special affection for him, and her café was Bebéi's favorite place. Few people in Paris had noticed when he left — perhaps the coworkers in the ministry, but only them. In his previous life, Bebéi used to take the subway to work, shop in the same supermarket, watch football, news, and movies alone in his apartment, and hardly ever talk to anyone. Probably no one in Malakoff, his Parisian neighborhood, noticed when he moved away, but in Santa Clara, it was different; everyone knew him, and he proudly greeted all his friends when walking with Zoubir through the streets.

"Did the Hungarian also greet the people he crossed?" Bebéi asked Ilona. This thought bothered him, turning and returning in his mind. "Would someone miss me if I ever disappeared?" Ilona smiled to reassure him, but Bebéi was worried. "Zoubir certainly would, but do people only know me for my dog?"

Pirilo listened to their conversation while drinking the beer Ilona had brought; he anxiously awaited the octopus risotto, his favorite dish. The lieutenant was also intrigued and mentioned his doubt: "Was he kidnapped or, even worse, was he killed?"

They continued the conversation until Jordi, still working as a waiter, brought them the two risottos. Pirilo said while grabbing his fork, "To believe that he just closed the apartment and disappeared does not make any sense."

Bebéi agreed, nodding, and Pirilo continued after enjoying the smell of coconut and garlic from his plate: "There's something else; no one leaves dishes in the sink if they are traveling. People only do that if they will come back soon, don't you think?" Bebéi again nodded, agreeing, and Pirilo continued. "But before he left, he turned off the electrical switch. Intriguing. A sign that he knew he would not return." Pirilo then paused to savor his risotto. "Where did he go?"

Ilona left their table to receive other clients, and they continued discussing some hypotheses, but the truth is that none of them knew what could have happened. They preferred to eat silently, enjoying the food and praising the blessed hands of Doña Cecy, the restaurant's chef.

After leaving the restaurant, Bebéi kept walking with his dog. He wanted to know more about the Hungarian. Besides Pirilo and Ilona, no one else seemed to care about him, not even Jordi. For Bebéi, the Hungarian was important; he was his neighbor and lived by himself like he did.

The urge to do something grew as he strolled through the deserted streets. The Cathedral was empty, with its doors still open. It did not seem right that everyone was ignoring his neighbor.

The Theater had its doors closed, but it was crowded. From the street, Bebéi could hear the applause of the local orchestra performance. Bebéi wandered along the boardwalk, looking at the crescent moon, and walked by the pier, which was silent at night.

With the Hungarian on his mind and the dog leading the way, he returned home. It was late, but he did not want to sleep. Zoubir stayed on the balcony guarding the seagull, and Bebéi returned to the Hungarian's apartment with a flashlight. He was going to look at each paper, object, and photo until he could understand why Arpad had left without warning, and he had to do it quickly since the following morning he would have to help Friar Bernard open his new pizzeria.

5

Thieves emptied the apartment. Friar Bernard was no longer a priest but was still very popular, and he was opening a pizzeria. He was profoundly religious and dedicated his life passionately to the poor. For many years, he had been responsible for Our Lady of Mercy Church and had made many friends, including the boozers who slept on the stairs, with whom he often shared a chalice of wine. His Sunday masses were crowded, and his only enemy was the Bishop, who disliked him for his open attitude toward gays and lesbians. Even the most traditional Catholics, such as the Mayor's wife, listened to and respected his opinion.

One day, however, he met Gigi, the heroin-addicted friend of Ilona. Gigi was a pale, skinny, and almost repugnant woman at that time. Only Ilona cared about her. However, after three years and many hours of conversation with the Friar, Gigi recovered to become a beautiful and pleasant woman. The only problem is that Gigi's recovery severely affected Friar Bernard's commitment to celibacy, and they decided to get married. Consequently, he left the Augustinian Order, kept Friar as his nickname, and planned to sell pizza to make ends meet.

He was born in Tuscany and learned to make pizza with his father as a child, but opening a pizzeria in Santa Clara was a long and arduous journey. He rented a property previously used as a warehouse, and with money he borrowed from the bank — with Ilona's guarantee — he refurbished the building and purchased the oven and all kitchen supplies.

Kay, the young Chinese accountant of every small business in Santa Clara, helped him with the documents and asked Bebéi's help to support the Friar in filing the paperwork. It was a collective effort. Rasta Bong, Grená's son, who had already opened numerous businesses in the city, gave him details of all he had to do, but it was not enough. The Friar was stubborn and had his way of doing things. That was the reason for the meeting. His friends were there, except Bebéi, who, surprisingly, didn't show up.

"I will not accept extortion," said the Friar, "I will not bribe anyone." He continued to speak vehemently, mixing some Italian words that did not seem appropriate for a former churchman. "I will not pay a kickback to the inspectors of the health department. They know that my refrigerator is new and works according to most modern standards. I will not give a penny to this bunch of *cornutti* from the labor department who already checked that all employees are registered and, even so, don't give me the license." And he kept repeating with anger, "I will not pay these mafiosi firemen who know everything is in order in my kitchen and refuse to authorize me to open. Neither to those *filli di putani* of the City Hall that still have not given me the license to use the building, despite all works concluded, nor to those *sporcci* from the Finance Department who have not yet released the documents Kay delivered to them two months ago. And you know what, *vaffanculo tutti questi scemi* who work with Historic Preservation. They know that I didn't change the facade but keep asking for a kickback to release the authorization."

Rasta, Kay, Ilona, and even Gigi tried to explain to him that without paying those "special commissions," it would take months or even years to get the necessary licenses. Still, the Friar insisted: "Paying bribes is as criminal as accepting them."

What was supposed to be a business meeting became a passionate debate on principles. Rasta Bong and the Friar were already shouting at each other when Ilona realized that it was senseless to continue the discussion. "We are done for today. Better to continue tomorrow, and Rasta, please stop by Bebéi's house to see what happened. It's not normal for him to miss an appointment." As Ilona never liked to wake up early, she added, looking at the Friar, "Let this one be the last meeting we do in the morning. You know that I have trouble thinking under the sun."

Rasta went to Bebéi's apartment, and the Friar followed him. They continued to argue. Rasta was pragmatic. When he smoked his joints at night, he cared about poetry, music, and colors. Still, during the day, he was a committed professional focused on the small businesses he established in Santa Clara by the Sea, such as the Rastafarian cooperative, the taxi service, the Gypsies' orchestra, and the barbershop he inherited from his father.

"With your fixation on questioning everything, you will not get anything," Rasta insisted to the Friar.

When they arrived at Bebéi's manor and were climbing the stairs, they finally stopped arguing. The door of the second-floor apartment was fully open. It seemed odd, but they kept walking up to Bebéi's apartment. They rang several times and noticed something unusual had happened from Zoubir's barking.

Rasta Bong called his brother Pirilo, who was also surprised. "Bebéi never leaves without his dog. He must be inside the apartment. Wait for me. I'll be with you in a minute."

Rasta Bong and the Friar went down to wait for Pirilo, and when he arrived, they climbed back up the stairs. On the second floor, Pirilo saw the door open and immediately entered; that definitely did not seem normal.

The surprise he had was even greater than on his first visit. The Hungarian's apartment was in total disorder. He went into the bedroom, and there the mess was even worse; the drawers were open, and everything that had been inside them had disappeared. He opened the bathroom door and found Bebéi gagged and tied to the sink.

Pirilo freed him, and Bebéi immediately reassured them: "They didn't hurt me. I'm fine," he continued gasping, "They were four." Bebéi explained that he had been checking the apartment to learn more about the Hungarian. He was inside the bedroom when he heard a noise and bumped into them. "They wore masks and gloves; that was all I could see."

The apartment was chaotic. All drawers were thrown on the floor as if the thieves had been looking for something inside them.

"They opened the doors without breaking anything," said Pirilo. "They probably had the keys."

"They had big trash bags," added Bebéi. "I saw them empty the cabinets in the bathroom and throw everything they found into big black trash bags."

The robbers took everything they found: clothes, papers, photographs, masks, and even the little objects the Hungarian had on the coffee table. They emptied the drawers entirely and even took the musical instruments. They just left the furniture and the piano.

"Why does someone steal pictures hanging on the wall? What the fuck are you going to do with them?" yelled Rasta Bong. Enraged, he took off the cap wrapping his dreadlocks, letting his braids fall, almost touching the ground.

"They were professionals," replied Pirilo, trying to organize his thoughts. "It was not a simple robbery. From what Bebéi told us, they had masks and gloves, and the marks they left on the dust do not present traces of shoe soles, meaning they were wearing some protection on their feet to leave no imprints. They were looking for something, and as they did not have time to find what they wanted, they took everything, probably to review elsewhere later." He also added a comment with a dazzled expression.: "It's amazing. The apartment was abandoned for ten years, and a few days after Bebéi discovered the apartment was still furnished, someone appeared to steal everything inside."

Pirilo then turned to Bebéi, sitting on the bed, still a little dizzy after spending so much time tied up to the sink. "I remember that the day we were here together, you took some kind of diploma from the wall, don't you?"

Bebéi confirmed. On that day, a sheet of framed paper caught his attention. He was not sure if it was a diploma or an invitation since it was in German, but it was framed and, in big letters, the name of Adolf Hitler appeared.

"That frame is the only thing left after the robbery," said Pirilo. With all the commotion Bebéi forgot to mention that before the robbers arrived, he had put the envelope on the floor at the apartment entrance into his jacket pocket.

"It's absurd," the Friar interrupted sarcastically after noticing the books remained intact on the bookshelf. "Not even thieves care for books anymore." After listening to his words, Bebéi surprised everyone, getting up with a giant smile and asking to take care of the Hungarian's library.

"I will take the books to my apartment; maybe I can learn something else about him by checking the books he read."

Pirilo could not understand how Bebéi could be interested in books after spending the night tied and gagged. But he didn't say anything. If Bebéi wanted the books, why not let him take them?

Some books were in German, others in French, and some had strange letters on the cover that Pirilo had not seen before. "It's Russian," clarified the Friar. "I don't know what they mean, but I can tell you for sure that it's Russian." Books had never attracted Pirilo's attention. For Bebéi, it was the opposite. Books, notebooks, and any kind of papers were remarkable, not only for what they told but also for what they hid.

Pirilo did not know that before the arrival of the four thieves, Bebéi had found a fascinating photo in one of the books. The picture was so particular that he chose not to tell anyone before he was sure of what it represented.

Pirilo called his assistants, instructing them to search for any clue, and Bebéi returned to his apartment to pick up the dog and take him for a walk.

Many thoughts were mingling in his head. They had stolen everything the Hungarian left; they took the pictures, the clothes, the masks, and even the papers and music scores. They emptied all the drawers, but luckily, they did not find the most critical thing: the books. Bebéi now had everything he needed, and he was only going to tell people when he found out who the Hungarian was, where he had gone, and especially why he kept hidden a picture of Bebéi's father in Algeria in one of the books.

31

6

He played for Hitler, he was a Nazi. It is not an easy task to explain who Bebéi's father was. According to his uncle, Bebéi's father was an Algerian who bravely fought alongside General de Gaulle to drive Nazis out of France. After liberation, he received a decoration from De Gaulle himself and was awarded French citizenship. He later married a young Parisian woman, and it was out of their love that Bebéi was born. When Bebéi was two years old, his father made a brave decision: after helping to release France from the Nazis, he returned to his country to free Algeria from its French invaders. Bebéi's mother joined him, and Bebéi remained in Paris, living with his uncle. The only news he had regarding his parents after that was when a woman dressed in black and using a cane knocked at the door of his uncle's apartment, telling him that the French army had executed both of them.

The few photographs his uncle kept of his parents were taken away by police a week later when they stormed the apartment searching for information. Only many years later, when a French newspaper published pictures of the prominent leaders of the Algerian revolution, did his uncle show him who his father was. That photo was the only image he had, and it was the same one the Hungarian kept inside one of his books.

Bebéi followed the unleashed Zoubir across the boardwalk; it was Saturday morning, and he had the whole day for himself. He was so intrigued that he didn't want to stop walking. He strolled toward the ruins of the old fort and reached the river from where he could see the poorer suburbs that tourists never visited. He craved more knowledge about the Hungarian, but the only thing he had was the framed paper that had been hanging on the wall — and it was in German. He could have asked for help at the embassy; many of his colleagues could translate it for him, but he didn't want to involve them. They would surely ask questions. Suddenly, seeing his dog freely running on the beach near the river, he recalled that Frida, one of the Brethren boozers, who was always at the church's stairs, was German. She could help him.

Frida was the nightmare of law enforcers in Santa Clara; she was always drunk and a renowned troublemaker. To make things worse, she was a strong and angry woman. For reasons that only people who lived in Santa Clara could understand, she liked the "chubby Algerian" who tipped his hat for her.

Grená, who knew all the secrets, had told Bebéi that when Frida was a young student living in Germany, she was a Trotskyist revolutionary and had set off a bomb at a train station in Stuttgart. Many things happened after that: she was arrested, spent a long time in prison, and somehow arrived in Santa Clara, first as a prostitute and later as an old boozer living on the steps of Our Lady of Mercy Church. Frida's reputation was intimidating, but Bebéi was not concerned; he knew how to deal with her. As he needed a favor, he had to reciprocate, and before joining her, he passed by the supermarket to buy a bottle of the vodka she liked.

Frida thanked him for the present, took two fingers of the bottle in a single sip, and shared the bottle with Null-and-void, the dean of the Brethren. She then read what was written on the framed paper and translated it for Bebéi — an invitation for a special dinner. *"On 19 March, 1944, at the Schloss Klessheim palace in Salzburg, Adolf Hitler the* Führer des Großdeutschen Reiches," — that, Frida explained, meant the leader of the great German empire — *"will receive for dinner Admiral Miklos Horthy, Regent of Hungary."*

The invitation also described what they would eat and mentioned that before dinner, *"To demonstrate the historic union between the two countries, the young Hungarian violinist Arpad Corvinus will perform the Hungarian Dance No. 5 by the German composer Johannes Brahms."*

"Son of a bitch," Frida snapped right after reading. "Your neighbor was a Nazi."

A rude remark that deeply troubled Bebéi. How could it be that his downstairs neighbor was a Nazi? A *sale cochon*, as his uncle used to say with anger. It could not be accurate. Bebéi left Frida shouting insults to the Nazis in German and ran to the bookstore of his friend Joseph, the Princess — this time, Zoubir was the one running to catch up.

Joseph had always exhibited a glowing personality. He only kept the bookstore open out of passion since few people bought books in Santa Clara. The Princess, as his friends called him, only resisted closure thanks to money borrowed from Ilona. Balancing the bookstore's budget had never been a significant concern for the Princess; the real big one was to hide from his friends his escapades at *La Gata Caliente*, the drag queen nightclub at the end of the docks where, every Tuesday and Friday, he performed old French songs dressed as his alter ego, Lola Marlene. One day, his secret was finally revealed and, surprisingly, it was Lola Marlene, with her exquisite taste in women's fashions, who saved Joseph's bookstore from bankruptcy. Now, the Princess is proudly out of the closet, splitting his time between the bookstore on the first floor — where he keeps trying to convince his neighbors to read novels and poetry — and Lola Marlene's fashion studio on the second floor — where he makes all the money he needs to live well and repay his debts.

When Bebéi arrived, Princess was at the fashion studio, discussing an outfit for a wedding party with the wife of the Argentinean ambassador. Bebéi respectfully waited, and when the Argentinean left, he showed Princess the dinner menu in German and explained what Frida had told him.

Princess was elegantly dressed in fluffy satin red pants, a white blouse with large red flowers, and a ravishing Asian scarf. He did not hesitate and went immediately with Bebéi to the bookstore to consult some Second World War history books. It took him only a few minutes to find a reference to the dinner.

"That banquet was very important," he said. "On that night, before sitting to dine with the regent, Hitler had instructed his German army to invade Hungary. Can you believe that son of a bitch? His troops invading the country while he enjoyed the music of your Nazi friend."

One more time, the Nazi accusation bothered Bebéi, but he wanted to understand. Princess, with the extravagant gestures of Lola Marlene, explained that in March 1944, things were starting to get tough for the Germans. "In Italy, the Allied forces were already attacking Rome, and the Germans struggled to resist. A complete nightmare for them! On the other side of Europe, the Soviet army had liberated Leningrad." Princess went on and on telling details of that period until he got to the crucial point. "Apparently, Horthy, the Hungarian regent, was betraying Hitler with some secret negotiations with the Soviets. That is why the Führer invited him to that dinner." Princess then added with a dramatic voice, waltzing around Bebéi, "The tanks were roaring and storming into Hungary while they were listening to the high notes of Arpad's music."

"So it's true that the Hungarian was a Nazi?" Bebéi asked resignedly.

"It seems so," replied Princess, regrouping his body in a strictly upright position and joining his hands in front of his chest in a *namaste* greeting.

That conversation confirmed the first bad news of the day, but there would be more. From the bookstore, Bebéi went to Ilona's Café, and once again it was Zoubir who had to run to catch up. Bebéi was profoundly disappointed and thought that perhaps eating a grilled sea bass covered with mushrooms prepared by Doña Cecy would help him recover his mood. At the café, however, he had another unpleasant surprise — from the door, his dog was the first to notice it. Ilona was playing with an adorable little puppy on the restaurant's terrace.

Bebéi's dog could well have been the reincarnation of a Buddhist monk, but when he saw Ilona cuddling the puppy, he lost his Zen posture and did not disguise his jealousy. Bebéi noticed and immediately showed his solidarity, leaving the restaurant. Ilona did not see them; she was so delighted with Wallace, her new Jack Russell, that she completely ignored her clients.

For Bebéi, the day was not over. That afternoon, he received a visit from a veterinarian, a friend of Jordi's, who had offered to see the seagull. The vet acknowledged that he had never before treated a gull, but he could look at the wound. Bebéi took him to the balcony, and while the vet was examining her, Bebéi answered questions from curious neighbors, shouting from the sidewalk.

The vet cleaned the wound with a cotton ball and presented his diagnosis: "From what I can see, it's a little cut, nothing that would prevent her from flying." Bebéi kept listening, puzzled. "Her wing is not injured, just dirty from what looks like oil. I'm sure she'll fly again at any moment," and he teased Bebéi. "If she has not done this yet, it's because you care for her so well that she is reluctant to leave."

Two pieces of bad news and a surprise in a single day: the Hungarian was a Nazi, Ilona had a new pet, and the wing of the gull was not injured. To complete the day, right after the vet left, one of Pirilo's assistants came to his door, informing him that the Hungarian's apartment was cleared and Bebéi could go there and get the books.

He immediately went downstairs; the Hungarian had left twenty-six books. For the thieves, they were just a heavy load that would have been a hassle to take away. Probably like Pirilo and his assistants, they were used to seeing books on shelves, and never worried about opening them. Bebéi, however, had the eyes of an archivist, and he immediately noticed that the books were organized in alphabetical order by the name of the authors. A book for each letter of the alphabet. And they were not there by chance:

The Shield of Achilles, W.H. **A**uden
Die verlorene Ehre der Katharina Blum, H. **B**öll
Heart of Darkness, J. **C**onrad
Justine, L. **D**urrell
The Hollow Men, T. S. **E**liot
The Crime of Sylvestre Bonnard, A. **F**rance
Die Blechtrommel, G. **G**rass
Siddhartha, H. **H**esse
Hedda Gabler, H. **I**bsen
Ulysses, J. **J**oyce
Der prozeß, F. **K**afka
Women in Love, D. H. **L**awrence
Eszter hagyatéka, S. **M**árai
Twenty Poems of Love and a Song of Despair, P. **N**eruda
1984, G. **O**rwell
Доктор Живаго, B. **P**asternak
Giorno dopo giorno, S. **Q**uasimodo
Briefe an einen jungen Dichter, R. M. **R**ilke
Az ajtó, Magda **S**zabó
Воина и мир, L. **T**olstoy
Niebla, M. **U**namuno
Aeneid, **V**irgil
Leaves of Grass, W. **W**hitman
La Montagne de l'Âme, G. **X**ingjian
Her Praise, W. B. **Y**eats
Germinal, E. **Z**ola

At first glance, Bebéi immediately suspected that the books were hiding a file. Before the thieves arrived, he had opened the first book, the one by Auden, and found his father's photograph.

Bebéi assumed that before he disappeared, the Hungarian had organized a file storing personal notes, letters, and photographs inside the pages of those books. He didn't know why, but he should certainly have a reason. Those books were probably hiding secrets, and he would find out. But he would not tell anyone; whoever had stolen the Hungarian's apartment could return and take those books away from him.

He also remembered that he still had the envelope he had found on the apartment's floor, a letter sent by someone, unaware of the Hungarian's departure, that the janitor had pushed under the door. Luckily, the letter was in French, and it bore only a few lines: *I am Morgen's daughter. I live in Kinshasa with my grandmother — my father's mother. From what I've been told, you may be my grandfather, too. If that's true, let me know, I want to meet you.* That letter had been written over ten years ago, and no one had ever replied.

The Hungarian who was gone had a granddaughter named Laurence. Did he know? Did he travel to find her? But the envelope was closed, and the Hungarian was gone before he received it. The letter had an address in Congo. Maybe the granddaughter still lived there?

7

Nothing could distract Bebéi. In the following days, Bebéi split his time between three major concerns: taking care of the uninjured seagull, understanding the Hungarian's files, and, last but not least, calming his dog's jealousy.

There was not much that he could do about the seagull. She was motionless on the balcony, enjoying the company of Zoubir, who was no longer sleeping next to Bebéi's bed but on the balcony beside his friend. This seagull had not betrayed him as Ilona had!

On the sidewalk, tourists kept taking pictures, and the seagull's popularity increased after the Portuguese placed another ad on local television stating that the seagull was so fascinated by the low prices of his supermarket that it was considering staying forever in Santa Clara. Rasta Bong, also always entrepreneurial, got inspired by the idea and started accepting bets at his barbershop on the exact date of the seagull's departure.

Understanding the bookshelf files, the second of Bebéi's problems, was just a matter of time. He was a sound archivist, confident that soon he would decode the Hungarian logic in filing his books. The problem was that some notes were written in languages that Bebéi did not understand. He could ask for help, but he wanted to be cautious.

He realized there was no direct relationship between the language of the book and the notes inside it. He also noticed that there was nothing inside the Xingjian book. On the last page, only a simple sentence was written in slightly hesitant handwriting: *My final book … what's the use to keep reading?*

There were no notes in Zola's book, only an envelope stuck between its pages with a key inside.

In four of the books, those of Hesse, Joyce, Lawrence, and Pasternak, the notes were in Hungarian, and luckily, Bebéi knew the archivist of the French embassy in Budapest. They had worked together at Quai d'Orsay in Paris for a long time, and he could ask him for help. The Budapest archivist did not know anyone in Santa Clara and would not pose any risk.

Inside D. H. Lawrence's book, there was an old photo of a Gypsy woman with a name on the back: *Lali*. Inside *Ulysses* by James Joyce was a letter signed by someone named Janus Corvinus, and in the book of Herman Hesse, some notes about Horthy, the Hungarian regent. They could indicate a relationship between the first letter of the book author's name and the subject of the notes stored inside it — Lali's L, Janus's J, and Horthy's H. It was too early, however, to draw any conclusion.

Bebéi could read the notes in French, Spanish, and Portuguese. In Paris, he took care of the archives of the Iberian countries and studied their languages. He would decide later on the others. What he needed most was to be patient; this was much more manageable than Zoubir's jealousy. The dog was infuriated.

Bebéi tried to take Zoubir to Ilona's Café several times, but the dog refused. Not even by the street of the restaurant was Zoubir willing to pass. Bebéi insisted that not only was he missing Doña Cecy's food, but he also needed to hide the key. He had left a copy of his apartment's keys hanging in Ilona's office, and he wanted to have the key he found inside the book with them. Nobody, except Ilona, knew that those were Bebéi's keys, and Zola's book key would be safe there.

Zoubir adamantly refused to enter the restaurant, but Bebéi forced him. Like it or not, the dog should accept that Ilona had her puppy. But it was not easy; Bebéi had to use all his strength to drag the pet inside.

He sat at the last table, always reserved for Ilona's friends, and tied his rebellious dog to his chair. Realizing what was happening, Ilona came over to pet Zoubir.

Bebéi ordered the sea bass, and when Ilona saw that Zoubir was relaxed, she brought her puppy to play with him. Bebéi watched silently when the little one started sniffing and licking the grumpy Zoubir under the table.

Ilona went to talk with other clients, and Bebéi ate alone. His thoughts were far away. He wanted to understand the Hungarian's files, and what intrigued him most was the photograph of his father inside Auden's book.

In the same book, Bebéi had also found notes referring to events in Algiers from 1958 until 1960 — when the Hungarian apparently lived there. There was no specific reference to his father, but the notes mentioned contacts from Arpad with Algerian revolutionary leaders.

Inside Quasimodo's book were a few papers, luckily all written in French: a Quebec address in Canada, a bank statement, and messages he could not understand mentioning someone named Walden. The book with the most notes inside was Conrad's *Heart of Darkness*, with a few letters, personal notes, and photos. All of them were related to Congo in Africa. From what Bebéi could understand, the Hungarian also lived in that country, and the notes mentioned people and places that Bebéi never heard before.

Although he did not wholly understand the notes in other books, they confirmed the relationship between the first letter of the author's name and the keyword of the file: Algeria for Auden, Congo for Conrad, and Quebec for Quasimodo. In Anatole France's book, some notes in Portuguese mentioned people and political problems in Angola and Mozambique. Still there was nothing related to the letter F. Patience, thought Bebéi; he was only beginning.

When he finished eating, he looked under the table and saw that Zoubir was now friends with Ilona's puppy. Good, he thought, one of the problems was solved. But what was still bothering him was Frida. She had told everyone that his Hungarian neighbor was a Nazi.

Bebéi could not accept that someone who had lived downstairs of his apartment; who had musical instruments in the room; and who was a teacher respected by Cristine and Jordi was a Nazi. But Frida insisted, and it was not only her. Every time Bebéi stepped in front of the Mercy Church, the boozers started to ask him about "his Nazi friend."

Among the photos he found in the Hungarian archive, there was one that would definitively prove that Arpad was not a Nazi, but how could he show it? No one in Santa Clara knew about the file. He left the restaurant pondering: he must do something to make Frida stop calling the Hungarian a Nazi.

8

The Mayor's revolutionary project. Now and then, there was a great novelty in Santa Clara and, in those days, everyone was talking about Lucia's Fitness Gym. Lucia was one of the most devout young Catholics in the city. She never missed the seven o'clock mass at Our Lady of Mercy Church — always wearing dark gray clothes. She worked arduously as the principal assistant to the Mayor's wife. After work, Lucia returned to church every day to feed the homeless. At twenty years old, she was the pride of the Catholic movement of Santa Clara.

Despite a pale face, she was healthy, but never felt comfortable walking in front of the Rastafarian Cooperative at the pier. Particularly when Chombo Zen, the yoga teacher, was there meditating with his legs crossed in the lotus position — a sinner image — shirtless, exposing his well-built chest. Lucia immediately started to sweat, feeling baffling anxiety that no doctor was able to explain.

Those symptoms persisted until a group of Rastafarians, including the handsome yoga teacher, took their clothes off on the boardwalk to protest against the Mayor. Lucia could not breathe when she saw them. She abandoned her virginity vow and traded her daily masses for private sessions of yoga with Chombo Zen. Her family tried to stop her, but it was impossible; Lucia had made up her mind. She became a determined woman and began to wear sensual and provocative outfits. Her father, the port administrator and chief of the local Masonic shop, could not bear seeing his daughter parading the streets in leggings and T-shirt while per-forming exotic activities at unknown places. As Lucia refused to give up, he proposed a compromise: he helped his daughter open her Fitness Gym and do whatever she wanted behind closed and private doors.

He rented an old warehouse that the port was no longer using for her and obtained all licenses and permits to open it in record time, paying the required kickbacks.

Lucia wanted to celebrate the opening with a modern dance show on the steps of Our Lady of Mercy Church, which initially bothered the boozers and ended up causing a great argument. The dispute only softened when Null-and-void proposed a tax on bottles of vodka that Lucia's father agreed to pay.

The Fitness Gym opened and immediately became a success among the youth, and a torment to Friar Bernard. Every day, when he got together with Rasta Bong to talk about the pizzeria, his friend would remind him, "Look how stupid you are! Lucia's father paid all bribes and is opening her gym, while you, with your principles, will never open the pizzeria."

The Friar was stubborn and didn't want to give up; he decided to ask for help from the Mayor's wife, who could not understand why someone would have to pay bribes to open an honest business. She insisted on accompanying him on a visit to the Mayor, who cynically said that he was shocked by everything he heard: "I can't believe this. I'll open an investigation immediately. You can rest assured that everything will be settled in less than a week." Kind words, expressed with a convincing attitude that conveyed the sincerity of the Mayor's intentions.

Nevertheless, what neither the Friar nor the Mayor's wife knew was that immediately after they left, the Mayor called his brother. "Who the fuck does this Friar think he is to bother my wife? Does he think that just because he is fucking the hot Gigi, he can do whatever he wants? Forget it! I want you to be tough with him. If there is no brown envelope with our money, he will never open his business," and the Mayor reaffirmed, fuming: "No exceptions are made on my administration."

Rasta Bong, who no longer knew what to do, complained to Ilona: "If the Friar does not pay what they are asking for, he will not open his business. Without it, he will not be able to repay the bank, and if this happens, we, as his guarantors, will have to pay for his stubbornness." Ilona listened and nodded resignedly.

Of all the kickbacks, the most disturbing one was for the fire department. The Friar was fully aware of the dangers of fire amid old colonial houses and insisted on using the most expensive and safest equipment; even so, the fire department refused to release his license. The Fire Chief, a cousin of the Mayor's, insisted that the assessment of the wood used on the little stairway leading to the warehouse still needed to be completed — this was just another excuse since the previous week it had been the exhaust outlet diameter, and the week before, the distance between the stove and the wall.

The Friar's anger went through the roof when a fire erupted at the ice cream parlor owned by the son of the Italian partner of the Mayor at the garbage business. According to the local TV news, the fire started in the electrical system, and the reporter pointed out that the shop didn't comply with most basic fire regulations. "How could it have been possible that they obtained their license in less than a week?" the Friar shouted in front of his still-closed pizzeria.

The Friar visited all newspapers telling his story. He also publicly asked in a TV interview for the fire department to inspect his pizzeria in the presence of journalists. The discussion widened, and the Mayor was forced to open an investigation. The fire department license of the pizzeria was finally issued, but it was just one of the many authorizations he needed. The Friar decided to go all in. He invited a television news team to visit the pizzeria and denounced, on video, how and who was extorting him. The response was so intense that he received an invitation from the National Association of the Chambers of Commerce in the capital to give a presentation at their weekly lunch.

The Mayor was deeply bothered and complained to his brother: "I can't believe this mess is happening now. I am ready to launch a mega neo-revolutionary project that will completely change the city, and this son of a bitch is talking about petty things such as corruption and bribes."

The idea of the Mayor's revolutionary project was familiar: some Saudi Arabians and an international hotel chain had previously proposed to build mega-hotels with casinos in the city, but the project didn't materialize. Most recently, however, the two groups were joined by Chinese investors and presented a broader super-mega project.

The first person to realize that something strange was going on was, obviously, Grená. According to what she explained to her customers, the driver for the Mayor's brother heard a private conversation about modern apartment towers to be built at the end of the boardwalk. From what the driver understood, the project would begin at the ruins of the Spanish fort, which would be transformed into a large hotel and connected to a large shopping center, with a new marina for yachts and four towers of fifty floors each for apartments and offices.

Grená's story worried many people, but it was just a rumor spread by the lottery ticket seller that might never turn out to be true. One week later, however, the whole story blew up when Carmela's brother-in-law, an engineer who before retiring had worked for City Hall, told everyone what he knew. He was in contact with some ex-colleagues still working for the Mayor, and he explained the whole idea in a meeting organized by Carmela at Ilona's Café Terrace.

"The total area of the new project would be three and a half times the built-up area of our whole city, and worse," he said, opening his arms as if preaching on a pulpit, "There is a project of a third casino hotel with a tower proposed by Russian investors on the other side of the city, that would also be launched as part of this new concept. With all those projects, big and modern buildings would completely engulf our historic town."

The engineer explained that the new movie theater to be built inside the shopping center would have eight viewing rooms, where almost a thousand people would be able to watch movies at the same time — a dramatic change compared to the City Hall Auditorium, which was currently featuring films every Tuesday and Thursday nights to no more than fifty people at a time.

"The project would also include a new six-lane avenue connecting our city to the capital," he explained to the group gathered at the terrace. "After the Fort, the river will disappear; all the water will flow through underground tunnels. Where the river now is, they will build the shopping center and the towers."

"Impossible," yelled Colonel Viera, a retired colonel who still believed he was an army member. "On the other side of the river, we have the army camp where we train our soldiers and officers. What are they planning to do with the training center?"

"They are going to transfer it to the north of the capital, where the new Muslims built the mosque," replied the engineer, almost causing the Colonel to have a heart attack.

The engineer also explained that the contractors would bring thousands of workers to build the new project and warned: "The project is very ambitious. Santa Clara will become one of the largest cities in the Caribbean, full of foreigners who are expected to come and live here."

His words were so astonishing that none of his listeners dared to ask questions. Ilona, who had been in a perfect mood since getting her puppy, didn't seem worried. "Let them do whatever they want. As long as they don't build anything in front of my terrace, and I can keep the restaurant for us, I don't mind."

Gigi, who was also there with the Friar, disagreed. "You've gone mad. Do you think all these people who come to your café today to drink, dance, and share stories will continue to show up if they build this madness? No way. The clients you like, those adventurous poets and dreamers, will not come here with all these new towers, hotels, shopping malls, and the boring people who love them. If they do this, we will never be able to get drunk and take a piss at the boardwalk watching the sunrise as we did yesterday. Wake up, woman; this is going to be hell."

"We might sell more pizzas," risked the Friar, trying to calm Gigi, who almost punched him.

"You don't understand that with the Mayor's project, we will have large chains delivering pizza, and we will have to work twelve hours a day to pay overpriced rent. Do you think that you will have time to feed the pigeons in the park as you do and to discuss philosophy with Diocles and his cats? No more! Forget your naps after lunch, dominoes with Pirilo, or the glass of wine you like sharing with the bums on the church's stairs. You will be working as a slave, and you will be tired at night. You will not be able to dance, drink, and make love to me, and worse, you will not bear my hangovers in the morning. No way. I want our life as it is now, and I don't want to live in this crazy city that the Mayor is promoting only to bring money into his pocket."

Bebéi was becoming confused with all the discussion. "Can we persuade the Mayor to suspend the project?" he asked naively, and the engineer immediately replied. "If the project is as big as they are talking about, the Mayor will earn so much money with kickbacks that he will never cancel it."

Diocles, the philosopher who was always careful and measured with his words, startled everyone by exclaiming: "If they go ahead with this project, I'm out of Santa Clara!"

Bebéi could not understand. If everything was going so well in the old town, why make a new one?

9

Could a Nazi take a picture with Guevara? The plans for the new city were already causing turmoil around the Mercy Church. People were packed around Grená's yellow umbrella, discussing the news. Even the boozers of the Useless Brethren were there, all of them shouting and debating. Colonel Viera, who before retirement had been one of the heads of the army — and after having an affair with a young woman, lost to her most of his pension and a lot of his dignity — was trying to convince the boozers to oppose the Mayor's plans. "We must resist" were his words.

Robespierre was so drunk that he kept dancing with two pigeons perched on a broomstick. Frida, who was relatively sober, wondered why a retired colonel would believe that hobos might care about the Mayor's plans.

Null-and-void, the eldest of the tramps, sympathized with the Mayor, probably because of the bottles of wine the Mayor used to leave at the church stairs in the middle of the night. He was also sober enough to know that there was nothing people could do to stop the plans of big international investors. He knew them and how they acted; after all, he had been one of them.

Bebéi couldn't understand the need for a new city. He listened to what people were saying just to be polite but without great interest. For him, the only thing that mattered was the Hungarian's file. Everything else was secondary at that moment. The notes on the Congo hidden in Conrad's book were written in French. They described the murder of someone named Patrício Lumumba and a dictator named Mobutu who, despite being an assassin, had received some help from the Hungarian.

Bebéi did not know the history of Congo and had a hard time understanding the content of those notes. His strength was filing documents. He had a photographic memory, and his mind could visualize all files as if they were on an open map displayed before him. That was his skill: filing and finding papers. Since he was a child, he could never focus his attention and read longer documents — his mind was constantly distracted by other things. No matter how hard he tried, his thoughts flew away. He needed help understanding what had happened in Congo and knew that Princess could help him, but how could he ask for help without explaining that the Hungarian's notes were in his apartment?

First, he tried to read the notes in Spanish, especially those in Henrich Böll's book. They mentioned African countries, particularly the conflict between Congo dictator Mobutu and a certain Agostinho Neto, who lived in Angola. Bebéi was also suspicious that Böll's book was where the Hungarian had filed notes about a Barbarroja, who seemed to be a Cuban involved in many African conflicts. Barbarroja — maybe that was the keyword for Böll's book.

In Magda Szabó's book, the keyword appeared to be Santa Clara. There, Bebéi found notes in Spanish about the Hungarian apartment in Santa Clara and the Miami law firm administering the Hungarian's assets. A third note referred to a property the Hungarian had bought in the city, but Bebéi could not understand it.

The most exciting notes were in Günter Grass's book. Bebéi found inside it an unquestionable proof that the Hungarian was not a Nazi. How can someone be a Nazi and at the same time be friends with Che Guevara?

There was a short note signed by El Che where he thanked the Hungarian for introducing him to Tamara. Apparently, she was a friend of Arpad's, and he introduced her to Guevara when El Che visited Leipzig for meetings with East German authorities in 1960. There were also other short notes where Guevara commented on some events in Congo, and on all of them, El Che included a paragraph telling news about Tamara. Most importantly, there was the photo of Che Guevara, and beside him, a young woman with a beret and a blond European man who was probably Arpad. The three were sitting at a restaurant table, and on the back of the photo, it was written: *Leipzig 1960 with T and G.*

Bebéi, who now understood the rationale of the Hungarian's files, looked at Tolstoy's book to see if there was any reference to Tamara. What he saw confirmed his suspicion; the name of Tamara appeared in all notes, indicating the first-letter connection — Tolstoy/Tamara — but they were written in German.

He desperately needed help; the Budapest archivist would help him with the notes in Hungarian, but he wanted Frida's help to understand what was written in German. He also needed Princess's help to understand what had happened in Congo and Africa. But how could he get all this?

He had sent a letter to the address on the envelope of the Hungarian's granddaughter mentioning he was Arpad's neighbor, and while thinking about that letter, Bebéi decided to lie. It might work. He would tell the others that the photo had been inside the envelope. It was not a big lie. That would contradict his moral principles, but just a white lie was not a big deal. It would save the Hungarian's reputation without exposing the whole file.

He put the photograph in his pocket and walked with Zoubir towards the Mercy Church. He was determined to put an end to the Nazi image of his neighbor.

He arrived, and Zoubir barked — as if announcing that Bebéi was bringing important news. Frida, who was in a good mood, welcomed them by singing "Raise the Flag," the Nazi anthem, with her right arm pointing straight forward as Hitler's salute.

Bebéi smiled; he was not upset anymore. He was ready to prove that there were no Nazis in his building.

He preferred talking to Frida alone and invited her into the church. He wanted to be discreet and keep the file in secrecy, but when Frida, a Trotskyist, saw Che's picture, she was elated. She immediately ran to the entrance and yelled to Null-and-void and Robespierre who were on the stairs in front of the church.

The two approached, but they could not see what she was showing. The picture was small, and they both needed glasses. Null-and-void tried to find his glasses, but he couldn't. Robespierre went to the barbershop to borrow a pair and got one from the Jewish Moses, who was having a haircut there.

When Robespierre, a nostalgic ex-revolutionary like Frida, finally recognized who was next to the Hungarian, he started to invite everyone who was entering the church to see the picture "of our honorable internationalist leader Che Guevara, that the companion and *tovarich* Bebéi had found."

Robespierre was so thrilled that he had tears in his eyes. He began to sing the Socialist International anthem and was joined by Frida, laughing to see the dazzled expression of Bebéi, who could not understand what was happening.

At the end of the anthem, Robespierre ran through the streets announcing the great news. Throughout the day a pilgrimage of friends and enemies passed the stairs of the church to see Che's photo, which Robespierre was proudly displaying.

The Hungarian, who until that moment was unknown by many in Santa Clara, became famous as a friend of Che Guevara, which for Bebéi seemed better than being a Nazi.

The tricky thing for Bebéi was when Grená and her son Pirilo asked the crucial question. "Where did you get this picture?"

"It was in the Hungarian's granddaughter's letter."

"What letter?" asked Grená.

"The one we found in the apartment. It was from his granddaughter."

"And what else did she say in the letter?" insisted Pirilo.

Bebéi shook his head, insinuating that she didn't say anything else, and Grená blasted him. "How come she didn't say anything? She just put the picture in the envelope with nothing else inside?"

Bebéi didn't want to invent more lies and started to stutter. Pirilo exchanged glances with Grena in silence. They both knew

Bebéi was hiding something and decided not to put pressure on him. Later, without people around, Pirilo would quickly discover what Bebéi was hiding.

What was important at that moment was that the Hungarian was not a Nazi, but a communist, which to Colonel Viera was the same crap.

10

A perfect day to chat at the park. Saturday, a morning to enjoy. That was what Diocles, the Santa Clara philosopher, had in mind sitting on the bench near the fountain in front of Princess's bookstore. The store was open but empty, which did not bother Princess. Whenever someone suggested that it might be better to close the bookstore, he would firmly reply: "How respectful is a city that doesn't have a bookstore?"

Bebéi, on his way to the park, passed by Grená's corner, where he heard the good news: Jordi was the first name on the list of approved teachers to be hired. Good news for him and bad news for Ilona, who would lose her best waiter, but Bebéi was happy; Jordi would finally do what he liked most. As soon as he arrived at the park, he explained to Diocles, who was cuddling a yellow cat: "Jordi will make less than what Ilona pays him, but she already told him that he can work at the café nights and weekends if he wants."

Bebéi sat next to Diocles and started feeding the pigeons pieces of bread he had taken out of his pocket while Zoubir ran with other dogs around the park.

Bebéi stayed beside Diocles in silence; he knew Diocles liked to think. They were only interrupted by La Pajerita. She slept at the boardwalk and spent days distributing useless pamphlets all over the town. That morning, she was handling invitations for a Uruguayan Theater performance that had happened three weeks before, and she made sure to give one to Bebéi and another to Diocles.

A few minutes later, Pirilo arrived. He pretended to be casually strolling, but the truth was that he wanted to talk to Bebéi and clarify the story of the photograph. Pirilo was concerned not because of Bebéi's lie; he knew that the archivist was a kind and harmless person. What was bothering him was the robbery at the Hungarian's apartment. Everything seemed so strange. According to Bebéi's description, they were professionals, but why would professionals break into an abandoned apartment? He had contacted his colleagues at the Federal Police, and they were also surprised. Even the Santa Clara Gypsies, who always knew what was going on in the underground, had no idea who had stolen from the Hungarian. The only clue he had came from a Romanian stripper who worked on Paris Street and heard from a Ukranian customer that someone had paid big money to clean out an apartment in Santa Clara.

How is it possible, wondered Pirilo, that someone would pay big money to hire professionals to steal personal belongings from a Hungarian whom no one knew and had been missing for more than ten years? Very weird! And there was more; why would the Miami lawyer come to Santa Clara in a hurry asking about the Hungarian? That well-dressed gringo, with a tie worth at least a month of Pirilo's salary, undoubtedly knew more than what he had told.

Pirilo sat on the bench and asked about the photo. Bebéi tried to insist on the story that the photograph had been inside the envelope, but he got so confused that he finally decided to tell the truth about the books.

Pirilo and Diocles listened patiently for almost half an hour to Bebéi's elaborations about the file and the notes. Pirilo even expressed interest in visiting Bebéi's apartment to see what he had found. Bebéi immediately stood up, ready to take him there, and Pirilo deceived him by saying, "Next week, perhaps."

The morning was so pleasant, and Pirilo could not believe that some papers stored in old books could attract anyone's attention other than Bebéi. He was convinced that the professionals hired to steal from the apartment were not looking for books, and he was also sure that it was not old notes and photographs that the gringo lawyer was interested in.

He thanked Bebéi and enjoyed the tranquility of the rest of that Saturday morning playing dominoes. The Asturian was probably busy preparing for Saturday family lunches, but he would find other partners willing to play. But why not be careful? Before he left the park, he called his assistants and asked for "special attention" to the security of Bebéi's apartment.

What he did not mention on the phone, but his assistants understood very well, was that "special attention" meant placing one of the new cameras. This would allow the lieutenant's team to monitor who came in and out of Bebéi's manor from their office at City Hall.

Surveillance cameras were a novelty in the city; only a few people knew of their existence. According to the Mayor's brother, who bought them, they should be placed in *strategic* points, and as Pirilo didn't know what was *strategic* in Santa Clara, he installed a couple to test the equipment.

He placed one at the entrance of Paris Street. That one got the primary attention of his assistants, who could now follow the movements of all the women working at the nightclubs. Another went in at the soccer field near the river, where gangs of young thugs met to plan their activities, and three more at the pier, at the boardwalk, where tourists were walking carrying expensive watches and dollars in their wallets, and on the park, not far from where they were talking. Since there were many cameras — it seems the Mayor's brother got a big commission on each acquisition — Pirilo had begun to spread them throughout the city. After that phone call, one was attached to the lampost before Bebéi's manor door.

Bebéi remained at the park, watching the dogs run around, amused by how well things were going in the city, and wondering why the Mayor had decided to change everything.

"I think it's a mid-life crisis," said Princess, who arrived at the bench with a hungover face. He, she — whatever — was conservatively dressed, wearing jeans and a Lady Gaga T-shirt. "Since the Jamaican lover left him for that handsome Ukranian who worked as a driver for City Hall, the Mayor is no longer the same. He spent some time fooling around with that blonde from the Chamber of Tourism, but she cuckolded him with a Spanish painter. And I will tell you something: that blonde might be beautiful and hot, but she's dumber than a door." Princess continued telling gossip that entertained Bebéi. "From what I was told, the Mayor is about to have cosmetic surgery to remove wrinkles and the bagginess under his eyes. Botox doesn't seem to be enough, and I will not be surprised if he does liposuction." Princess then concluded, smiling, "I think it's his age. That's why he invented this story of a New Santa Clara."

Colonel Viera, who had arrived while Princess was speaking, also added his opinion: "It's not the Mayor, it's his Serbian assistant."

The Colonel was not the only one to mistrust the Serbian. Many people in the city, including Grená, attributed to her all the neo-revolutionary strategy that had increased the Mayor's popularity. The Serbian didn't show up on the streets and rarely talked to anyone, but according to Pirilo, who often saw her at the Mayor's office, she was bright and a hidden influence behind the Mayor.

"Forget the Serbian," yelled Null-and-void, who was not yet drunk and was walking, holding his pants barely tied around his waist. He was constipated, and walking was an excellent incentive to his bowels. "It's not the Mayor or his assistant," he said, with a lengthy fart and a pleasant smile. "This New Santa Clara is a huge project. You can be sure that the Mayor, his brother, and his friends will make a lot of money out of it." The others on the bench listened attentively since, on money matters, Null-and-void, an ex-banker, was undoubtedly knowledgeable.

Bebéi added that he had heard a comment within the embassy that the Arabs had hired a French public relations company to help them with the project. With his naive sincerity, he also added that the new ambassador, a woman, had been instructed by the government to support the Mayor.

"The only thing that interests that woman," added Priscilla, a hairdresser who was Lola Marlene's friend and had just joined the conversation, "is the meditation classes that the Chombo Zen gives her at night. And from what she said yesterday while I was doing her hair, she is furious with Lucia's new academy. The young girls seem to be having too many private sessions with Chombo Zen, and the poor guy is always exhausted when he meets her."

Rasta Bong, hurrying to his barbershop, also commented that the Rastafarians were worried about the project. "We just opened the Haile Selassie Center with a huge reggae concert hall, and from what we heard, the new center is right where they want to build the shopping mall." Rasta Bong concluded earnestly, "Rasta brothers used to like the Mayor, but this new town is a bad idea!"

Bebéi stayed a little longer, but when he realized Zoubir was tired, he bade farewell to his friends and headed for his apartment. He had a mission. Bebéi loved gossiping but preferred working on the Hungarian's file for the rest of the day.

To his surprise, Colonel Viera joined him when he started to walk toward home. "You must be careful. They have already robbed the Hungarian's apartment, and now they will try to break inside yours. They have microphones everywhere. You can be sure that tomorrow, the Mayor and the Serbian will know everything we discussed. You must be very careful with everything you say in the park."

Bebéi listened, suspecting that Colonel Viera was getting to be as mad as Robespierre.

11

A story that sounded like a movie. Another surprise awaited Bebéi in his apartment: an email from his Budapest archivist friend had just arrived on his computer. While he printed it to read it comfortably on his armchair, he poured water for Zoubir, glanced to ensure the seagull was still on the balcony, and filled a glass with his favorite Porto wine. The letter was long:

Dear Friend Bebéi, I miss those times when our desks faced each other in Quai d'Orsay. I learned a lot from your questions. Sometimes, they seem naive, but they are always meaningful. Reading in your letter that a key was hidden within the books, I remembered that you always kept an extra copy of my desk's key. We never needed it, but as you said, if by chance something happens, a copy was there. The story of your Hungarian neighbor is fascinating, and I will start by saying he was a Gypsy.

His mother, Lali, or Lalika, as Janus, his father, called her, was a Gypsy dancer — as was the Emerald from the movie The Hunchback of Notre Dame *that we watched together. Do you remember? Lali danced in the streets, and her son, Arpad, played the violin and passed the hat. Arpad's name was not a Gypsy one, and that was the only concession Lali made to his father, Janus Corvinus, a young man from a traditional Hungarian family who fell in love with her.*

From what I can understand, she also fell in love with him, but Janus lived in a palace, and the world of Lali was the streets of Budapest. Her two passions were music and soccer. Apparently, she used to go to the stadium when the Ferencvárosi team played, and she was friends with

Sarosi, a great player of the Hungarian national team in the thirties. She wanted her son to be a player, but Arpad never showed the slightest ability to play soccer, and as a second option, he ended up being a violinist. Lali taught him to play, and at five he was already playing at her side in the streets. Lali danced so well that she was invited to perform in theaters. The papers you sent me include a clipping from the leading Budapest newspaper at that time commenting on the success of her performance at the Erkell Theater. Lali was a beautiful and free woman.

From what Janus tells us in his letter to his son, he thought about giving up his diplomatic career to live on the streets beside her, but he was never brave enough. As he acknowledged in his letter: "I will take this remorse with me through the last day of my life."

Janus, the father, was one of the young Hungarian idealists who worked with Admiral Miklos Horthy. They all shared the dream of reuniting the Great Hungarian homeland divided by the Trianon Treaty. Arpad's father worked for over twenty years with Horthy; he held various important positions and became one of his principal advisers during the Second World War.

At eleven, Arpad was living with his mother, trying to play soccer to please her, and performing with the violin as an angel. He learned to speak as many languages as are heard on the streets of Budapest: the Romani of the Gypsies, Hungarian, German, Romanian, and Slovak. He never attended a school and only learned to read and write much later, but as his father wrote, "Arpad could understand words even if they were spoken in a language that he had never heard before."

In 1937, his mother fell ill — tuberculosis — and on November 19, she died in the hospital. As Arpad wrote, he was so devastated that it took him a long time to accept her death. He met his father for the first time at the hospital — Janus had promised Lali that if anything happened to her, he would take care of their son. Arpad attended the funeral, and in the afternoon of that very same day, he entered for the first time into the sumptuous palace where his father lived. Everything there was new. Arpad carried only the violin that he played with him. His father took him to the Franz Liszt Academy of Music in Budapest, an academy respected throughout Europe. As his father wrote in his letter, "He barely began to play, and they offered him a fellowship to study with them."

The academy and classical music had such an impact on him that his father gave up the idea of a traditional education and resigned himself to the fact that the only thing his son would do in his life was to play the violin. Arpad practically lived with the violin in his hands; touching it was almost an obsession that helped him to live after his mother's death.

Only in June 1938, when his mother's friend Sarosi's telegram arrived, telling him that Hungary had lost the final of the world football championship to Italy, did he finally understand that he would never be able to see a football match with his mother again. At that moment, all sadness for her death exploded in his heart. As he wrote, he spent weeks depressed until he went to her graveyard and promised to play better than anyone else the Hungarian Dance No. 5 of Brahms, Lali's favorite piece of music.

He dedicated his life to that objective, so a few years later, when Horthy went to Salzburg for dinner with Hitler, he took Arpad with him to impress the Führer.

Can you understand how significant that dinner was? Hitler was the mighty lord of Europe, and Horthy was doing everything to prevent him from invading Hungary. Arpad played at Horthy's request to demonstrate what a Hungarian could do while playing a German composition. At that banquet, Arpad probably had to quietly listen when Hitler told Horthy that the Hungarians should be more active in eliminating Gypsies and Jews. As he was a violinist, Arpad responded with his music. That night, Arpad did not play for Hitler as a Hungarian, much less as a Nazi, something he never was. He played as a son of Lali, a Gypsy, like many others that Hitler was eliminating throughout Europe. At that dinner, he celebrated his mother's life, dancing barefoot through the streets of Budapest by playing the most Gypsy of the German songs composed by Brahms. The Gypsy Dance, as her mother used to call it, might have never been Hitler's favorite, but that was the tune that reminded Arpad of his mother.

That's why that invitation was so important. For Hitler, that dinner might have been just a farce; when he invited Horthy to the Schloss

Klessheim palace in Salzburg, he had already secretly instructed Operation Margarethe, the Hungarian invasion. But to Arpad, that was the night that, as a Gypsy, he challenged the murderer responsible for the death of twenty-eight thousand Gypsies who lived in Budapest. That invitation certainly deserved a prominent and fancy frame on his wall.

Another thing I noticed from the notes was that besides being a Gypsy, he was sympathetic to the Jews. In 1943, when he was only seventeen, he married an older woman from a Jewish family named Eszter Bider. In Hungary, the Jews were not as persecuted as in other European countries, and although it's not mentioned in the notes, he probably married her to protect her from the Nazis. Curious, isn't it? The virtuosity with which he played the violin allowed him to survive as a Gypsy and to protect Eszter. Imagine how well he played!

The papers you sent me also included a note his father wrote after watching him play in Salzburg: "Even if I might live for a thousand years, I will always keep the sadness I felt when I listened to your violin tonight. I followed selfish dreams my entire life, ignoring my heart, and all I found was unhappiness. Tonight, you made me cry as a child. Your violin still keeps our Lalika alive, and I thank you and congratulate you for it."

Then came the end of the war and, in 1945, Hungary was invaded by the Soviets. Horthy managed to escape with life, but the Soviet troops executed Arpad's father. Arpad was banished to the Soviet Union and then to Kolyma in Siberia. Why was he deported? Hard to say. Maybe because he was the son of Janus or perhaps because he played for Hitler, but we will never know. Six hundred thousand Hungarians were exiled to Siberian concentration camps, and only two hundred thousand returned.

Among the documents, there was also a note that Admiral Horthy sent him in 1952, indicating what happened after the war. In the note, Horthy congratulates him for Morgen's birth. Horthy also mentioned that "after everything that happened in Kolyma," without explaining what this was, "you cannot continue enchanting everyone playing your violin, and that is why it is imperative to accept the work that our friend the ambassador is offering." In the same letter, Horthy reflected on all the Hungarian nation has suffered since the end of the First World War and wrote:

"Although you can no longer defend your homeland by playing the Hungarian Dance, your father would be very proud to know that his son is fighting to regain the freedom of all Hungarians." From the note, it's impossible to know what kind of work he was talking about or what Arpad did afterward. I tried to find some record of his presence here in Budapest, and I found none.

I understand that Arpad returned from Siberia to live in Berlin with Eszter, and their daughter Morgen was born. However, I could not find out what he was doing there. If you discover something else, please tell me; these notes made me curious about what happened to your neighbor Arpad. How could he live if all he knew was to play the violin and could not play it anymore after Siberia? Only you can find out. Cheers, my friend.

PS: I could not read the notes marked with the letter P of Pasternak; they are not in Hungarian; they are in Czech, a language that I do not know.

Part Two

THE SPY

12

Bebéi wants to play the detective. The letter explaining what happened to the Hungarian — who was a Gypsy — confirmed Bebéi's theory about the files. Each book on the shelf was used as a binder where the Hungarian filed papers that somehow were special for him. Why he did it was not clear. Was he hiding a secret? But if he was, why did he save all the information? And for whom had he organized those files? Those questions were still unanswered.

Bebéi was sure that the first letter of each author's name was associated with a keyword. He read the notes in French and knew that A from Auden's book was for Algeria, C from Conrad's for Congo, and Q from Quasimodo's for Quebec. Among the notes in Spanish, Böll's book contained notes about a Barbarroja, but Bebéi did not know yet who that could be.

The letter D from Durrell's novel seemed to be from the Dominican Republic, and the notes inside referred to a Juan Bosch and some events of 1963 in that country. The letter G from Günter Grass's book was for Guevara and included notes sent by Che Guevara describing events in Africa and about Tamara.

The notes in Szabó's book were also in Spanish and related to Santa Clara, indicating that the S was for the city's name.

The books of Eliot, Márai, and Tolstoy contained notes in German, and considering what Bebéi already knew about the Hungarian's life, he suspected that they referred to Eszter Bider, who was his wife, Morgen Corvinus, his daughter, and Tamara, who was a relative or a close friend. There was a fourth book, Orwell's, where the notes were in German, but those notes, Bebéi did not know to what or whom they were related.

Two books didn't have notes; Xingjian's novel had only a sentence on the last page indicating it was the final book. Bebéi even considered reading it to see if he could understand why it was the last, but the book had more pages than his attention could manage. Zola's novel did not have notes, only the mysterious key Bebéi had hidden in Ilona's office.

He had yet to find the keyword for the other alphabet letters. Some notes were in Russian, Czech, and English. With the Russian notes, he would not have problems since Ludmila, Rasta Bong's wife and a former stripper, was Russian and could help him. Bebéi only had to wait for her return from a trip to Moscow, where she had gone to see her father. He didn't know, however, anyone in Santa Clara who could understand Czech. For the English notes, he was unsure. Moriarty, another of the Useless Brethren members, could be an option to translate them, but the old hippie was permanently stoned and miles away from reality. Bebéi wanted to be cautious, and he would rather wait.

To ensure that nothing was forgotten, he prepared a table indicating the language in which the notes were written and the most probable keyword. Once he finished, he realized that the table was still full of question marks.

A - Auden - French - Algeria
B - Böll- Spanish - Barbarroja ??
C - Conrad - French - Congo
D - Durrell - Spanish - Dominicana?
E - Eliot - German - Eszter?
F - France - Portuguese - ??
G - Grass - Spanish - Guevara
H - Hesse - Hungarian - Horthy
I - Ibsen - English - ?
J - Joyce - Hungarian - Janus
K - Kafka - English - ?

L - Lawrence - Hungarian - Lali
M - Márai - English - Morgen?
N - Neruda - Russian - ?
O - Orwell - German - ?
P - Pasternak - Czech - ?
Q - Quasimodo - French - Quebec?
R - Rilke - Russian - ?
S - Szabó - Spanish - Santa Clara
T - Tolstoy - German - Tamara?
U - Unamuno - English - ?
V - Virgil - English - ?
W - Whitman - English- ?
X - Xingjian - The last book?
Y- Yeats - Russian — ?
Z - Zola — !!!

The next step was clear in his mind: he had to translate the notes from German, and there was a single option for that. He knew telling Frida about the files would be risky, but she was the only one who could help him. Out of caution, he took only part of the notes inside Eliot's book — two letters signed by Eszter Bider and a third one with Eszter's name in the first paragraph. A fourth note, the longest among all books, also seemed to be about Eszter, but Bebéi decided to keep it with him. He knew that when Frida was in a bad mood, she could throw everything in the street, and he did not want anything to happen to that note.

The following morning, while at the embassy, he received a phone call from the law firm that managed the Hungarian apartment. Apparently, they had been informed that Bebéi had received a letter from a relative of the Hungarian, and they wanted to send someone to look at it. Bebéi was suspicious and called Pirilo, who immediately reacted: "Do not give them anything. How did they know about the letter? Bring me what his granddaughter sent, and tell them to call me." After a pause to calm himself and regroup,

Pirilo added, "Do not tell them that you wrote to her. Let's wait and see if she answers; then we'll decide what to do." It seemed an excellent idea to Bebéi.

That afternoon, when Bebéi passed by City Hall to leave the letter with Pirilo, Bebéi crossed paths with his friend, the Lady from the American embassy. The Lady, an exuberant and very decisive woman, was accompanying some American businesspeople on a visit to the Mayor.

"I heard you're now a communist," she said, smiling at Bebéi. "Is it true?"

Bebéi quickly tried to explain that he was neither a communist nor a Nazi and that Hitler's invitation and Che's picture were from the Hungarian.

"I'm just teasing you," she reassured him, "It's been so long since you've come for a visit that I thought you had forgotten me."

The rumor was that the Lady was an important CIA agent responsible for operations in the whole Caribbean. She loved Santa Clara but particularly liked three people: Lola Marlene, her fashion adviser; Grená, with her gossip; and Bebéi, with his simplicity.

It was only late in the afternoon that Bebéi finally had time to look for Frida at the church stairs. Zoubir was also impatient; Bebéi was so busy that he almost did not have time to take him for a walk.

When Bebéi was crossing the street toward the church, he heard someone yelling his name. It was Hector, a retired teacher and maestro of the Municipal School Band. Hector was at the barbershop and wanted to see Che's picture.

Bebéi, who had it with him as proof that the Hungarian was not a Nazi, showed it to Hector.

The old teacher looked at it with emotion on his face. He was a veteran communist and, for him, Che Guevara was legendary. Hector recognized the young Arpad, whom he had known as a music teacher, but what struck his attention was the young woman sitting between Arpad and Guevara in the picture.

"She is Tamara Bunke."

His comment surprised Frida, who had approached them. "Who the fuck is Tamara?"

"She was an East German activist," answered Hector. "She met El Che after the Cuban revolution. Some people say that she was Che's secret lover and others that she was an undercover agent of the Stasi, the Eastern German secret service. What we do know for sure is that she lived a while in Havana and then went with him to Bolivia, where she ended up being arrested and executed."

Hector told what he knew with evident pride in his knowledge. As head of the communist cell of Santa Clara — with four members — he had never taken any action, but he did not complain; at least he had enough free time to study what was happening in the world of socialism and even to know who Tamara Bunke, Che's secret lover, was.

Bebéi, to be gentle with Hector, mentioned that the Hungarian had some letters from El Che, which immediately intrigued Hector and Frida.

"And how did you get these letters?" asked Frida.

"I do not have them," replied Bebéi, still trying to keep the file secret. "The Hungarian granddaughter has them and sent me a few." To avoid further questions that he could not answer, Bebéi quickly took from his pocket one of the letters signed by Eszter Bider and passed it to Frida to translate.

The translation took slightly longer than expected since Frida needed glasses to read, and Hector's were not strong enough. Null-and-void had a better pair, but they could not find it. Robespierre was there with a humongous hangover and was sent to Moses's clothes store to borrow his.

When the glasses finally arrived, Frida started to read in silence. After the first few lines, she asked: "Was your Hungarian friend in some prison camp?"

Bebéi told her what the Budapest archivist had written him.

When he was finishing, Colonel Viera approached them with a strange pair of binoculars in his hands. Hector welcomed him teasing: "Colonel, when we used to meet at the park, nothing interesting happened. Now that I've retired, you guys get involved with Nazis and even with Second World War mysteries," and Hector finished by smiling, "I'm also impressed that you, a well-known orthodox fascist, now talk to people who knew El Che."

The Colonel chose to stay silent, pretending he didn't understand the sarcasm.

Frida, who was also in a good mood, poked him: "What kind of paranoia explains that now you walk all over, looking around with a pair of binoculars?"

Colonel Viera was about to explain when Null-and-void, who had just woken up, approached them. After releasing a huge fart that stuttered down the stairs of the church, he complained, "My goodness, how could anyone concentrate on farting with all this yelling."

Bebéi realized that translating the notes with Frida's help would be more challenging than he had imagined.

13

No one would stop the revolution. The plan for a Great Santa Clara was not just a rumor. While Bebéi mobilized his friends' support to translate the Hungarian's file, the Mayor gathered his team to discuss the final details of the project. The Mayor's meeting was at a secluded cottage inside a beach resort owned by his Italian partner. The place was also used by them for holding private retreats with women from Paris Street.

The Mayor was there with his brother, the Italian, and also a Romanian, who managed all sorts of shady businesses in town and had been responsible for bringing the young women, all beautiful blondes from Eastern Europe who could barely understand what they were speaking and were invited to serve drinks and, if requested, to provide other types of intimate amusements.

The Serbian assistant was with them too, but not for the women since her preference was strong young men, but rather because she liked to be around when the Mayor discussed his political strategy. Another special guest on that Saturday afternoon was an Egyptian who was acting as the representative of the Saudi Arabian investors.

"We cannot underestimate the opposition," said the Mayor, with a wave of the long cigar in his right hand. He spoke and walked in circles around the terrace bordering the pool, wearing a swimsuit that covered his knees. As he disliked walking barefoot, he also had long white socks and black sneakers.

The Italian was listening, lying in a hammock. The others were seated in comfortable straw chairs with colorful cushions, all of them surrounded by palm trees. The atmosphere was informal, and the Romanian divided his attention between the Mayor's words and a Lithuanian woman, who was bare-chested and sitting on his lap.

The Mayor's popularity was skyrocketing thanks to the Serbian's new revolutionary strategy, which could be summarized in three words: populism, lies, and profits. The implementation was an absolute success: the economy was growing thanks to tax reliefs for his friends and an increase in public investment funded by long-term loans. "You don't need to be worried," he always reassured his partners. "We will all be living comfortably in Florida when the loan repayments are due."

Almost everyone in Santa Clara was pleased with him. "Always tell them what they want to hear," was the Serbian's main advice to him. "People don't care about the truth if you give them what they want," and the Mayor was an expert in lying.

Following her advice, he awarded the monopoly of tourist transportation on Santa Clara Bay to the Rastafarian Bobo Ashanti Cooperative.

Initially, he objected to it: "I hate those Rastas with their filthy and disgusting hair."

"But they vote," replied the Serbian, "and everybody loves their parties and music." As he was unconvinced, she added: "Remember what happened when you forced them to pay taxes, and they took their clothes off at the boardwalk in protest? It was a media nightmare. Granting them the monopoly will imply no cost for you and make them happy."

She was right. Thanks to the monopoly and the instructions that the Mayor gave Lieutenant Pirilo — to turn his head every time a Rastafarian was smoking a joint — the Mayor became the living reincarnation of Haile Selassie, praised with speeches at every Rastafarian party.

Also, per Serbian advice, the Mayor joined, with infinite patience, the events of the League of the Catholic ladies, led by his wife. He went even further, and despite an appalling track record of extramarital adventures, he publicly adopted a conservative position against abortion, supporting sexual abstinence among the youth, and making his wife proud.

The Mayor loved to talk and be applauded. Every other day, with no exceptions, he attended a town hall meeting at the park, entertaining his supporters by sharing ludicrous stories and telling whatever they wanted to hear. He promised all thinkable things at those meetings and blamed his opponents for not letting him deliver on his commitments.

The city economy was booming, and City Hall awarded a great number of licenses to hotels, restaurants, and nightclubs — which were only released after a not-so-small financial contribution was paid to his brother. The Mayor's personal wealth was increasing exponentially, forcing him to split his money into several secret accounts in neighboring tax haven countries.

Once a week, he played dominoes in the park with the retirees, and one evening, realizing that the park was dirty, he returned with a broom in his hand to clean it. Of course, he was received by a television crew from the local network that had been previously alerted by his public relations assistant: a Venezuelan woman who, according to Grená, was already in line to be the First Lover after the Jamaican cuckolded him.

He was doing his best to please his supporters, and in return for the work done, he was embezzling money from all city contracts. His partners were also having their coffers filled, so they were quiet that evening, listening to his explanations and enjoying the young models.

"Our Serbian strategist," continued the Mayor, "is worried about Friar Bernard and the whole mess he created complaining about our commissions, but to be honest with you, I have my doubts." He said that mischievously, looking at the Serbian. "The Friar has blue eyes, and I've seen how our Serbian looks at him."

The Serbian didn't change her expression, ignoring his comments, and he continued. "I don't care if he is handsome or not. I want him to shove his pizzeria up his ass, along with that junkie Gigi." Looking again at the Serbian, but now with a strong-minded expression, he added, "If he doesn't pay us, he will not open his business."

The Serbian could not understand the Mayor's behavior. He usually accepted her suggestions, but when she proposed being more lenient with the Friar, the Mayor got angry. She suspected that the reason was Gigi. The Mayor had invited Gigi many times for private dinners, and she had never accepted. But since the Serbian was an experienced woman, she didn't question him publicly and preferred to remain silent.

"We must help the Rastafarians with a new space," the Mayor continued. "Those filthy bastards like what they have now, but we need to relocate them. I have already discussed it with my brother, and we will give them the warehouse that City Hall has at the end of Paris Street. I know that the Koreans were willing to build a casino there. Still, according to the wise advice of our Serbian, it's much better to hand over the place temporarily to the Rastafarians. Later, we will find something for the Koreans." After a theatrical pause, he punctuated: "As you all know, the important thing now is to keep everyone in peace."

The Mayor was excited, and he continued with his considerations about the project: "We've already proposed to the army that they could build a new training center near the airport. With the new center, they will have twice as much space as they have now, and it will not cost us too much. I believe that with this agreement, we have the whole issue of land solved."

The Mayor then opened his arms, smiling, and his friends applauded.

Looking at the Egyptian, the Mayor asked, "Is it true, El Wahun?

"No doubt," replied the Egyptian, who was a little distracted, his hands caressing the tits of a Ukranian who was bored and sleeping on his lap. "We already have almost all the land purchased."

"Did you say all or almost all of it?" The Mayor asked, upset. "Most of it is not enough. We need it all! What if we are missing a piece? How will we build the whole project if we miss a land plot right in the middle?"

"There is no reason to be worried," insisted the Egyptian, waking up the Ukrainian and almost dumping her on the ground. "We have already identified all the lots that were missing, and we are about to sign the agreements. We will not have problems. You can be sure that everything will be settled next week, and we will be able to begin construction."

"That is essential," insisted the Mayor, looking straight into the Egyptian's eyes. "I do not want this land problem to hinder our project."

After a few steps to reorganize his thoughts, the Mayor continued, "The issue about historic preservation of the fort was already settled. Wasn't it?" asked the Mayor to his brother, who was having his nails polished by a young Russian with long legs.

"For sure," replied the brother, "I already lubricated them all. That fort is now in ruins, but thanks to our project, it will be the eatery of the shopping mall where all food franchises will be located." He said that looking at the Russian, who could not understand a word of what he was saying, "Can you imagine? To eat a Big Mac viewing the fort and the yachts at the marina. It will be amazing!"

"That's the idea," completed the Mayor, "to build modern buildings around the old city with hotels, casinos, and shopping malls," and he continued proudly. "We will also widen the boardwalk and let the Saudis build the office and apartment towers. Santa Clara by the Sea will become a great city, and the Spaniards will also help us, building a new resort where wealthy Americans will play golf over the cliffs with an exquisite view of the bay." He continued, excited as if talking to a crowd, "On the other side, after the Paris Street and the new Rastafarian Reggae Hall, we will let the Dutch build their hotel and casino. With all these, we will have two thousand new five-star rooms for tourists and almost a thousand new apartments to be sold to foreigners, particularly

American retirees. Can you believe it? Today, Santa Clara has a thousand houses. Our new city will be four times bigger. And in the heart of all this, the old town, the main tourist attraction, full of fancy shops and restaurants."

He was proud of his vision he could not stop talking. "We'll start with the park in front of the Cathedral. Today there are eight thousand square meters there, squandered with pigeons that dump shit on tourists' heads. And not only that; there is also that bunch of old useless retirees playing dominoes and noisy little kids running and screaming with their dogs. A total waste! Let's surround the park with restaurants and fill it with restaurant tables for tourists. And I do not want El Cheap ones. I want the expensive ones to delight and attract rich tourists." And he continued, looking to the Serbian. "Those living in the city today will have to move away." When he said that, he opened his arms to his friends as if asking for their endorsement. "What else can we do?" As nobody answered, he went on, "It's progress. They had the city for so many years and didn't do shit. Now it's our turn, and we will make Santa Clara a great town. We will do in four years what they could not do in five hundred."

The Mayor was excited, which was understandable; he had already agreed with the Saudis that the construction companies he owned with his partners would participate in and profit from the entire construction.

"The main embassies," he continued, "are already on board. Even the French are happy. In their holy naivete, they think they will decide from whom we will hire the services. Bullshit — we will be the ones to choose. The Americans also support our strategy, and I promised them heaven and earth. Of course, I will not give them everything they want, but it will be too late when they realize it. We must, however, keep our eyes wide open to the Lady of the Secret Service; she has now become some kind of protector of the old city. It's true that she can't do anything against her government's instructions but, anyway, it's better to keep our eyes open. The Spaniards are quiet; they will have their hotels, and the Italians, we leave them in the hands of our friend here," and he pointed to his Italian partner. "He is negotiating a good agreement for all of us. What we have to do now is to force the legislators to pass the new laws that will facilitate local residence for rich foreigners and cancel international deportation agreements that our country has signed in the past. It is essential to create conditions for all wealthy people, thieves or not, to come and live here. Let's not ask where they came from or how they made their money. If they want to live in Santa Clara, no problem, we will protect them." He then added, smiling, "Of course, as long as they pay us a nice commission."

While all this was happening at the resort, in the old town, the local opposition to the project also gathered at Ilona's Café. There were ten in all. Friar Bernard tried to persuade Ilona and Rasta Bong to rent a good printer so that he and Jordi could launch a weekly newspaper. The amount of money needed for the printer was not very large, but it represented an expense, and the Friar was trying to justify it: "If we don't do it, we will never be able to resist the Mayor's plans."

14

The Hungarian saw the Germans playing. It was only on Tuesday that Bebéi finally gathered Frida and Hector in his living room to go through the notes written in German. He had made little progress during the weekend and invited his two friends to his apartment. There, they would drink good wine, a condition Frida imposed to accept the proposal and have all the quietness they needed. The seagull and Zoubir were on the balcony, peacefully watching the city lights.

For Hector, as an old communist, helping Bebéi understand notes describing El Che with details of his relationship with Tamara was far more interesting than anything he had done in two decades as head of Santa Clara's secret communist cell.

After reading the first note, Frida explained, "At the war's end, Arpad was deported, and his wife Eszter fled to East Germany to live in Berlin with her mother."

"Imagine what Berlin would be like," Hector commented excitedly. "I once saw a great Rossellini movie, _Germany, Year Zero_, showing the city completely devastated ..."

Frida interrupted him. She was unwilling to waste time talking about movies: "From what I understand from the second note, Eszter joined the Communist Party to find Arpad. She knew he had been deported to the Soviet Union and wanted to know where he was. From what she wrote, it was thanks to the Communist Party that she managed to survive and find out where your Hungarian neighbor was detained."

She continued reading a few more lines and then explained: "This is a letter Eszter sent at the end of 1947, and as Arpad was deported in 1945, it means that your neighbor spent at least two years freezing in a gulag prison camp. The letter was written during the winter, and I can't conceive how that woman traveled to Kolyma in Russian Siberia to search for him, but what we know for sure, from a note written by Arpad, is that she found him."

"But how did he write it," Bebéi interrupted. "My friend from Budapest said the Hungarian never went to school and only knew how to play the violin."

Frida tried to answer: "I believe he learned it later when he returned to Berlin and went to live with Eszter. On another note in 1954, he mentioned that since he could no longer play the violin, he had to learn a new profession. And he also wrote *Eszter taught me everything I had to learn to work.*"

Frida continued patiently explaining in an unusually good mood — probably thanks to the quality of the wine Bebéi was serving, a Christmas gift he had received from the French ambassador. "I don't know what learning means, but I imagine it includes how to write." Frida smiled and made an observation. "Can you believe what a German woman is capable of? She crossed Siberia to save her man, supported him, taught him how to work and even to write."

Hector took advantage of Frida's comment to ask her if there was anything in the notes about El Che and his lover. Frida didn't like to be interrupted, but she answered his question, clarifying that there was no mention of Tamara in Eszter's letters but that Arpad mentioned her in one of his notes: *"In 1952, the Bunken arrived in Berlin to live with us."* And there is something else before that," Frida added, "In 1951, Arpad and Eszter's daughter was born, and they called her Morgen. He even wrote, *Although she is the daughter of a German-Jewish mother, Morgen has all the features of her Gypsy grandmother and the same color of skin and hair.*"

Frida paused for a second to check Bebéi's reaction and continued. "Morgen was born in 1951, Tamara arrived in '52, and in '54,

Arpad returned to Budapest to watch a soccer match. The Magyars, as Arpad wrote, were the best soccer team in the world and were going to play against England for a World Cup preparation match."

Hector and Bebéi looked at Frida, surprised. How could a soccer game be so essential as to be saved in a personal file?

"From what your friend from Budapest wrote," Frida continued, "the two things that reminded him of his mother were the violin and soccer. Arpad wrote in this note,

I will never forget the notes of the Hungarian Dance and the line up of Grosics's team; Buzanski, Lorant, and Lantos; Bozsik and Zacharias; Toth, Kocsis, Hidegkuti, Puskas, and Czibor.

Frida was delighted by that unexpected mention of a soccer team and continued translating word by word the notes, including one that Arpad wrote to Eszter:

I know that, for Otto, it seems absurd to return to Budapest for a soccer game, and I thank you and him for helping to fulfill my dream. I felt it would be necessary. We won before at Wembley, but the game now was in Budapest, in our Hungary. Before going to the stadium, I walked through the streets where I played with my mother. I'm sure she was also there with me to watch the game. I've never seen a similar celebration in that city. All recollections I had from Budapest are memories of sorrow: my mother dancing, the Soviets arriving, the street where they executed my father, and the building where they seized me, but yesterday was different. People rejoiced on both sides of the river, and you can't imagine how it was! The stadium was not full, there were many restrictions, and many were afraid, but many people like me wanted to celebrate and shout joyfully for our country. Our Magyars did not disappoint us. From the beginning until the end, it was a Hungarian game. We scored seven goals and the British one. After the game was over, we went out to celebrate. How I wish I could have played my violin. I am sure Lali would come from wherever she is to dance with me in the streets of Buda. That's all I can say. Let me forget politics for a moment; the Soviets are everywhere. Nagy tries to make some reforms, but there are few hopes.

"Who was this Otto?" Bebéi asked anxiously, and Frida tried to respond.

"From these notes, it seems he was a friend who helped them both. Eszter had worked for him since her arrival in Berlin, and it was Otto who helped her find Arpad in Siberia. It was also him who later got a job for Arpad when they were already living in Berlin and helped him return to Budapest to see the Hungarian team defeat the British."

"Curious," Hector said, "getting out of East Germany and going to Budapest then was not easy. If Otto helped Arpad, he would be someone powerful. He would probably be one the young activists that emerged in Germany right after the war." Hector then added. "This Nagy mentioned in the note was the Hungarian who led the 1956 revolution against the Soviets."

Bebéi was listening and thinking that Otto was probably the keyword for the notes inside Orwell's book.

"Soccer gave the Hungarian joy but also great sadness," said Frida, interrupting Bebéi's thoughts. "Look what he wrote," and she translated,

After the Budapest game against the English, the Hungarian team traveled to Switzerland to play the World Cup, and we were the favorites. In the first phase, we easily beat the Germans, the Koreans, and the Turks. Then, we defeated the two great South American finalists of the 1950 World Cup: Brazil and Uruguay. Only one game was missing; we would become world champions if we beat the Germans.

"The game was in Bern in Switzerland," Frida explained. "Arpad again went to watch the game thanks to Otto, and to that game, he took Eszter with him. According to his words,

It rained, and what they played was not soccer but a war. The first half ended tied. The Hungarians attacked with all the strength of Puskas and Czibor, but the Germans resisted, and the second half was a nightmare; six minutes before the end, Rahn scored 3–2. The Hungarians still scored a goal, but according to the referee, Puskas was offside. We were the favorites, but the Germans performed a miracle in Bern. Germany became the world champion. Unbelievable! Regardless of what I suffered in Siberia. I think that match was the worst day of my life, and I was impressed by Eszter's reaction. She had every right to be happy because she was German like them, but she was sad and hugged me. When we left the stadium, we walked for hours, and she took me to the train station, where we returned home. I don't remember anything else that day. I remember that when we arrived in Berlin, the Germans were partying, but Eszter was sad at my side.

"From what we understand," said Frida, completely entangled by Arpad's story. "The great passion of your Hungarian neighbor after he returned from Siberia was soccer. He did not play the violin anymore, but we still don't know why. Eszter and he continued to work for Otto, but it was unclear what they were doing. Our only mention is that Arpad was more interested in soccer than politics."

"I think that is quite understandable," interrupted Hector. "After living through the Great War and seeing his country invaded by the Germans and the Soviets and spending many years in a concentration camp in Siberia, I'm not surprised that he was not interested in politics."

"The one who was interested in politics seemed to be Eszter," interrupted Frida, "but it's curious that from what Arpad wrote, she was a rebellious communist. Look what he wrote about her:"

Initially, she defended what was happening in East Germany, but Soviet interference was overwhelming. She didn't talk about this with anyone, but I can see that she frequently argues with Otto.

At that moment, they had to interrupt their conversation; Jordi arrived at the apartment to visit Bebéi and the seagull. He was also bringing good news: Ilona and Rasta Bong had agreed to pay for the printer, and they were ready to publish the newspaper.

Jordi was happy, but Frida, Hector, and Bebéi were too curious about the Hungarian's fate to be interested in anything else. There was still the long letter Bebéi had kept to himself, which he finally gave to Frida. It was a letter written by Arpad to Otto that for some unknown reason had never been sent — or perhaps had been sent, and, for some reason, had returned to Arpad.

Before reading, Frida asked Bebéi to open another bottle of wine. The letter looked promising. It was written at the end of 1956 and described how Eszter died.

15

Eszter died confronting the Soviets. It's almost ironic to think that in Bebéi's living room, reading that letter, there was a drunkard who, in his youth, tried to change the world by bombing train stations, an old communist who hoped to build a better society, but had only managed to be a good husband; and Jordi, young and a firm believer in the power of political demonstrations.

The Hungarian had never been popular in Santa Clara, and the few people who noticed him walking silently on the streets could have never imagined that the lonely and shy man who lived on the second floor of the amber manor had gone through what that letter described. *My dear friend Otto* — that's how the December 1954 letter Frida translated that evening began.

It's not easy for me to write, but I have no other choice. I am not brave enough to meet you and look into your eyes. You knew that we disagreed with some of your ideas and positions. Many times, I witnessed you and Eszter arguing. But despite our differences, we had no right to deceive you. The truth is that we betrayed you, and everything turned out very badly. I know that if it were not for your support, we would not have been able to leave Budapest and return to Berlin. Thanks to your friendship, I survived, but Eszter did not. She is no longer with us, and before she died, she made me swear I would tell you that you have always been as valuable to her as Morgen and me. She said more. On the train, wounded when we returned, she said that only the future would tell us the truth, but whoever is right, and no matter where in the universe each of us will be, our friendship, gratitude, and respect will be eternal. Eszter also asked me to tell you everything that happened, which explains why I am writing this letter.

We were in contact with friends from Budapest for a long time, and we did it behind your back. They believed, like Eszter, that our countries needed to be freed from Soviet rule. She told you many times that we could never follow relevant policies for Germany since we are compelled to favor what is essential for them. We were following from afar the struggle of our Hungarian friends against the Rákosi government and in July when he resigned, everyone's enthusiasm, especially Eszter's, was contagious. She spent many days looking for someone to tell us the latest news from Budapest. I presume you now understand why you were arguing so much. Eszter did not tell you what she was doing. She knew you would not be able to keep it a secret; your loyalty is evident. But you must understand that her heart was with the fight of our friends in Budapest. And you know as well as I Eszter's strength and determination. Whenever she wanted something, no one could ever stop her. Hitler did not want her because she was Jewish, and she resisted. Horthy did not want her to be a Communist, and she ignored him. Soviets wanted me dead, and she saved me, and even though you, our dearest friend, wanted her to be a disciplined communist and respectful of the decisions of the Party, Eszter was a rebel. She never accepted other's impositions. I even think that she had some of my mother's Gypsy blood, and probably that's why I loved her so much.

With the news arriving from Hungary, she became restless, and I'm the one who proposed we travel there. She was so excited that we decided to go even though we knew it was risky. Tamara could care for Morgen, and our friends would help us cross the borders. We did not tell you; you would never have allowed us to travel. We knew that it was a betrayal, but she thought that by going to Budapest, she would better understand what it meant to be free from the Soviets. Maybe then she would be able to convince you. She knew you could never do what we were doing, but deep in her heart, she believed you had the same doubts. But your discipline and the German attitude, as she used to say, would never allow you to question the Party.

Once the decision was made, we spent months preparing for our trip. Only in October could we leave and travel by train to Prague and, from there, to Budapest. We arrived on the morning of October 22. Can you imagine what it was like for Eszter, after so many years out of Hungary to return to Budapest exactly on that Monday? Luckily, we had slept on the train. After that day, we barely had a night's sleep. We arrived very early. I had been in Budapest for the soccer game, but Eszter hadn't. She spent the rest of the morning strolling by the riverside. By early afternoon, it was impossible to keep walking. The excitement in the city was enormous. Everywhere, young people were gathering to discuss the list of claims made by the students from the Technical University; everything the Hungarians wanted and never dared to say was there. The first point called for the withdrawal of Soviet troops from Hungarian territory, and it also proposed to have secret elections for all party positions and direct elections for the National Assembly. As you can imagine, Eszter was euphoric since that was precisely what she wished for Germany. The sixteen-point document also proposed to bring to justice those who had committed crimes against democracy and included two emblematic issues: the immediate destruction of Stalin's statue and the removal of the communist star from the Hungarian flag that represented the Soviet dominion over the country.

Since our friends were journalists, we spent the first night at their Union Headquarters, making plans for the next day. They were planning a joint demonstration with the students in front of the statue of General József Bem, one of the heroes of the Hungarian Revolution of 1848.

We woke up early on Tuesday to prepare for the demonstration. Those who were extra optimistic were saying that we could assemble a thousand people in the park, and in the early afternoon, when we got there, we could not believe what we saw. More than twenty thousand people were already there, and in whatever direction you looked, people were arriving. Veres spoke first for the journalists, and then a group of university students read the sixteen points of the statement one by one.

Emotion took over the park, and more people were joining us with flags in their hands. It was as if all Hungarians were united in their thoughts, and the city once again belonged to us. It was impossible to control the euphoria that took hold of the people when the loudspeakers began to broadcast the verses of "Nemzeti Dal," the poem written by Petöfi after the revolution of 1848. "We were slaves up till now," we shouted all together, "Cannot rest in a slave land." Eszter, your German and Jewish friend, stood beside me in tears, reciting, "By the God of the Hungarians, we vow. We vow that we will be slaves no longer!" And all of us, euphoric, waving our flags after years of resignation and silence in which we let the Soviets command our country as if we had no dignity at all. We were there that day as strong as the sun that illuminated us, boldly defying the Soviets who executed my father, who deported me to Siberia and kept my country in captivity for more than ten years. My chest burst, and Eszter was all tears and joy at my side.

Listening to everyone in the park recite the verses of Petöfi I felt as Puskas and the Magyars on the soccer field defending our national team. Our Hungarian homeland, of which my father spoke so much and that was destroyed by the Treaty of Trianon, was there at that park proudly saying: Here we stand!

Near us, a young student cut the Soviet star at the center of his flag with scissors. We saw him do it, and when he began to wave the flag with that hole in the middle, everyone imitated him. In a few minutes, all over the park, we could see the Hungarian tricolor flags with no Soviet star blossoming and flying above our heads. There were so many! You could look at the river and see flags waving on all bridges and even on the Pest side.

Eszter wanted to cross the bridge towards the Parliament, and they announced on the radio that we were more than two hundred thousand people demonstrating in the streets. Can you believe it? After years of oppression and silence; two hundred times more people than we expected that morning. It was different from those demonstrations we have here in East Germany organized by the Party when you know exactly how many people are there, who they are, and until when they will stay. In Budapest, the demonstration was not an imposition but a roar coming from the people's hearts.

At eight o'clock, we heard on a small radio the speech of Gerö condemning the movement. Listening to him say he did not recognize what we claimed in the streets enraged us. We, the people in the streets, decided to take justice into our own hands. One of the sixteen points had already been achieved: the Soviet symbol had been excised from the Hungarian flag, but another one was missing: to overthrow the statue of Stalin. What very few would have dared to imagine that morning happened right before our eyes on that evening. The crowd put down that colossal statue. It was not yet ten o'clock, and the icon was already on the ground. Eszter, your dear friend Eszter, was one of the women who put the Hungarian flag without a Soviet star fluttering in what were once the boots of the dictator's image.

Every minute, someone approached us, telling us about a new confrontation, and we realized things were taking a violent turn. We heard shots, and the first police vehicles were burned. I do not think anyone in Budapest slept; it was a long night of battles between demonstrators and police. What we did not know by then; it was also the night when Gerö asked for support from the Soviets to suppress the opposition.

At three in the morning, we finally sat in an apartment owned by a dentist we met that night. I do not remember his name, and I doubt he remembered ours, but we share a piece of cheese and bread — the first thing we ate that day. It was only then that we noticed, from the terrace of the apartment, the Soviet tanks entering the city. The radio did not announce it, and no one knew what to do. We remained there, waiting for the morning sun, before venturing back into the streets. When we left the apartment, everything was silent. The Soviet soldiers and their tanks were waiting for us at every corner, and the city was completely taken.

We thought our battle was lost, but when we met our companions, we quickly realized that no one was willing to accept the dream was over. Little by little, the first barricades appeared, and the students took the initiative. All they had known since childhood was the Great War and the Soviet invasion. For the first time, they were experiencing the sweet taste of freedom and were not going to surrender. You will not believe what happened; nobody was worried about dying. I confess that I was afraid at times, but I think I was one of the few. Everyone there wanted to fight until death, and now I realize this was the feeling that moved Eszter.

Someone told us that students were distributing weapons stolen from a police station, and without time to think, we were already at one of the barricades, preparing and distributing Molotov cocktails. Eszter, at my side, had a pistol with her. At every minute, someone was telling us about a new victory, a burned tank, a street picked up, and it seemed that no one would stop us. We did not know that among the Soviet troops, there were instructions to avoid confrontations, and we mistakenly believed that we were the ones who were intimidating them.

When the sun returned and the morning fog dispersed, Eszter and I were at a barricade before the Parliament. There, we heard that the Hungarian Government had fallen, and the principal ministers fled to the airport and Moscow. It sounded like another dream. We heard from the radio that the opposition was forming a revolutionary government led by Nagy. You know very well that Nagy's ideas represented a new hope for Eszter, and she was not the only one. An enormous enthusiasm took over the streets and parks of Budapest. Tanks could not easily move through the narrow streets where Molotov cocktails were thrown from apartment balconies. As the Soviets had no authorization to fire back, they could not protect themselves. Many chose to seek defensive positions in sheltered places.

The street fighting continued throughout the weekend. No one knew who was giving the orders, and everything was chaotic, until on Sunday, they announced a ceasefire. On Monday, after a whole week fighting in the streets of Budapest, Eszter and I finally slept in a room with a bed just for us.

We woke up the following day happy, and Eszter was exceptionally beautiful. We had breakfast with a woman named Lusja, an elementary school teacher who was celebrating that she was finally free. At that breakfast, Eszter and I decided that we would go back to Berlin, get Morgen, and return to Budapest to live in a socialist country without having to follow the Soviet Politburo's instructions.

Life slowly returned to normal. By Tuesday, most of the Soviet tanks had left the city. We attended meetings with members of the new government to discuss the organization of the whole town. We debated who would take care of the new schools, the militias, and even who would collect the garbage. We were all euphoric, ignoring that while we were dreaming, the Soviets were regrouping their army for a new invasion, but this time with much more organization and much more strength.

We worked the whole week as if we were citizens of Budapest, and we even sent a telegram to Tamara saying that we would return to get Morgen. Then, the bloody Saturday came. The Soviet army invited a delegation from the new government to negotiate the terms of their complete withdrawal from the country. To everyone's surprise, however, when the commission met them, they were all arrested. On Sunday, November 4th, Soviet tanks invaded the city again. The militia were headless after the main leaders were arrested. The confusion and anxiety went on all night. At six in the morning, we listened to Nagy making a desperate plea on the radio. The country was being taken, and we no longer knew what to do.

Some tried to resist; if we had defeated the Soviet tanks once, we could repeat it. We did not know that the soldiers' orders were now to strike without pity. The few people who tried to approach the tanks with Molotovs were hit, and among them, our Eszter. I cannot tell you how it happened because I was not by her side. I went with a group to get weapons for our militia, and when I returned, she was wounded and bleeding. What happened next, you already know. I got in touch with you and, thanks to your help, we managed to take a train to return. But the bullet that was in her chest had come very close to her lung, and she could not resist. We arrived in Prague on the 8th, where I heard that János Kádár was taking over the government with the support of the Soviets. The next day, Eszter died, before arriving in Berlin, before embracing Morgen, and before even asking your forgiveness for our betrayal.

16

Tamara and El Che in Africa. "Who would believe it?" was Hector's comment. "The Hungarian who was shy and nobody paid attention to was a great violinist who played for Hitler, a prisoner of war in a Siberian gulag, and a revolutionary who fought on the streets of Budapest."

Jordi was even more surprised. "We thought that he only cared about his music lessons." After a pause, he added, "I must tell this to Cristine: her music teacher, who seemed clumsy, made Molotov cocktails on the barricades to burn Soviet tanks."

Frida, who was not a bit impressed by the Hungarian's revolutionary past, shot with disgust: "I'll tell you what I think, and I know you're not going to like it, but this Otto was from the Stasi."

Hector understood what she was saying, but Bebéi and Jordi had no idea what Stasi meant. Hector explained: "The Stasi was the East Germany Secret Service, but secret service agents were not as friendly as the Lady of the American Embassy in those days. They were harsh, distrustful, and controlled everyone's movements."

"If *he-ah* was from the Stasi," said Frida, beginning to show that the bottles of wine were confusing her words, "it means that Eszter was from the Stasi too and that your *neighborror* who was not a Nazi was an even greater son of a bitch working for the Stasi."

Bebéi was alarmed by the comment, and Hector tried to clarify: "Better not to rush to conclusions. We know that the Hungarian loved Eszter and that she died in 1956. We are not sure that he was Stasi. We know he worked for Otto and probably lost his job after this letter. We also know that he could no longer play the violin, that he liked to watch soccer games, had a daughter called Morgen, and was friends with Tamara."

Bebéi and Jordi were listening to Hector, but Frida was showing signs of restlessness. Hector tried to convince her to look at the notes that mentioned Tamara Bunke; they were brief notes written by Tamara herself. There was also a photograph of her, still a child, and on the back was written *Tamara was born in November 1937, the same month that Lali died.*

"Tamara was a beautiful woman, *hic.* Your neighbor probably fell in love with her after Eszter's death," Frida commented.

"I do not think so," replied Hector. "Arpad was in his thirties, and Tamara was only eighteen."

"You are a moron and an old moralist," Frida replied, barely keeping her sobriety. "Don't forget that El Che was about the same age as this son-of-a-bitch Stasi neighbor of Bebéi."

Hector insisted that Frida translate Tamara's notes, but Bebéi was worried. He knew that when Frida got drunk, she was unpredictable and violent.

"There is a note from 1954," she said. "I believe it was written when Arpad and Ezster went to Switzerland to watch the soccer game." Frida paused for a moment before reading it. She seemed dizzy.

Enjoy the game. Thanks for trusting me and leaving your daughter with me. She is a charm, and like her grandmother and her mother, she is rebellious and loves freedom. I have already discovered that it is absolutely impossible to tell little Morgen what she should or should not do.

As the wine bottles were empty, Frida started drinking from a bottle of scotch Bebéi had bought for his guests.

"Another note from Tamara, and this one is from 1957," said Frida, burping.

How are the Algerians? Do they look like the Argentineans I described to you? Morgen is a lovely girl. We are all happy to have her with us. Do not worry about anything. I still think you'd be better off here in Berlin, but Mr. Otto told me we must respect your decision.

Bebéi interrupted Frida to explain that from the notes in Auden's book, he understood that after Ezster's death, Arpad went to Algiers. Hector also clarified the mention of Argentinians, explaining that Tamara was born and lived in Buenos Aires until she was fifteen.

"Was it this Stasi bastard son of a bitch who sent Arpad to Algiers?" asked Frida, expressing an aversion for Otto.

"I don't think so," interfered Jordi, getting engaged with the stories he was hearing. "The note from Tamara implies that Otto wanted him to stay in Berlin."

Bebéi then recalled that in the letter of his archivist friend from Budapest, there was something about Admiral Horthy wanting Arpad to accept the work his friend, the *ambassador*, was offering. "Maybe he accepted that job?" said Bebéi.

"But what kind of job was it?" Hector asked.

Bebéi went to pick up the letter and reread the passage:

It is imperative to accept the work that our friend the ambassador is offering. ... although you can no longer defend your homeland by playing the Hungarian Dance, your father would be very proud to know that his son is fighting to regain the freedom of all Hungarians.

Hector repeated, trying to understand: "A job offered by the ambassador where he would fight for freedom. What work could this be?"

Frida was clearly becoming impatient, so Hector decided to focus her attention on translating Tamara's notes, leaving all digressions about the Hungarian's job for later.

"There's another note from 1959," said Frida.

How nice to know that you are coming to Berlin, but I am sad to hear they transferred you to another African country. I confess my sadness is not because of you; I know you are doing your best to overcome Eszter's loss, but I feel sad for Morgen. She's very special to me. But do not worry; you are doing the right thing. Although I love that quarrelsome and rebellious girl, it's better for her to be close to her father.

With that note, Frida's patience was over. There was one more note where Tamara mentioned El Che, but it was impossible to hold her there.

"So far, I've behaved very well." With those words, she stood up, walked staggering toward the door and explained before leaving, "Your seagull might be delighted to stay inside your apartment, but I'm like Lali, *hic*, and I'd rather feel the sweet smell of piss in the street."

Bebéi didn't question her; at least they had made progress. They didn't know yet what sort of work the Hungarian had done, but they knew that after Eszter's death, he went to live alone in Algeria. From there, *they* transferred him to another African city, Kinshasa in Congo — which Bebéi knew from Conrad's book notes — and he took his daughter Morgen with him.

"But who are 'they' who transferred him?" asked Bebéi, and neither Hector nor Jordi could answer.

"We also know," mentioned Hector, "that in 1960, he returned to Germany, at least for a short time. That is when they took a picture of Tamara, Arpad, and El Che at that restaurant in Leipzig."

Hector was enjoying learning about the Hungarian's life. Arpad had been his colleague at school; Hector led the band and Arpad was the music teacher. They had several times discussed musical arrangements. Hector's genuine interest now was not Arpad but Guevara. Frida was no longer there to translate the notes inside Günter Grass's book, but Hector had done a few notes with her that allowed them, at least, to understand what some messages signed by Guevara were about. On the first message of '61, Guevara wrote about Tamara in Havana. On the message of '64, he mentioned that he was going to Congo and wanted to meet Arpad. Finally, on the one of 1966, he thanked Arpad for everything he had done to help him *even from afar* and ended up saying *Too bad we did not achieve our dream.*

With those notes in hand, Hector made a passionate speech that Jordi followed absorbedly, explaining that Guevara went to

Congo, leading a Cuban internationalist army to support the Simba movement against the dictator Mobutu.

"Maybe Arpad and El Che were in Congo at the same time," suggested Jordi.

Hector could not answer. He needed to check the dates. Bebéi suggested they talk to Princess. "He knows everything," Bebéi assured his friends. "When he is not singing as Lola Marlene, he is always reading those books he sells."

Before they left Bebéi's apartment, Jordi explained his plans for the newspaper. For him, opposing the Mayor was even more critical than understanding the Hungarian's adventures.

"Our idea is to launch a weekly newspaper. We need it. Those national newspapers don't deal with issues that are important to our city. Friar Bernard wants to denounce the Mayor's bribes, and Carmela and I are mainly concerned about the New Santa Clara project. If the Mayor goes ahead with his plans, we will all be forced to move away." Jordi continued excitedly, "We will begin with a four-page newspaper. We can print it on one page and fold it. It has to be simple because we have no money. We will print two thousand copies and have the money to finance the first issue. We are storing our material in Carmela's house, printing it in the back of Rasta's barbershop, and using Gigi and Friar Bernard's apartment for our editorial meetings."

"It might not be enough to challenge the Mayor and his friends, but it is surely a good beginning" was Hector's comment.

From there they walked to Princess's apartment but he was not there. "It's Tuesday," Bebéi said, recalling that on Tuesday night Princess always performed at La Gata Caliente, the harbor's drag queen cabaret. "I can tell you. It is useless to go there. Princess is the main star and is always surrounded by his admirers. Let's talk to him tomorrow."

17

For whom did the Hungarian work? The following evening, after work at the embassy, Bebéi met Jordi at the park with Zoubir. Hector could not join them; the former head of the communist cell had to help Doña Lourdes with the groceries.

Princess/Lola Marlene received them at his fashion atelier and was pleased to know they had questions. Designing clothes made his life more comfortable, but his passion was the books and everything inside them. The bookstore was doing relatively better. Following a suggestion of Rasta Bong, he had bought an Italian machine and was serving coffee for clients at small tables placed on the sidewalk. As he explained, "If they do not buy books, at least they feel the pleasure of having a good coffee while looking at them."

Princess realized that the conversation would be long. To be more comfortable, he changed Lola Marlene's elegant turquoise and yellow attire for something more appropriate for a history discussion: a pair of old jeans and an *almost* subtle white shirt with little pink flowers.

Princess suggested they sit around one of the sidewalk tables. From there they would watch Zoubir playing with his dog friends at the park.

Princess was thrilled to talk about Africa: "Better start with Congo in the sixties," he said, sipping his cappuccino from a tall, elegant glass. "I understand from what you told me that it was during that period that the Hungarian, who was Che Guevara's friend, lived in Kinshasa." Princess smiled, excited by gossiping about such a celebrity. "If you want to understand those notes, I will have to tell you what happened when the North Americans and Soviets sought to increase their international influence as part of the Cold War."

Princess then explained, talking loudly, hoping he could attract the interest of some young students sitting beside them. He loved crowds. "At that time, the world was split between the first world of the capitalist countries; the second of the Communists led by the Soviet Union; and the third, comprised by the least developed nations including the whole continent of Africa."

Bebéi was a bit confused by those sophisticated explanations. He knew, however, that for Princess, it was essential to describe the context where everything had happened.

"The Congo," continued Princess, "was one of the first African colonies to seek independence and one of the countries that suffered most in its fight." With Bebéi's papers in his hands, he continued. "The first note in Conrad's book is from 1960. From what I understand, someone close to the North Americans wrote it. The note mentions Patrice Lumumba, the first African leader to rise against colonialism.

"The Congo was a Belgian colony, and Patrice led the fight for independence. He was brilliant, and the note that the Hungarian kept inside the book confirms it by recognizing that *Patrice was an intelligent man capable of leading the newly independent nation of Congo*. I believe, however, it is a note written by someone from the North American side since they proposed his elimination after speaking well of him. Ironic, no? According to the note, *his ideas of creating a democracy where everyone had equal rights had approached Lumumba from the Soviets*. The curious thing is that the same note mentions another Congolese leader, but regarding this one, the note only mentions negative things — someone incapable, corrupt, and violent. The note even says *some people consider him a beast, and probably they are correct, but at least he is our beast*. That is why I'm sure someone from the American side wrote it. The note even mentions that the other guy *would not be able to lead the country, but he can help us to liquidate Lumumba,* adding, *Then we will find some-one to take care of him.* After saying that, Princess stopped and added with a mischievous look, "That leads me to a bigger question. Did you find out what the Hungarian was doing in Congo?"

"When he was in Germany before he went to Africa, we suspect he was working for the Stasi," was Jordi's reply.

Bebéi did not say anything; he was confused by everything he was listening to. Lumumba was good and had to be eliminated, and the other guy was a beast but was *our beast* and should be supported. Had he got it right?

"That sounds strange," said Princess, opening his arms theatrically. "First, I do not believe the Stasi was active in Africa. Among Communists, it was the Soviets with their KGB who took care of Africa; the Stasi was an agency focused on preserving communism in East Germany. This letter was probably written by someone working for the CIA, the agency our friend the Lady works in. They were the ones coordinating American political activities in Africa at that time."

After making this comment, Princess paused with an exaggerated suspicious look. He did not say anything and continued reading the second note from 1965. "This note is even more curious. From what you have told me, the Hungarian was a friend of El Che. I know for sure since I read a book Guevara wrote about it, *The Congo Diary,* that Guevara was in Congo in 1965 supporting the Simba Revolution. This note seems to be written by the North Americans and describes several executions Congo's government authorities ordered against his opponents and the need to support them. It also mentions *the importance of convincing the Tutsis to support Mobutu and fight against the people of Pierre Mulele.* Princess was getting intrigued. "This note was not written by a Che Guevara friend. It's evident. It was precisely Pierre Mulele's group that Guevara was supporting with its Cuban fighters."

Princess changed his expression, and again, with mischievous eyes, he provoked his listeners with a not-so-innocent question:

"Was the Hungarian working for the Stasi, or did he work for the CIA?"

Bebéi and Jordi kept looking at Princess, speechless.

Princess insisted with a childlike smirk, "Even worse, was the Hungarian a double agent?"

Bebéi looked at Jordi, hoping he would say something, but Jordi was as confused as himself.

Princess was proud; his comments had attracted the students' attention, and he ordered another cappuccino. "This is more interesting than a Le Carré novel," and, looking to his newly acquired crowd, Princess added with overdone gestures, "Please tell us, what else do you know about this Hungarian, since I'm already in love with him?"

Jordi tried to answer, a little embarrassed to speak to some students he didn't know: "Bebéi has a letter from Admiral Horthy, regent of Hungary, where he suggested that Arpad accept the job that an 'ambassador' was offering him, but we do not know who this ambassador might be."

Princess walked inside the bookstore to check a few books about the Second World War and brought with him a notebook to look at few sites on the internet; puzzles like these enticed Princess — particularly if there was a crowd watching. "Horthy's great friend was the American ambassador John Montgomery, which reinforces my suspicion: "Was Arpad working for the Reds or the North Americans?"

Jordi immediately mentioned Che's letter where he had written that Arpad had helped in Congo and used the expression "from afar."

Princess insisted, "I believe the Hungarian was a double agent."

Bebéi's imagination started to fly higher than the seagulls. How many books had he read telling stories of international spies, and now he discovered that a double agent from the Cold War had lived in the same building. It did not matter that he was gone and Bebéi had never met him. Arpad lived in an apartment like his. And all his books and notes were now in Bebéi's apartment. He immediately recalled the key. What mysteries could the key stored in Zola's novel unveil, but he prudently didn't tell, since with all those mentions of spies and the CIA, more than ten young students were surrounding their table. They were so many that Zoubir approached the table to check if Bebéi was okay.

They were all engaged but couldn't continue. Princess had to get ready for a special performance. "Some rich Arabs were extremely impressed by my performance singing Edith Piaf songs last night, and invited me to make a private presentation on their yacht."

Bebéi and Jordi went with him to his apartment, hoping to quickly review the three notes inside Conrad's book while Princess did his makeup.

The first one, written by Arpad, described a plan to support the development of a city called Kisangani. It quoted the priority actions to develop the whole region between Kisangani and Bukavu, on the border with Rwanda.

"Kisangani is the name of the city where Laurence, the Hungarian's granddaughter, lives," commented Bebéi, explaining that he had written her a letter.

The second note criticized a plan by the Soviets to encourage the fight between two African groups, the Hutus and the Tutsis, to destabilize North America's control of the country.

"Whoever wrote it," Princess said, "proposed 'neutralizing the Soviet influence within the Hutus by helping the Tutsis to attack them.'"

The third was from 1974 and described the importance of persuading Mobutu to fight the MPLA forces in Angola. According to the note, *Agostinho Neto, the head of the MPLA, was close to the Soviets.* The note also mentioned it was essential to convince Mobutu that *if Agostinho Neto gained control over Angola, he would sell the oil from Cabinda to the Soviets.* It also pointed out: *Although this will never happen, since we are negotiating with Angolans to ensure the access of US companies to the oil, it's crucial to persuade Mobutu to fight against him.*

That's all they could accomplish. After finishing his makeup, Princess went inside his bedroom for a few minutes and returned wearing an elegant black dress. On the street, a white limousine was waiting for her.

Bebéi and Jordi stayed a few more minutes walking at the park, watching Zoubir run with his friends, and Bebéi commented, "After all these adventures, he came to live in Santa Clara, where he had no friends, and nobody noticed when he vanished. Who can understand this?"

18

*A **Gypsy played the accordion.*** Every Friday night, the high school band performed at the park's bandstand, and, as usual, Bebéi was there. But that evening, he was alone. Zoubir insisted on lingering next to the seagull on the balcony, and nothing could change his mind. Bebéi even suggested a pleasant walk through the boardwalk after the performance, a proposal always received with considerable wagging. The dog flatly refused, which turned out to be exceptionally fortunate since, as absurd as it might seem, someone tried to break into Bebéi's apartment that evening.

The first signal was the barking at the balcony; something was disturbing Zoubir. People in the street noticed, and neighbors decided to check. The apartment door was locked, and as the barking was unusual, the Asturian of the Tavern walked to the bandstand to warn Bebéi. They returned together, running to his apartment, and Pirilo, who was also watching the performance, noticed and followed them.

When they got to the manor, the door was locked, and everything seemed normal. Nobody was on the stairs, and Bebéi's apartment door had not been forced. When they got inside, Zoubir stopped barking but was still shivering, the seagull motionless, as if scared, behind him.

Until that evening, Pirilo had paid little attention to the surveillance cameras, but he went to his bunker at City Hall to review the video recorded in front of Bebéi's manor. In the video, he could see two people entering the manor using a key, but curiously, they never left after that.

He returned to the manor and checked the four apartments, including the one that belonged to the Hungarian. The two visitors were not there. He examined the wall at the back of the manor and realized the protective fence had been cut off. Strange! "If they left by jumping the wall after Zoubir barked, they were doing something wrong."

Pirilo went back to City Hall and gathered with his assistants. He wanted to review all surveillance videos around Bebéi's apartment. It was in moments like this that Pirilo missed Cristine the most. Jordi's girlfriend had worked for him briefly and she was, by far, his best assistant until the Mayor decided to send her away with the fellowship.

On a camera positioned on the boardwalk, Pirilo identified the two men who had entered Bebéi's house, walking and meeting with a third man.

Pirilo rechecked the video at Bebéi's manor's door and noticed the third man had passed there twice. On the first, he just walked by. But when he passed again, he stopped for a few seconds looking at the balcony; his movements were tense, probably because Zoubir was already barking.

"I know what happened," Pirilo concluded. "There were three; two got inside the house using a key, and the third stayed outside, waiting. They were probably trying to break into Bebéi's apartment, assuming Zoubir was with him at the park. When Zoubir started to bark, they jumped over the wall and walked to meet their third friend at the boardwalk."

It was impossible to recognize any of them from the videos. The three were wearing dark sunglasses and hoodies covering their heads. By how they were dressed, they did not seem to belong to any known gangs in Santa Clara.

Pirilo was intrigued. In Santa Clara, there were never robberies like this, only kids bag-snatching and pickpocketing tourists' wallets and cell phones. But since Bebéi had discovered the Hungarian's apartment, two break-ins happened in a few weeks. On the first, they emptied the apartment, but what were they looking for now? Was it something that was inside Bebéi's apartment?

"It could be that they were looking for the seagull," said Bebéi, trying to cooperate. And he insisted, "I know it seems crazy, but Zoubir didn't want to go to the concert. He predicted that something would happen and chose to stay on the balcony, protecting the seagull."

Absurd! But the truth was that Pirilo was lost. No one would break into an apartment to steal a seagull, but what could interest them? If they had emptied the Hungarian's apartment, and only the books were with Bebéi, what could they be looking for? Could it be the notes?

To avoid further surprises, Pirilo reinforced Bebéi's apartment protection and proposed keeping the Hungarian's notes in a safe at City Hall. Bebéi accepted Pirilo's suggestion but didn't tell him about the key hidden in Ilona's office. Pirilo put all the notes inside blue folders, one for each book, and took them to his office.

Pirilo was getting upset. All these events had changed his routine, and he did not have time to play dominoes with his friends. He had to manage his time and activities more efficiently. He didn't want to be stuck discussing a dead man's notes. As his assistants were having problems handling the new technological paraphernalia of security, he decided to look for help with the Lady of the American Embassy. They were friends, and they had exchanged information in the past.

Pirilo visited the American embassy and told the Lady about the new attempted robbery. She was concerned and sent a few experts to work with Pirilo's assistants. They could find an image of the three men inside a car from one of the cameras placed on the main avenue leading to the capital. From the car tags, they also discovered that it was a rental car, and the rental had been made with forged documents.

The Lady sent professionals to inspect the vehicle. They found fingerprints and checked them against the American intelligence files: one belonged to a Peruvian living in Miami.

All this happened on Saturday, and on Sunday morning, in Miami, the Peruvian was detained and confessed that he had been hired by a Cuban who lived in Little Havana.

That same afternoon the Cuban admitted that he had been contacted by another Cuban, a restaurant owner known for delivering "special" jobs.

On Sunday night, forty-eight hours after the incident, FBI agents broke into the house of the restaurant owner, who was quietly eating a pizza with his family.

To avoid further problems, the Cuban confessed that a law firm had commissioned the Santa Clara services — the same law firm that was managing the Hungarian's assets.

They did not make any arrests since no crime had been committed. All information was kept confidential. As the Lady explained to Pirilo, "We did not use traditional methods of investigation, and it's better not to let people know about them."

Pirilo understood, but all this information made him more intrigued. "What is so important there?" he asked his assistants, and none of them answered. Jordi's girlfriend was the only one who could answer those questions, and she was not there.

Pirilo didn't know he was not alone in looking for answers. When the Lady left the City Hall, she asked her chauffeur to drive around and find Bebéi, who was walking his dog on the boardwalk.

It was Sunday night and the boardwalk and the streets were almost empty. The Lady got out of the car and joined Bebéi on his walk. She did not ask questions; she just walked beside him from the boardwalk to the park, where they both sat on the same bench where Diocles was feeding and cuddling his cats.

In the park, a few couples were listening to a Gypsy accordionist play on the steps of the bandstand, with Diocles's fat yellow cat at his feet.

The Lady listened to the music and let Bebéi vent everything that was bothering him. She had a hunch that something important could come out of it. Bebéi told her about the letter from his archivist friend from Budapest about Lali, Eszter, and the Magyars' soccer games. He also told her about Hector's suspicions that the Hungarian worked for the Stasi and even mentioned that according to Princess, whom the Lady preferred to call Lola Marlene, the Hungarian could have worked for the CIA. Bebéi also told her about his father's photo in Algiers, the Congo letters, Hitler's invitation, and Che's picture. The Lady listened patiently, sympathetic to Bebéi's enthusiasm for discovering who his lonely Hungarian neighbor was.

From a practical point of view, nothing seemed relevant, since they were just past stories from the sixties and seventies, when the Berlin Wall still split the world and the Cold War was the primary concern of the Americans. Anyway, she listened attentively and even committed herself to helping him find out if Arpad had worked for the CIA. She was puzzled, however: What were the Miami lawyers looking for? Undoubtedly, the robbery had nothing to do with the soccer stories Bebéi had told her. Why had they hired professionals to clean out the Hungarian's apartment, and what else were they looking for? If they had hired experts, there was something there that was worth money. What could it be?

She left, and Bebéi remained in the park with Diocles and Zoubir. It was late, but he still had another problem to solve, and perhaps Diocles could help him. Bebéi did not know anyone in Santa Clara who could speak Czech, the language of the notes filed inside Pasternak's book. He showed the note to Diocles, who told him that one of the Paris Street women, who often crossed the park after attending clients at the Spaniard's hotel, was Czech. Diocles kept the note with him. Maybe she could help?

19

The Santa Clara Barrel Organ. Rasta Bong convened a meeting, and the subject was the pizzeria. Rasta was still worried about Friar Bernard's insistence on denouncing bribes; they were delaying the opening. Since he knew that the Friar listened to Ilona, he proposed holding a meeting at the Café, and avoiding the same mistake as last time; Rasta suggested it be in the evening hours to be sure that Ilona would be fresh and awake. Gigi, Diocles, Bebéi, and Jordi were also there, along with Ilona, Rasta Bong, and the Friar.

"You can't continue to be stubborn," complained Rasta to the Friar. "You got the fire department's license, and I know that the historical conservation is about to issue the authorization thanks to the pressure made by Lola Marlene, who knows the head of the agency from the drag queen cabaret. The only one missing is the license for alcoholic beverages; please, pay the bribe they are asking, and start to sell pizzas."

The Friar listened but replied firmly: "All the kitchen equipment we got is first rate, the same as Ilona has but brand new, and it took them months to approve them. And to deny us the alcoholic beverage license is a shame; we will only sell a few glasses of beer with the pizzas. Our drink sales for a whole month will be smaller than Ilona's in a single night. Why are they refusing the license?"

Rasta insisted, "Juanita also had equipment as good as yours, sells even fewer beers at her taco place, and had to pay the 'commission.' Our cooperative has life preservers on all boats, but we must pay a 'tax' to the port supervisor weekly. Once, we forgot the payment, and he made us take the life preservers out of the boats and put them on the pier to count them; we were forced to suspend all morning tours, enraging the tourists."

"That is exactly why I am resisting," insisted the Friar. "We can't continue to accept this corruption."

Rasta looked at his friends, begging for help, but they offered none. Ilona never questioned anyone's judgment. "Each one has his own head, thinks what they want to think, and does what they want to do." Diocles, sitting on the other side of the table, didn't say a word. Everyone there knew that the old philosopher greatly supported Friar's moralization crusade. Rasta even looked at Gigi, desperately begging for help, but she also chose to remain speechless. Rasta was disappointed, but there was not much he could do. As everyone remained silent, Jordi began talking about the newspaper that did not have a name.

Rasta Bong had proposed *The Lion of Judah*, but no one accepted. Already frustrated with the fiasco of the pizzeria discussion, Rasta stood up and went to the terrace's corner to light a joint.

Ilona refilled the wineglasses. She was excited about the newspaper idea and proposed a name: *The Seagull.*

Friar Bernard did not like it. "A seagull is always flying, and it does not reflect those of us who, no matter what happens, resist and stay firmly in the city."

His comment triggered a discussion about what represented the city of Santa Clara the most.

"Its architecture, with the narrow cobblestone streets and the large colonial mansions," said Gigi, and Jordi replied that many other towns had similar historical districts.

"The serenity," argued the Friar, and Jordi again retorted that this was a common element to every small town.

Everyone shared their opinion, and no progress was made until Ilona asked Bebéi, who was quietly following the conversation.

"And for you? What's the first thing that comes to mind when someone talks about Santa Clara by the Sea?"

Bebéi thought for a moment and then answered: "The song of the 'L'Orgue de Barbarie.'"

No one understood what he said, and Ilona, the only one there who could understand French, explained: "The barrel organ."

For almost a full minute, everybody stayed close-mouthed.

Ilona was the first to break the silence. "I like the barrel organ, too. There are days when I feel like killing all of you, but when I hear the sound of the ice cream seller's tricycle, it's as if all anger fades into the air."

The Friar mentioned that the barrel organ was nostalgic and showed their wish to keep Santa Clara serene and preserved. Everyone commented and, surprisingly, all opinions were favorable.

Rasta, who was coming back to the table with his eyes gleaming, heard the name and immediately reacted: "Cool ... the barrel organ ... One love." He then started to laugh so infectiously that everyone there, without understanding why, began to laugh too.

Jordi supported Bebéi's suggestion: "Our newspaper must stir emotions, and I think *The Barrel Organ* would be a great name."

After a few other expressions of approval, the name was consensually chosen. Jordi even added, "With this name, every time anyone listens to the barrel organ music of the ice cream stand, they will remember our newspaper."

Rasta Bong, still laughing, interjected: "A newspaper promoted by an ice cream seller. So crazy — I love it!"

The meeting did not go on for long — Rasta Bong was too high — but the name had been chosen and the next day, after Grená had spread the news from her corner, *The Santa Clara Barrel Organ* became the talk of the town.

Grená confessed under her umbrella that she waited for the ice cream tricycle every morning and that its music cheered everyone around it. Diocles commented that every time the ice cream tricycle stopped at the park, everyone celebrated it: the retirees suspended their dominoes, those in a lousy mood started to smile, and even those in a hurry paused to listen. Jordi confirmed that the name was well received among younger people and was surprised to realize that everyone — from the most privileged who attended Lucia's fitness academy to those who lived in the impoverished area beyond the river — shared the allure of the barrel organ music. Even the Useless of the Brethren agreed; whenever the tricycle stopped over there, Robespierre halted his insults, and Null-and-void tried to control his farts.

Rasta Bong was a fan of barrel organs. He was the one who had proposed and financed the ice cream seller to attach a barrel organ to his tricycle. Even before the discussion of the newspaper name, Rasta was planning to build similar tricycles with barrel organs to take tourists on strolls through the streets, and he suggested to Jordi, "What if I postpone the construction of the tricycles and ask the carpenter to build a stand-alone barrel organ? We could have it in front of the Cathedral in the morning and at the boardwalk every afternoon. I'm sure tourists will love it, and we can have someone selling newspapers next to it."

The barrel organ was nothing more than a set of pipes playing musical notes, and the simple ones, such as the one belonging to the ice cream seller, played twenty notes. The pipes were fed by bellows, like the accordion of the Gypsy, and as the crank was turned, the bellows' air passed into the pipes, playing the notes programmed by the cylinders.

It was almost all woodwork, and the carpenter's son, who was repairing the cooperative's boats, had learned how to make them and was working for Rasta. The bellows were the same as in the accordion, and the Gypsies knew where to order them. The last component, the cylinders, were made by an artisan blacksmith, copying those found in an abandoned manor. They could easily and quickly finish the construction of a colorful barrel organ to promote the newspaper, but there was still a problem: Who would turn the crank?

The cylinder must be rotated, and on the ice cream tricycle, there was a mechanism by which the pedals activated the bellows and the cylinders. A similar device was to be installed on the tricycles for taking tourists, but if they built one to stand alone, somebody would have to turn the crank.

Hiring someone would be expensive, and they would not be able to afford it. It had to be someone willing to help them and who had nothing to do during the day. And, although it seemed odd, it was not easy to find someone with spare time in Santa Clara: Diocles had to walk through the streets observing people; Chombo Zen had to meditate and entertain his women, and the drunkards had to get drunk. None of them could spend the day under a tree before the Cathedral. They almost gave up the idea when Bebéi made a berserk proposal: "What if we ask Arcadio?"

Rasta and Jordi were bewildered, but Bebéi insisted. "I know everybody in town hates Arcadio. He also hates everyone, but what if we ask him and see what he says?" Bebéi concluded with an original thought: "He has nothing to do. If he accepts, no one will have a reason to hate him, and, who knows, maybe he will stop hating us."

Arcadio was a beggar who did not drink but robbed everything he could. No one — absolutely no one in town — would consider talking to him. He stank, was always angry, and was the last person anyone could imagine turning the crank of the barrel organ, but Bebéi proposed it. What seemed irrational became something that, according to Jordi, was worth trying.

The Friar loved the idea, reminding them that tolerance was a sign of wisdom, and Diocles strongly backed him. Bebéi, as the idea's author, was tasked with talking to Arcadio, which was challenging. Arcadio lived in the ruins of the old fort, and when Bebéi arrived, the beggar barely let him speak. Arcadio uttered the most horrible words Bebéi had ever heard and sent him immediately away.

"And how did it go?" asked Diocles when Bebéi returned.

"Well," Bebéi answered, surprising everyone with his optimism. "Let's wait a day or two. I believe he'll take it."

They did not have to wait that long. Late that same afternoon, Arcadio walked into the park and sat down next to Diocles, asking if it was true what Bebéi had proposed to him.

"Well," said Jordi, pleased when Diocles told him, "now we have a barrel organ, someone to turn the crank, and the newspaper's first issue is almost ready. We will launch it next Saturday." Too bad, he thought, that Cristine would not be here to share this new adventure.

20

Unveiling the trash price. The first edition of *The Santa Clara Barrel Organ* featured two articles. The first was a three-page article about "How Much Your Trash Costs" written by Jordi, in which he denounced the benefits the garbage company owned by the Italian was receiving from the city.

The first perk was the acquisition of new trucks for trash collection by City Hall, transferred at no cost to the Italian's company. The Mayor's excuse was that it was essential to have modern equipment. As the Italian did not have the resources to do it, City Hall would buy it: "Our trash collection will be second to none," the Mayor announced, and according to all independent polls, citizens approved his decision.

The other benefit was the paying off of all employees dismissed by the downsizing implemented by the Italian. The Mayor, showing appreciation for the working people, decided to keep paying their salaries, making the employees still available to work for the garbage company. "We will keep those people employed at any cost. It's our humanitarian obligation," he said. Another demagogic strike that increased the Italian's profits and further improved the Mayor's popularity — regardless of the fact that the decision dramatically increased City Hall's debt.

The third was related to a compensation fee that City Hall agreed to pay and was calculated in secrecy by the Mayor's brother as city treasurer. The reason, which the Mayor explained in a television interview, was that "Unfortunately," and he said that emphasizing his disapproval, "many people do not pay the tax collection fee, and this undermines the sustainability of the garbage company." That is why his brother had invented a formula defining how much people should pay each month, and if, for some reason, the fees collected did not reach the expected level, City Hall would transfer to the Italian's company the difference.

No one ever had explained how these numbers were determined. Still, the data Jordi obtained through a secret informant was that City Hall was paying an additional twenty percent to the company every month. The rumor was that half of that twenty percent, the Italian did not even see since it was going straight to an account in Grand Cayman the Mayor shared with his brother. Jordi did not mention the Mayor's cut since he could not prove it, but he clearly denounced the twenty percent.

The other article was the story of Lais, who survived for many decades selling empanadas from the window of her apartment in the green manor. Everybody in Santa Clara knew her and enjoyed her empanadas. The picture of Lais proudly smiling at her window was displayed on the front page.

Jordi decided to refrain from mentioning the New Santa Clara project. "First, we need to build up credibility," he said. "If we start by criticizing the Mayor's plans, they might deny it, and we will look like idiots. The corruption inside garbage collection is something that we know, and no one can deny what we wrote."

Jordi made two thousand copies of the newspaper; almost all were gone on the first day. He was responsible for the distribution and walked from house to house, delivering copies. By evening, when the boardwalk was filled with tourists, Jordi went there to distribute copies, and later, since there was a piano performance in the Colonial Theater, he stayed in front of it, handing out newspapers until the last guest had entered the theater.

The newspaper was also available in two fixed places. The first was at the barbershop, where Rasta Bong left the papers stacked next to the manicure chair, where anyone could get their copy. The second was at the coffee shop of Princess's bookstore, a distribution point mainly aimed at younger people.

Everything went so well that Jordi was considering printing a thousand more copies and was running around trying to raise the necessary funds. They considered charging for advertising, but to do it, they would have to register and legalize the company publishing the newspapers. This would lead them to the same litany of bribes, commissions, and annoyances that the Friar faced with the pizzeria. Perhaps later, thought Jordi.

Inside City Hall, the reaction to *The Santa Clara Barrel* was immediate: the Mayor summoned his advisers to an extraordinary meeting. He was outraged. The Serbian tried to calm him, but she couldn't; the Mayor wanted revenge on the Friar, Jordi, and all those funding the newspaper.

He made it clear: "The pizzeria license for alcoholic beverages can be entirely forgotten, and I want you to investigate right now if we can deport that Friar son of a bitch. I was told he had a visa to work within the church. Now that he is no longer a friar, I want him to return to Italy and take his fiancée with him." The Mayor continued furiously, "That Jordi was hired as a teacher, and I will open an internal investigation and dismiss him for political activism. Until we finish the process, he will remain suspended without a wage."

The Mayor was so angry that the Serbian could not appease him. She tried to convince him to adopt a more intelligent and less passionate stance, but he was furious and was saying things that might leak and create problems.

And that is precisely what happened; on Monday, everything the Mayor said at the meeting was repeated in front of Grená's yellow umbrella: "The Mayor wants to deport the Friar and fire Jordi for what they published in *The Barrel Organ*."

The immediate consequence was that everyone who had not read the paper ran to find a copy, and the whole town started to talk about garbage collection. So many people began to look for the newspaper that Rasta decided to finance the printing of additional copies and asked the manicurist to leave his clients waiting to help Jordi print them at the back of the barbershop.

When Gigi heard that the Mayor wanted to deport the Friar, she immediately called a lawyer friend of Ilona's and came up with a pragmatic proposal: "The Friar needs a residence permit, and he can have one if we get married."

The problem of Jordi, however, was more complex. The Mayor had grounds to start the investigation. Jordi was a full-time teacher and was not supposed to be writing articles for a newspaper. The teachers' union backed him with a lawyer, who warned that it would not be an easy battle.

Jordi's support grew in the next few days and came mainly from students. He was honestly trying to work, and many of them knew him from the school where, besides being an excellent soccer player, he had been, along with Cristine, one of the best students. Jordi had to stand out to the selection committee and legitimately earn his position, and now he would lose his job for exposing facts of public interest. This was neither fair nor acceptable. The students were outraged and proposed a strike that started on Wednesday.

On Friday the carpenter finished assembling the barrel organ, and the decision was to launch it immediately. Rasta Bong rushed to organize a Gypsy band presentation for that same evening at the bandstand. At the end of the show, attended by an enormous crowd of students and teachers on strike, Bebéi — who had been chosen to make the announcement — climbed the stairs of the bandstand followed by Zoubir and solemnly introduced the barrel organ. Next to him, the "gentleman" responsible for turning the crank, Arcadio, was dressed in a tailcoat forgotten at the Colonial Theater by a magician. He had his hair well cut, his beard trimmed, and he carried the scent of a welcome shower.

It took a long time for people to realize that it was the same Arcadio that everyone hated, but that evening, he did not steal, and for the first time in his life, townspeople looked at him with a smile. He turned the crank, and the barrel organ music filled the park in a duet with the Gypsy orchestra. After that presentation,

Arcadio never stopped amusing people and distributing the local newspaper.

21

The Serbian knew Machiavelli. The Mayor's problems really began when his wife stormed unannounced into his office like a hurricane. "How can you even think of deporting Friar Bernard?" After saying that, she continued to unload so many horrible things that the only one the Mayor could remember after she left was "The only reason I am still married to you is the work I do with the Friar. If he goes, I'll leave you."

And it was not just her; all her friends, including those who rarely left their homes other than for weddings, burials, and Sunday mass, gathered during the week in the Mayor's house, insisting that Friar Bernard should not be deported from Santa Clara.

Everyone understood when the Friar was expelled from the church. He explained that he would not hide his love for Gigi and, despite being still committed to his faith, the church did not want him as a priest. He made it clear that he would continue his social work, not as a Friar, but as an assistant to the Mayor's wife. The pizzeria was to make ends meet. "The restaurant will not take much of his time," the Mayor's wife reassured her friends. "His priority is to help the neediest." But now it was different; nobody knew about Gigi's wedding alternative, so they thought he might be deported forever.

If all the Catholic ladies came out in Friar Bernard's defense, even greater support came from those living in the impoverished areas who depended upon his work. The resentment was widespread.

When the Mayor attended the town hall meeting that week, he faced angry questions: "Do you believe in freedom of expression, or is your support of public debates hypocritical?" asked an old nun who had come expressly to challenge the Mayor.

The Serbian advised him to remain in silence for a few days. Still, he insisted on going to the Colonial Theater on Saturday for an orchestra performance celebrating the International Day of Music. It was raining. As soon as he left the car, he was received by teachers' union activists and students with banners supporting Jordi. Inside, in the lobby, people started to boo him. The situation did not worsen thanks to the Serbian, who instructed the theater manager to begin the orchestra presentation immediately.

The next day was even worse: a respected national newspaper published an opinion article in its Sunday edition: "The Hypocrisy of a Mayor," accusing him aggressively for falsely saying that Santa Clara welcomed tourists while expelling foreigners doing socially relevant work for the people.

To make matters even worse, the Mayor had an event at the pier that morning. He had been announcing for several weeks the reforms that would give a modern look to the old marina — new protection fences, restrooms, and a cafeteria, as well as water and power installations for all boats anchored there. Still, it did not seem to matter since City Hall had financed the cost with another loan, and the first payment would only be made six years later.

When the Mayor arrived, the pier was completely taken over, not by tourists but by students and people with banners defending Friar Bernard. The Mayor tried to approach them, relying on his friendly smile, but the protesters were in a bad mood, and the heckling was so loud that his security insisted that he withdraw.

A nightmarish Sunday was beginning: In the morning, the booing at the pier; later, at a lunch previously scheduled by the Catholic ladies, he had to listen to an endless stream of criticism for the Friar's deportation, which was completed in the evening by a scolding from the Serbian for his impulsive actions. And as if all this were not enough, at night, as soon as he went to bed, he was awakened by a call from Pirilo: "Two cars are burning across the river. They belonged to the engineers making the measurements for the new project and were parked in front of the Arab's warehouse."

The Mayor was appalled; things like this had never happened in Santa Clara. He instructed Pirilo to pick him up and quickly dressed to go with him and check what had happened. When they got there, the fire was extinguished, but the two cars were completely burned.

The Arab investors had rented a warehouse across the river to house their engineers. The whole thing was very discreet. They had three cars without any external identification, and the fire had destroyed two of them; the third one was spared, as some engineers were traveling in it.

What worried the Mayor the most was a note hanging on the warehouse's door with two very eloquent words: *Get out!*

The Serbian was right; it was the first thought that came to his mind.

"You have to focus on what's important," she had told him that afternoon, "and the important thing is to build New Santa Clara. With this project, you will make all the money you need to retire as an Arabian prince. The criticism in the newspapers is irrelevant; with two significant events that we can easily organize, everybody will forget them. The problem is the Friar and Jordi, who permanently turn people against you. The pizzeria and *The Barrel Organ* are only creating problems for us because of your attitude. You are jealous of Friar Bernard; he is young, handsome, and attracts many women, but if you insist on being stubborn, you will have serious problems. Keep in mind that if you lose the support of the poorest and the young, they will destroy you and your project."

The Mayor was fuming and wanted to make "that Friar, son of a bitch, eat shit," but that would have to wait; the new project was more important, and he could not risk everything just to screw the priest. That same night, he sent a message to his partners and advisers:

Tomorrow at the very first hour, an emergency meeting in City Hall.

They were all present at dawn, but the only one who spoke was the Serbian. The Mayor preferred to remain quiet at her side. "Today, the Mayor will visit the Friar's pizzeria at 12:30 p.m. Along with him, we will have the treasurer, the chief fireman, and all those responsible for health, work, and beverage licenses. All permissions for the pizzeria will be approved before the end of the afternoon. With no exceptions." And she added, "Please, I ask those of you who will join the Mayor to shave yourselves and wear sober and elegant clothes. Television reporters will be there."

Everyone remained silent, and she continued: "At three p.m. the Mayor will receive in his office young Jordi to inform him that his suspension is revoked and that he will begin to give classes next week. For this meeting, the Secretary of Education must be with the Mayor in his office." The secretary nodded while all others remained speechless, and the Serbian continued: "Lieutenant Pirilo told us we had a fire, probably caused by someone who carelessly threw a cigarette out of the window of a vehicle, and two cars were burned. The good news is that we had no casualties, and the vehicles were fully covered by insurance." She then warned: "Any rumor that criminals provoked the fire must be vehemently denied since it could impact our city's image among investors. The city has already issued an official press release, and none of you should comment or answer any question about it." The Mayor nodded with an unsmiling expression to highlight the importance of what the Serbian had said.

"It is important," she continued, "that you all be aware that tomorrow at noon, the Mayor will visit Cathedral Park, together with young Jordi, to announce that a group of investors has just made a significant financial contribution to *The Santa Clara Barrel Organ*." And she added seriously, "As you all know, the Mayor strongly values freedom of expression."

She did not say anything else because everything had already been said. Next to her, the Mayor closed the meeting by saying, "You can all go back to work."

At twelve-thirty sharp, the Mayor arrived at the pizzeria and he was not alone. All his top aides were there with journalists, television cameras, and two vans filled with forty pizzas ordered from a pizzeria in the capital. The Mayor got out of his car smiling, hugged Friar Bernard, and, in front of the cameras, reported: "As it is taking so long to open, I decided to bring the pizzas and all my staff to see what we can do to open this place as soon as possible." He then posed, smiling, next to the Friar for the photographers. "Santa Clara by the Sea urgently needs a pizzeria." The image of his arrival hugging the Friar and distributing pizzas was shown on the main television news channel.

The following day, also with reporters from national newspapers and television networks present, the Mayor made a powerful speech defending the freedom of all citizens to express their opinions and handed Jordi a check to ensure at least three months of newspaper publishing. The image that everybody saw on their televisions that night was of the Mayor turning the crank of the barrel organ next to Arcadio.

"The crisis is over," the Mayor said to his advisers at the end of the day. "Let us now focus on our New Santa Clara project."

22

The Cold War confused Bebéi. With all the excitement of those days, Bebéi had not made any significant progress with the Hungarian's files. When he walked by the bookstore and saw Princess sitting behind the counter reading a book, he felt it was a good time to resume his investigations. He went to Pirilo's office to take a few folders: the one of Auden's book with the information from Algeria and Conrad's file, including notes on Congo. All notes in these files were in French, a language Bebéi knew very well, and that Princess had learned singing Edith Piaf's songs. He also took the folder of Durrell's book, with notes about the Dominican Republic, and Böll's book mentioning the Barbarroja, with notes in Spanish, a natural language for Princess, born in Santiago de Cuba.

When Princess saw him approaching with blue folders in hand, he got so spirited that he strutted elegantly in his direction, wearing pink pants, a white blouse, and a fluffy white, gray, and red scarf. He invited Bebéi to sit with him at one of the tables on the sidewalk and ordered two cappuccinos.

That morning the park in front of the bookstore looked like a dream, with pigeons fleeing from tourists, kids playing with dogs, and Robespierre dancing, eyes shut, to the music of Arcadio's barrel organ.

"Your old secret notes excite me," explained Princess. "The scent of old paper moves me even more than the glitter of the sequins."

Bebéi did not understand, but Princess's smile made him interpret that was something positive, and he passed him the folders. Princess immediately opened the first one.

In that folder, from Auden's book, there was a newspaper clipping with the photo of Bebéi's father among men in uniform. According to the excerpt, they were all founders of the National Liberation Army, the military arm of the National Liberation Front that led Algeria to its liberation in 1961.

Princess commented that Bebéi's father was a handsome man and said he suspected Arpad was a double agent. As far as Princess could see from another note, Arpad's job in Algiers was merely to observe what was happening and keep his bosses informed. It was impossible to identify who his bosses were, but Princess guessed they were not Communists. The notes he read discussed how far the leaders of the liberation movement were involved with the Soviets, and one of them even read:

For the French, Algeria's independence is a passionate subject, which is leading them to lose their rationality. For us, it's not essential to know whether Algeria is a free country or not; what we do not want is a red Algeria.

The other note written by Arpad showed he was learning French, and there was a note from Arpad to Otto.

Bebéi interrupted with a question that was intriguing him: "Inside several books, I found notes written by Arpad to this Otto, and I don't understand; if he sent them, the notes should be with Otto and not within Arpad's file."

Princess only listened; he didn't know what to say. He took a sip of his cappuccino and read the note:

They do not ask me anything. I just keep them informed. I miss Eszter and Morgen very much. But when I think of going back to Berlin, I feel an even greater pain; I know that I will see Morgen, but I will experience the sorrow of not having Eszter with me. Here, at least, I can daydream that they are both waiting for me at the Biders' house. Life in Algiers is enjoyable. Drops of sweat become part of your skin, and strong scents remind me at every moment that I am far from Europe. The food and music are excellent, but the soccer they play is terrible.

"Arpad apparently spent little time in Algiers," continued Princess. "By the end of 1958, he was transferred to Congo," After thinking for a moment, Princess continued: "That makes me wonder. In Algeria, the situation remained very tense until 1962, and if they sent him to Congo in 1958, his work in Algiers was irrelevant. And we should also consider that for Americans, the Congo was much more critical in their struggle for Africa's political control."

Princess was increasingly interested in the Hungarian puzzle, and Bebéi approached his chair to better see the notes Princess was reading.

"In the notes inside Conrad's book," said Princess after reading a few of them, "it's possible to see that Arpad had a more meaningful participation in Congo. He also took an interest in what was happening in other countries. See this note, for instance."

I'm in Kinshasa, but I'm keeping my eyes open to follow what is happening in the Dominican Republic, Jakarta, and Eastern Africa. It's as if the whole world is exploding at the same time, and unusual things are happening everywhere.

Princess explained that the CIA was heavily involved in all these countries, and when Arpad had mentioned Eastern Africa, he was probably referring to Eritrea, Ethiopia, and maybe Chad, where there were also revolutionary movements in the early sixties.

"All this," said Princess, "seems to confirm that Arpad worked for the CIA. In the sixties, the Americans were concerned about the Congo revolution — Che Guevara and the Cubans supported the rebels. At that time, the CIA was also supporting the effort to bring Juan Bosch back to power in the Dominican Republic. The Americans believed that another revolution like the one of Cuba in the Caribbean would destabilize the entire continent in favor of the Soviets."

Bebéi listened carefully to everything. Princess made an effort to avoid losing Bebéi in all the information. Bebéi's immediate interest was only in understanding what the Hungarian had to do with all this, and Princess didn't want to confuse him more.

"The notes in Henrich Böll's book," explained Princess, "are fascinating. They mentioned the Barbarroja. He was a well-known personality. Manuel Piñeiro Losada — his real name — coordinated all the Cuban government's activities in Latin America and Africa. From what I read in one of these notes, it was Guevara himself who introduced Arpad to the Barbarroja in a meeting they had in Algiers."

After silently reading the notes about Barbarroja, Princess made a definitive comment: "Here it's clear that your Hungarian friend was playing a double game. He worked and received a salary from the CIA to inform them of everything happening in Africa. At the same time, out of his friendship with this Otto, and perhaps to El Che, he also kept Barbarroja informed of all he knew, not only in the Congo but also in the Dominican Republic, Indonesia, and other countries that were tense spots of the Cold War."

Bebéi told Princess about his conversation with the Lady and explained that she had promised to find out if the Hungarian had worked for the CIA. Princess replied, smiling, that she probably would not be happy to know that the Hungarian sympathized with the enemies.

After reading a few more notes and pausing to arrange his elegant scarf, Princess continued: "After 1966, things calmed down a bit in your friend's life. The Americans, with their troops, backed Balaguer's election in the Dominican Republic and the elimination of all Juan Bosch supporters. In 1967, Suharto, another North American puppet, took over power with full control over Indonesia, and Mobutu consolidated his power in Congo."

Princess continued to read the notes silently while Bebéi patiently waited; Bebéi was so focused that he had not touched his cappuccino.

"As shown by these notes," continued Princess, "it's during this period that Arpad started to work on a project with the Tutsis. If I understood correctly, he was doing it for the Americans who wanted to prevent the Tutsis from supporting the pro-Soviet revolutionaries. From what Arpad wrote, it seems to be a major project to develop agriculture. Arpad participated in the design, and his daughter Morgen was also involved."

Little by little the notes were revealing the Hungarian's story.

"At the end of the sixties," Princess continued, "while living in Kinshasa, Arpad seemed to go often to Kisangani, the city where you told me his granddaughter now lives, and also the region of the project.

"There is something else," Princess suddenly mentioned after reading a note including references to a Francisco who worked in Angola and Mozambique.

Bebéi interrupted him to clarify that in the book of Anatole France, some notes, written in Portuguese, mentioned Angola and Mozambique. Maybe Francisco was the keyword for that file. Bebéi also commented that other notes in English could help them understand everything the Hungarian was interested in. In Ibsen's book, there were few notes on Indonesia, and inside Kafka's novel, notes signed with a K — Bebéi suspected the keyword for the file was the city of Khartoum.

The two enjoyed working on unraveling the puzzle but had to interrupt their conversation when Jordi arrived. He pulled up a chair and sat, a worried expression on his face.

"I think I'll have to publish *The Barrel Organ* alone." He paused as if thinking and added, "I cannot ask Friar Bernard to help me."

Bebéi and Princess were intrigued, and Jordi explained.

"On the same day that he visited the pizzeria, the Mayor privately mentioned to the Friar that he would support his application for a resident visa and that his wife was willing to be the sponsor. It would not be fair now to keep asking him to help us to bombard the Mayor."

Bebéi and Princess nodded, agreeing, and Jordi continued, "The truth is that the Friar no longer has time for the newspaper. He must open the pizzeria and now, more than ever, it's important for him to continue with his social work. That is why so many people are fighting for him. But you don't need to be worried," Jordi added, "I can handle the newspaper, and Cristine has promised me that when she returns she will help me."

At that precise moment, the three stopped talking; an unusual and unexpected couple was approaching their table. Diocles was walking toward them, serene as ever, with his long white beard and thoughtful expression, dressed in the same old gray raincoat he had worn from the first day he arrived in Santa Clara. At his side, however, was an astonishing surprise: a blonde and beautiful woman over six feet tall with a very tight dress and a voluptuous body.

Princess and Jordi were even more surprised when Diocles politely introduced the blonde who accompanied him.

"My friends, this is Mrs. Dusanka," and then, looking at her, "Lady Dusanka, these are my friends Mr. Bebéi, Mr. Princess, and Mr. Jordi."

Dusanka was the Czech who entertained clients at the hotel and would help Bebéi understand the papers inside Pasternak's book.

She had already read the notes Diocles gave her and explained that they mentioned an apartment where a woman by the name of Natasha lived as well as the name of a law firm in Andorra. The other note had the number of a mailbox that supposedly belonged to Natasha.

Bebéi immediately thought that the keyword for the notes inside Neruda's book could be Natasha. Still, he would only be sure when Ludmila, Rasta's wife, who was expected to arrive soon in Santa Clara, could read them since they were written in Russian.

There was not much else they could do. Bebéi asked Mrs. Dusanka to help him write a letter to the address of Natasha's mailbox, telling her he was trying to figure out what she knew about Arpad Corvinus. She did it right there, seated at the table and observed with an obnoxious look from Princess.

As she left, she kissed each of the four, who then followed her hip movements with their eyes until she got into a taxi and left.

"She has varicose veins" was Princess's blunt and jealous comment.

Part Three

AN AFRICAN HEIRESS

23

The Heiress's surprising arrival. Bebéi's investigation made his Hungarian neighbor famous in Santa Clara. On the window where Lais was selling empanadas, Princess was telling Hector and Colonel Viera that the Hungarian was, for sure, a double agent. In Lieutenant Pirilo's office inside the City Hall, the whole discussion was about the attempted robbery and the words they heard from the CIA Lady: "They were looking for something worth money; we must find out what it is."

On Grená's corner, in front of Our Lady of Mercy Church, the stories were endless: "I always distrusted the Hungarian," said a Japanese woman with a vegetable stand in the market. "He always bought the same things, never asked questions, and never complained. He paid for everything and never discussed the price. Nobody is like that. I always knew that he was hiding something."

At the Asturian Tavern, after lunch, Pirilo played dominoes with his friend the owner, who told him the obvious: "Something strange happened there and, since his first visit, you mistrusted the gringo lawyer. Now you know that he hired the thugs to break into the apartment, and you must do something. Without Cristine, your assistants can't help you find an elephant hidden inside the park. You have no choice; you must find out what's going on by yourself, and the only person who can help you is Bebéi, no matter how crazy his notes are."

Pirilo did not find spending time reading notes appealing, but he summoned Jordi, Princess, and Bebéi to a meeting in his office.

It had to be done, and the rules should be strict: only four of them, and the doors closed. They would stay there until they understood what could be worth money in all that Hungarian's story.

They got together the same evening; the lieutenant did not want any interruption, and asked the Asturian to prepare a fish paella and send an Albariño wine bottle with it. On the table of his office were all the blue folders and four copies of a sheet prepared by Bebéi updating what he knew about each folder.

A - Auden - French - Algeria
B - Böll- Spanish - Beardman
C - Conrad - French - Congo
D - Durrell - Spanish - Dominican Republic
E - Eliot - German - Eszter
F - France - Portuguese - Francisco
G - Grass - Spanish - Guevara
H - Hesse - Hungarian - Horthy
I - Ibsen - English - Indonesia?
J - Joyce - Hungarian - Janus
K - Kafka - English - K or Karthoum?
L - Lawrence - Hungarian - Lali
M - Márai - English - Morgen
N- Neruda - Russian - Natasha?
O- Orwell - German - Otto
P- Pasternak - Czech - Prague
Q- Quasimodo - French - Quebec
R - Rilke - Russian - ?
S- Szabó - Spanish - Santa Clara
T - Tolstoy - German - Tamara?
U - Unamuno - English - ?
V - Virgil - English - ?
W - Whitman - English- ?
X - Xingjian - The last book?

Y- Yeats - Russian — ?
Z - Zola —

Bebéi suggested starting with the letter from the Budapest archivist and explained to Pirilo all Frida had told him about Eszter and her search for Arpad in Siberia.

Then they read the notes in Spanish supporting Princess's theory that the Hungarian was a double agent.

Jordi, who knew a little English, commented that the notes in Ibsen's and Kafka's books confirmed the theory that the Hungarian was a double agent. "One of the notes in Ibsen's book mentions that Americans had prepared a list with names of members of the Indonesian Communist Party, the PKI, and handed them over to General Suharto. And in Kafka's book, several notes refer to CIA-backed executions of leaders of nationalist and Muslim movements who aligned themselves with the Soviets."

Princess started to explain the political situation of those countries, and Pirilo interrupted him: "I know that all this history thing is important, but I want to know what, among all these papers, could attract the attention of a Miami law firm."

His comment intimidated Princess and Jordi, but not Bebéi: "The robbers were looking for something hidden in these notes, and if we do not understand them, we will never know what they were looking for." Pirilo lowered his head, resigned.

Bebéi then proposed to look at the notes inside Anatole France's book. He could understand Portuguese, and he had read them. They were unsigned notes, probably from that Francisco who was mentioned in other files; all of them very critical of CIA activities. The first was from 1966 and mentioned that someone called Agostinho Neto had met with Guevara and that his group, the MPLA, was receiving support from the Barbarroja and East Germany.

"Agostinho Neto was the main leader of the revolutionary fight in Angola and became its president," explained Princess, and Bebéi continued translating the note. *The Portuguese, with all their internal problems, would not withstand the pressure, and probably Agostinho Neto would assume control of the country in alliance with the Soviets."*

The note Bebéi read also reproduced an instruction that Francisco had received from his bosses:

You must do everything possible to prevent the alliance between Agostinho Neto and other revolutionary movements. Dividing them is essential. I recommend you seek support from your friends from Kinshasa to position those of the Enclave of Cabinda against Angola. It is essential to involve Mobutu in this; the greater the tension between them, the harder it will be for them to control the oil. Do whatever you can to support Golden and the FNLA; they are a disaster, but that is all we have. Savimbi is fascinated by the Chinese. We cannot prevent the Soviets from taking control, and for this reason, we have no alternative; the only thing we can do is collapse the country.

After translating the note, Bebéi paused and asked, looking at Princess: "I don't understand. Did the Americans want to destroy the country just because this Agostinho was a friend of the Communists?"

Princess found that answering would be distracting and avoided the question by asking Bebéi about the other notes in the F folder.

"The other records are from Mozambique," Bebéi responded, "Francisco wrote the instruction he received":

> *To support Dhlakama, no matter what our colleagues in the State Department think. They are trying to convince Samora Machel to ally with us, but it is essential to weakening the government and the country.*

Bebéi was astonished. In his romantic vision, international spies protected freedom and didn't destroy countries. Princess noticed Bebéi's confusion, but the purpose of that meeting was not to discuss the ethics of international politics nor to judge what the Americans had done. Pirilo's instructions were quite clear: They must discover what, within those notes, could be worth money.

"Arpad lived in the Congo," Princess said, "but he made several trips abroad and was interested in other countries. We already know that he traveled to Algeria, where he met Barbarroja. He also discussed the Dominican Republic in a meeting — we don't know where it occurred, but I suspect it was in Havana. I also believe, from the notes Jordi read, that Arpad went to Khartoum and Addis Ababa. We also have indications that he was somehow involved, or at least interested, in what was going on in Jakarta and that he kept in contact with this Francisco, with whom he discussed Angola and Mozambique. In summary, the Hungarian was not a simple John Doe. He worked with almost every country in Africa around where there was a revolutionary movement. And we know that while working for the Americans, he had no sympathy for many things they were doing."

They then went over the question marks on the list. They agreed that Frida was the only choice for the still untranslated notes in German, and as Bebéi was the only one who could talk with her, he would be in charge. For the notes in Russian, Pirilo would ask Ludmila's help, Rasta Bong's wife. She would arrive that same night, and they would be able to talk with her the following day. The only doubt remaining was about the notes in English. Princess and Pirilo were unsure about asking the Lady of the Embassy; perhaps the notes had something that the Lady wanted to hide, but they had no options.

"There are twenty-six books and only twenty-four folders," Pirilo commented before ending the meeting. "Why?"

It was only then that Bebéi told about the line written at the end of Xingjian's book. *"My final book ... what's the use to keep reading?"* None of them understood.

The other missing folder was from Zola's book, and Bebéi was forced to acknowledge that there had been a key inside the book.

"Maybe it's the key the lawyers are looking for," Pirilo said, finally excited by something.

"I hid it," said Bebéi, and when Pirilo insisted, Bebéi answered firmly, "It's well hidden, and until we know what that key opens, I'd rather leave it where I know that no one will find it."

There was no way to convince him otherwise. Pirilo was frustrated, but at least there was something concrete to focus the investigation on: a key. And if there was a key, there was a safe, and in the safe, eventually, the money. That was probably what they were looking for.

After the meeting, Bebéi returned to his apartment, where a surprise awaited him. At the door, he found a message written in French:

I'm here. At the Backpackers' Bed
and Breakfast.

Laurence.

The Hungarian's granddaughter had not answered to his letter but had taken a plane to meet him in Santa Clara. Bebéi just headed inside his apartment to pick up Zoubir and went to the inn.

Laurence was a pleasant surprise; a nice and friendly woman. She told him that her father was Tutsi and, although she was tall and extremely handsome, her face had a timid expression. Her skin had the color of cinnamon, and her eyes were a shining blue, her mother's legacy. Her eyebrows had something strong and exotic about them, possibly Gypsy or perhaps Jewish, certainly something from the Mediterranean.

They began to talk on the inn's porch, and after just a few minutes, Bebéi was charmed. Laurence was in her early thirties, spoke perfect French, and had studied at the University of Grenoble in France. But even more importantly, she was curious about his grandfather's life.

She said that Morgen, her mother, rarely mentioned Arpad. It was as if he had not existed. It was only when her mother was debilitated by tuberculosis, a few days before she died, that she told her, "Maybe I was wrong denying your grandfather a chance to explain what he did, but it was impossible to forgive him."

Laurence never understood what his mother was saying.

Bebéi told her everything he knew. He said that Arpad had disappeared ten years earlier and someone else was interested in finding out what he had left in his apartment. He also told her about the books where Arpad kept his notes and that they were now in Lieutenant Pirilo's safe.

After thoroughly discussing, Bebéi took her to the Hungarian's apartment. There was little for her to see, but everything there was now hers. They also went up to Bebéi's apartment since he wanted Laurence to see the seagull, and as soon as he opened the balcony's glass door, Laurence sat on the floor to cuddle the bird.

Curious, the seagull stopped staring at the sea for the first time since it had landed and turned his beak toward her.

Laurence continued to caress the seagull's neck, and it seemed her affection was the only thing still needed for the seagull to regain the desire to fly. When Laurence stood up, the seagull surprised them, finally flying away.

Zoubir barked, wagging his tail, and the moonlight allowed them to follow the bird's circle before the terrace and toward the sea.

The seagull was finally cured, and with the touch of Arpad's granddaughter, it had flown again. The only one sad was the Portuguese from the supermarket, who would have to cancel his promotion.

Bebéi remained on the balcony, wondering: Had the seagull been just waiting for Laurence to arrive?

24

Stories of Banyamulenges and Kisangani. After long minutes lingering on Bebéi's balcony, Laurence realized that she had not eaten yet, so they went together to Ilona's Café. It was a short walk, but Bebéi was intrigued that all the men stopped talking and turned their heads when Laurence passed.

Ilona clarified, whispering in his ear: "Do not repeat what I'm going to say, especially to Gigi. She would be jealous, but Laurence is the most beautiful woman who has ever been in my restaurant."

A modest comment if compared to what Lola Marlene said that same night as she got into the café exuberantly dressed for her show in the cabaret and came across Laurence: "Are you a woman or a goddess who came to earth just to spread envy among us?"

Laurence smiled and lowered her eyes as Bebéi translated the comment for her. It was remarkable how Laurence combined beauty with shyness, which starkly contrasted with Lola Marlene's effervescence.

Laurence quickly captivated everyone. While dining on the terrace, she showed several pictures and told the little she knew about her grandfather, Arpad. "He worked for the North Americans and was responsible for a major USAID-funded project for the Banyamulenge." She explained that this was the name by which the Tutsi Congolese who lived between Kisangani, the town on the top of the Congo River, and Bukavu on the border with Rwanda, were known.

"My grandfather's project was why my mother moved to Kisangani."

She said that her mother, Morgen, lived and studied in Kinshasa, but since Arpad was responsible for the project, she started to join him on trips to Kisangani. Morgen became fascinated by the place. They went so many times that Arpad decided to buy a little house there for them.

"When my mother was sixteen, they had their first fight. My grandfather wanted her to go to the university in Germany, and she lied, telling him she had sent all the documents for registration. The truth is that she didn't want to go. She wanted to stay in the Congo. When Arpad discovered that, it was too late; the course had begun, and my mother was not enrolled. My grandfather tried everything he could, and with the help of a friend from Berlin, he even managed to get her accepted, but she refused to go." Laurence continued telling her story with Zoubir at her feet: "After a big fight, my mother decided to move permanently to Kisangani, and that was in 1969."

Laurence explained that there was considerable boat traffic in the Congo River between Kinshasa, the capital, and Kisangani. However, there were only mountains and the jungle from Kisangani to the Rwanda border. "That part of the country few foreigners know, but my mother knew every inch. Every place and every family — all who lived there liked her. Not only for what she did but mainly for her energy, traveling everywhere, and helping everybody. My grandmother from my father's side told me that sometimes my mother vanished for months, traveling into the mountains. Her great passion was the Maiko region, and according to what everybody says, when she was nineteen, my mother went personally to ask President Mobutu to sign the law creating the national park there."

Laurence's words bewitched Bebéi, and it seemed he was not the only one.

"The falling out with my father happened later," Laurence continued, mostly looking at Bebéi. "Not even my grandmother knows why. Something my grandfather did made my mother stop talking to him."

Doña Cecy, the cook, abandoned her kitchen to stay on the terrace listening to what Laurence was telling. "My mother continued to live in Kisangani but never worked with my grandfather again. It was around that time that she met my father, and they made a partnership. He had an old boat transporting goods between Kinshasa and Kisangani, and since my mother had the money saved to finance her studies, she bought a new boat, and they set up a joint transport company. My father still carries cargo with the boat they bought, but my mother never worked with him. All she wanted out of their business was the money she needed to live, and to continue to help the Banyamulenge. She even created a foundation to receive donations to fund their projects. A foundation that still exists."

Those places and towns had no significance to all those listening on Ilona's terrace, but it was alluring to hear Laurence talking.

"A couple of years later, my parents married, and I was born. All my childhood memories are beside my mother. I never went to a real school as a child; she taught me everything I know. We always traveled together, and she made me study every night, no matter where we were. With her, I learned French and German. I learned math, history, and everything else." Laurence paused before explaining, "The mountain region near the border has always been dangerous. There were Simba's guerrillas there, but we never had problems. We traveled all over where the Tutsis lived, and my mother's great concern was the conflict with the Hutus."

The mention of Tutsis and Hutus sharpened Princess's attention. He knew about the conflict between those two ethnic groups. Was Arpad involved?

"She died in 1991," Laurence continued, "I was sixteen then, and after her death, I stayed with my grandmother in Kisangani. It was sad, but my grandmother was sweet with me. She made me apply for a French government scholarship. No one believed I could pass. I had never attended a single class in school and only studied with my mother, but I got the highest grade. Thanks to my mother, I won the scholarship and went to study in France." Laurence said that, smiling. "When I was at the university in Grenoble, I tried to find my grandfather and discovered he lived in Santa Clara. I sent him a letter, but as no one answered, I suspected he had died. I finished my studies, returned to Kisangani, and worked at the foundation, trying to do the same job my mother did, but things are getting worse. While I was in France, the foundation grew thanks to donations we received, but it was also the period of the civil war and the Tutsi massacre in Rwanda. Today, it's almost impossible to travel to the border. Clandestine hunters and guerrillas control the mountain region. But then," she said, looking at Bebéi, "I received his letter and took the first flight to come to Santa Clara by the Sea to meet all of you who knew my grandfather."

Nobody made any comment. Laurence was happy, and it was not the time to tell her that no one there at the café's terrace had ever talked with Arpad.

Early the next day, before going to the embassy, Bebéi took Laurence to Pirilo's office; the lieutenant had not been at Ilona's Café the night before. Bebéi wanted to introduce Laurence to him and show her the blue folders inside the books of Márai, Orwell, and Tolstoy. Laurence could speak German almost as well as Frida, and what was inside those folders might help her understand what happened between Arpad and her mother.

At the meeting, Bebéi was surprised that Pirilo showed some trouble organizing his thoughts. Pirilo basically remained silent, and only when they were leaving did he mention to Laurence with a formal, strange posture, "I still do not understand what these lawyers want, and the truth is, I don't trust them. If they call you, please do not talk with them without me. Call me. It can be any time of day or night; it doesn't matter. Call me, and I will be with you."

Bebéi got the impression that something was bothering Pirilo. Contrary to other meetings at his office, he had not asked questions and had let Laurence freely talk. Was Pirilo also impressed by her beauty?

Pirilo's advice to Laurence was prophetic. That same evening, the lawyers called her. Somehow, they had discovered she was in Santa Clara and wanted to meet her.

Following Pirilo's recommendation, Laurence proposed a meeting on the next day in City Hall. "Lieutenant Pirilo insists he wants to participate," she said on the phone, displeasing the lawyers.

How did they discover that she had arrived? It was the first thought on Pirilo's mind. Do they also have cameras installed in the city?

Pirilo asked her on the phone about the places where she had been. There were only a few of them: the bed and breakfast, Arpad's apartment, Bebéi's apartment, and Ilona's Café. How had they discovered her presence so quickly? Was he becoming paranoid? Paranoid or not, he asked his assistants to check for cameras in all the places visited by Laurence. Maybe someone was following Bebéi's movements? After giving these instructions, he sat at his desk smiling. It was good that she trusted him. Something about Laurence's personality differentiated her from the women he knew. Probably because she was a foreigner, he thought.

That afternoon, Bebéi and Laurence returned to Pirilo's office. It was Laurence's idea. She called Bebéi saying that she wanted to explain what was inside the notes in German she read before they met the lawyers.

As soon as they arrived, Bebéi realized that Pirilo was again using the same formal and controlled posture of the morning. Could it be that the experienced bachelor was intimidated by her?

Laurence described what she had discovered in Márai's book. The notes on Morgen confirmed that Arpad felt for her mother. "He felt guilty that he had taken her to Africa. It took a long time for him to understand that she was happier there than in Berlin. The notes also confirm that he did everything he could to send her to Berlin and that a friend named Otto pressured the university for her to be accepted without previous enrollment."

Bebéi commented playfully to Pirilo that Otto could solve any sort of problem, from trips to soccer matches to late university applications.

"The problems between the two deepened later," said Laurence with a worried expression. "It has to do with his work. According to what Arpad wrote in a note, *Morgen never understood why I do my job, and I do not blame her. I never understood it, either. The difference is that I have long stopped asking questions, and Morgen goes on digging.*"

"Curious," interrupted Bebéi, "your grandfather did not seem proud of his work."

Pirilo continued silently. No questions, just observing Laurence.

Laurence commented that she had gotten the same impression after reading the notes. She then translated another one:

What happened in Burundi was horrible, and I could not avoid it. I did not know what they were planning. When I realized it was too late. Morgen never forgave me. She knew who was behind it, fomenting their rebellion and giving them their weapons. Morgen knew that I had blood on my hands.

Pirilo was having trouble focusing on the discussion. He seemed unexpectedly distracted by Laurence's presence and was not helpful. Bebéi suggested inviting Princess to join them, so at least with him at the meeting, they would be able to understand what those notes were saying.

Pirilo agreed and called Princess, saying it was an emergency.

Princess was elegantly dressed as Lola Marlene, receiving a group of ambassadors' wives at his fashion atelier. As it was an emergency, she did not have time to change her clothes.

She crossed Cathedral Park rushing in high heels, wearing a full white floating skirt underlining a tiny waist — in the style of Grace Kelly in *Rear Window* — with a black fitted bodice and a plunging neckline.

The whole City Hall stopped when she arrived. Laurence was thrilled, and it took them a few minutes to calm Princess, who was breathless.

After almost an hour of reading and rereading notes, they finally understood what had happened. Apparently, Arpad's project was an attempt by the Americans to get closer to the Tutsis. Their interest was not just to help; the Americans were trying to persuade the Tutsis to fight the groups opposing the Mobutu government.

The question was even more complex, explained Princess. "According to the notes I read, the Soviets were, for their part, trying to organize the Hutus to confront the Tutsis," he added with a displeased expression. "Both Americans and Soviets were doing exactly the opposite of what Morgen wanted. While she was trying to defuse the tensions between the two groups, Americans and Soviets were firing them up, throwing Africans against Africans, with the sole purpose of increasing their own domination as part of the Cold War."

Laurence accepted Princess's explanation and, to back it, she described Morgen's concern before she died. "From what my mother said, there was a lot of tension, especially in the region of the Rusizi River, which stretched from Lake Kivu to Lake Tanganyika. Tutsis lived in the Congo but also in Rwanda and Burundi. My mother always said that they didn't fight in the past, and it was the outsiders who convinced them to fight. She never explained who did it. All that happened before I was born." After pausing Laurence continued, with tears in her eyes, "I remember talking about the great massacre in Burundi, but I could never imagine that my grandfather was involved. Still, this note he wrote confirms it." She then translated it with sadness.

Morgen always said that we should not hand over weapons to the Tutsis because that was not what they needed. She was correct, but my people thought it was important to arm them to fight the Simba movement, and it all ended in a great tragedy.

There was another note explaining his actions, and Laurence translated it:

My mother taught me how to delight people with the sharp notes of the violin, and all that my hands do today are dirty reports of blood.

When she finished reading these lines, Laurence proposed to interrupt the meeting. There was too much information on her mind, and she felt drained. She needed to walk around before talking to the lawyers at the meeting late that evening.

When leaving, she commented, "My mother knew that after the massacre in Burundi, it was important to calm the spirits. If the Hutus decided to seek revenge, they would massacre the Tutsis. She perceived that the massacre the Tutsis perpetrated in Burundi could cause the genocide that later occurred in Rwanda, and she regretted that my grandfather worked for those who had fostered the conflict."

25

Pirilo was an excellent poker player. Later that evening, they met the lawyers. The meeting was at City Hall. Bebéi also attended, and the lawyers' team included the young lawyer from the local office and the lawyer from Miami, who had arrived the day before and was wearing another elegant and expensive tie.

The first question they asked was whether Laurence could prove that she was Arpad's granddaughter. She presented her mother's birth certificate issued in Germany and a birth certificate from the Democratic Republic of Congo.

The Miami lawyer took the documents in his hands and, with an arrogant expression, argued that they would have to obtain the necessary certifications and that he anticipated some complications in attesting the validity of documents issued by the Democratic Republic of Congo, particularly the records released from a city with the name of Kisangani.

Laurence listened with the same humble attitude she had demonstrated since her arrival. When he concluded, she replied, "I also have the document that my mother got, anticipating that someone could question the validity of my birth certificate." She showed them a birth certificate issued by the German Democratic Republic and explained, "Even if I have never been in Germany, I have German citizenship by virtue of being the daughter of Morgen Corvinus."

The lawyers could not hide their disgust.

Bebéi had a humorous thought; he realized that at that table, everyone suspected everyone.

After seeing the documents, the two lawyers did not have further questions. They made a few quick comments, and the meeting seemed to be ending. Pirilo even asked, "Anything else you'd like to discuss?" The lawyers declined.

Pirilo patiently waited until the three had stood up from the conference table. Only then, still seated, did he ask a new question, looking at the senior lawyer: "When I was in your office for the first time, your local lawyer referred to another estate belonging to the Hungarian. Don't you think it would be convenient to talk about this property, too?"

The Miami lawyer was not a good poker player; his expression denounced that he was bothered by the question. "I didn't think it necessary to mention it. For the time being, we do not yet have a clear indication that Mr. Arpad Corvinus is dead. So far, we continue to manage his estate and financial assets just as we have always done."

"I agree, and we are all thankful," said Pirilo without disguising his irony, "but as Mr. Arpad disappeared more than ten years ago, I think it would be useful to inform Ms. Laurence, his heiress, what assets her grandfather had. Don't you think?"

The lawyers returned to their seats. The younger one opened his case and grabbed a document he read with an annoyed expression.

"In addition to the apartment in the amber manor, we also manage a savings account with approximately one million dollars and a plot in Santa Clara by the Sea of twenty-six thousand square feet where there is currently no construction." The Miami lawyer immediately added, "We will continue to administer his assets with the same care and dedication until the situation of Mr. Corvinus and his eventual heir is clarified."

There was another silence, and Pirilo decided to provoke them further: "I imagine you are aware that after the apartment was robbed, three people came from Miami to invade Mr. Arpad's residence. Do you have any idea what they were looking for?"

Pirilo spoke while closely watching the two lawyers' expressions, and, oddly, the local lawyer was surprised. He turned his face to the Miami lawyer, who answered , making an effort to remain calm: "We only knew about the theft of Mr. Arpad's personal objects. We never heard of this second attempt."

Pirilo was a good poker player and was having fun taunting the lawyer and his expensive tie. He even tried to go further by asking: "Were they looking for a missing key?"

The two lawyers gave the clear impression that none of them had any idea of what key Pirilo was speaking about.

Little more was said and, when the lawyers had left, Pirilo made a comment to Laurence. "Now we know that you are not only beautiful but also very rich."

They continued chatting, and Bebéi asked Laurence: "Who was that friend in Germany who helped you with the birth certificate?"

"I never knew him," Laurence replied. "I only know that it was someone who had known my mother since she was a child, and lived in Berlin."

"Probably Otto," Bebéi said to Pirilo, and they both explained to Laurence their suspicions about Arpad's work. Otto was probably from the Stasi, and Arpad was a double agent working for the CIA, and also for the Stasi and the Soviets.

Amazingly, Laurence was not surprised: "The notes inside Orwell's book confirm your suspicions. From those, I could see that Otto had always been a great friend of my grandfather. They kept in touch until my grandfather left Congo in 1976." She made the same comment that, since the beginning, had intrigued Bebéi. "What is curious is that Arpad had kept with him letters that he sent to Otto, and I do not understand why he is the one who has them and not this Otto."

Laurence then translated the notes that were inside Orwell's book. The first one was from Algeria, where Arpad mentioned:

I want to distance myself from everything, but I do not know what else I can do. I know that you would always help me in Berlin, but I cannot live there; everything in your city reminds me of the sadness of the war and the heavenly life I lived with Eszter.

Laurence continued, "I know, since my mother once told me that my grandmother Eszter worked for the Stasi. It was the price she had to pay to get the confidence of the Communist Party and get the help she needed to save my grandfather from the Soviet gulag camps. But I also know that she had always been a rebel. Otto could have been a close friend of the family, and it's difficult to say what exactly he did. There is another note where Arpad talks about his work. A letter that Arpad wrote to Otto where he explains his remorse.

All I have seen is how Americans and Soviets played with the lives of Africans. Among the people I know, the only person who really cares about Africa is Morgen, and because of that, she abandoned us all and broke with me. She did what everyone who loves Africa should have done. I continued to take advantage of my job, and the only thing I achieved is death and destruction.

Bebéi was following her words and writing what he was hearing in his little notebook, so as not to forget it.

"In the notes where Arpad writes his personal remarks, there is a reference to Otto," continued Laurence. That note seemed so meaningful that she handed it to Bebéi after translating.

January 1977: the last time I met Otto. He's always been by my side, but now I must stay alone. I cannot have him beside me. Now I'm going to do what I should have done before.

After looking at all the notes in Orwell's book, they still discussed Tamara's notes inside Tolstoy's novel. Pirilo seemed to be more relaxed. There was a note that Frida had not translated. It was a very personal note from Tamara, where she talked about the problems in Bolivia. It was written in 1965, the same year that Guevara went to Congo, and it said: *I told our friend that he should not approach you.*

"Tamara knew that Arpad was a double agent," said the lieutenant, becoming interested in the Hungarian's life. "The fact that El Che should not get close to him reinforces what we thought about Che's note when he said that Arpad was helping from afar."

Much had been clarified, but Pirilo still had a crucial doubt: "What did your grandfather Arpad do after 1977? What is the meaning of this phrase: 'I'm going to do what I should have always done?' Arpad only arrived in Santa Clara in 1986 to be a music teacher. We are still missing ten years of his life, and maybe what happened in those years explains the key that was stored inside Zola's book."

26

What was clear turned confused. Little by little, the questions were answered. It's true that they still did not know why the Hungarian vanished, much less what the key was for. Pirilo suspected that the key was the cause of the robberies, but he could not be sure. On the positive side, they at least knew what the Hungarian had done before he moved to Santa Clara: he had been an important CIA spy who was also a double agent feeding Cuba and Berlin information on African countries.

At least, that was what they thought until the Lady called Bebéi, proposing an encounter in Lola Marlene's atelier. She would check some new outfits specially designed for her and wanted to talk about the Hungarian. Bebéi mentioned the meeting to Pirilo, who also decided to go, and what they heard that afternoon was a complete surprise.

"Arpad Corvinus briefly worked for the CIA. He was in Algeria for two years and then went to Congo, where he worked for fourteen years. But there, he only did intelligence work, or espionage, as Bebéi likes to call it, for a couple of years. He was then transferred to our development agency, the USAID. It seems that the work of intelligence didn't attract him, and he never impressed his supervisors. His work in Congo was more of a bureaucratic kind. He visited Burundi and Rwanda on account of development projects but never worked outside those countries."

"You mean, he was not an important spy?" Bebéi asked, disappointed. The Lady replied, "Sorry, but no."

Lola Marlene, who was also there, disagreed. She told the Lady that the information they gathered showed unmistakably that he was involved with important events in several countries, not just in the Congo.

The Lady listened politely but reaffirmed that Arpad was not an agent, but to be kind to her Santa Clara friends, she offered to visit Pirilo's office that same afternoon and look at the documents they had.

Bebéi left the meeting frustrated; Arpad was not an international spy. How could that be? As he had asked for a half-day leave from the embassy, he took Laurence for a tour around the city.

The first stop was the corner of Our Lady of Mercy, where he introduced Laurence to Grená. The lottery ticket seller asked some questions, and Bebéi helped them to understand each other.

Frida and Null-and-void, who were drinking on the church's steps, also approached them. Frida was happy to speak to someone in German, but Null-and-void was wasted. He could hardly stand up. When he finally greeted her and looked at her face, he recovered his energy and instructed Bebéi with authority. "Tell your beautiful friend that from now on, she will live in Santa Clara," and added with determination, "Forever. It's my decision!"

Ignoring Null-and-void's comments, Frida kept talking in German to Laurence, who translated to Bebéi. "She said that both my grandfather and Otto were working for the Stasi and that she didn't like them for that."

From there, they went to Rasta's barbershop, where Bebéi welcomed Ludmila, Rasta's wife, still recovering from the long flight from Moscow she had made. Bebéi handed her the folders with notes in Russian. Laurence stayed at the door watching the ice cream seller and his little monkey while Ludmila read one of the notes in Rilke's book.

Bebéi was respectfully waiting at the door with Zoubir when Ludmila began to cry, which was not unusual since she had become pregnant. In between sobs, she translated to everyone a note that

Arpad sent to Eszter written in Russian, thanks to the compassion of a concentration camp soldier who helped Arpad to write it.

I would give any part of my body if I could preserve my hands; it was with them that I played the violin for my mother, but the cold here is so devastating. When I arrived, I could not protect them. They only gave me a pair of old gloves; one of them, the one for the left hand, was torn and had only two fingers. First, I tried to put all my fingers inside those two glove fingers, but it was impossible. As they forced me to work, I had to separate my thumb from the other fingers to hold the shovel. I put my thumb in one of the glove fingers and two fingers, the index and the big one, in the other. The two smaller fingers remained exposed to snow, and they froze. When I returned to the dormitory at night, they were just two black things that seemed stuck to my body. I lost my fingers — exactly the two I needed to play the highest notes in the violin. Those were precisely the notes that had enchanted Lali and made her dance in the streets of Budapest. The only thing I know is how to play the violin, and my music was forever frozen beneath the snow of Kolyma.

In the folder, there was also a photo of Arpad with Eszter in Moscow in front of the Kremlin that Ludmila showed everyone. It was probably taken when Eszter found him, since he appeared extremely frail and sick.

Those inside the barbershop — where, despite two roof fans, everyone was sweating, thanks to a scorching afternoon — started exchanging passionate opinions about how someone could survive in the snow that they only knew from calendar photos and movies.

While listening to the discussion, Ludmila took a quick look at the notes in the book of Neruda, and her expression suddenly changed. She went on reading a little more, then, unexpectedly, told Bebéi that she could not fully understand what was written and preferred to go home and read them calmly.

Rasta Bong noticed that her behavior was unusual. Ludmila walked away with the note, and as soon as she got home, she called Pirilo. "You should come here. We must talk right now."

Pirilo understood it was important, but he was waiting for the Lady in his office. He promised to go and see Ludmila after the meeting, and she insisted. "Please come as soon as you can. What I must tell you is much more important than all your domino games."

Pirilo noticed that Ludmila was tense, yet he was curious to meet the Lady. He was sure Arpad was a double agent, but he knew the Lady was well informed.

Laurence and Bebéi were also in his office when the Lady arrived, and Princess/Lola Marlene came with her since he/she was also curious to hear the Lady's reaction to the Hungarian's notes. Even though Laurence was the most beautiful one there, Lola and the Lady were both unbeatable in exquisite elegance, Lola in yellow and the Lady in blue.

The first thing Pirilo showed the Lady was the notes about Congo and Francisco. She read them carefully, and her only comment was that both the Hungarian in Congo and Francisco in Angola were not happy with the work they were doing. The Lady also explained to Laurence that it was a period of great political turmoil, and many regrettable blunders were committed.

Pirilo also handed her the notes in English from Ibsen's book referring to Indonesia, and her expression started to demonstrate some concern. She insisted that she did not believe what was written. The notes were saying that someone Arpad knew had access to a list prepared by the CIA, including names of members of the Indonesian Communist Party, which was handed over to General Suharto for execution. Clearly, the note indicated that Arpad was sharing the list with the Soviets so they could try to save some of the people included in that death list.

The Lady reaffirmed that it did not seem to be true and was interrupted by Lola Marlene: "My dear, I love you to death, but do not even try to say that the Americans were saints in Indonesia. History tells us that at least five hundred thousand Communists were exterminated there by General Suharto." Lola Marlene then added, waving a Spanish fan she had brought, "What is in the past stays in the past, I accept that. But that is what happened, and you can't deny it."

The Lady did not reply and continued reading the notes until she learned that there were copies of the Indonesian lists, and that they were "well kept," and that, *if needed, they would be forwarded to the newspapers.*

"Could the Hungarian have more documents hidden in his residence?" she asked.

The lieutenant thought for a moment and replied that he did not believe it; the thieves had already taken everything, and his team had checked the apartment.

"They did, but they did not realize what was inside the books," recalled Bebéi, which led the Lady to believe it would be convenient to do a new and more detailed review of Arpad's apartment.

Then she read the notes from Kafka's book, and as she was reading, she explained that they mentioned someone called K, who was a contact of Arpad and lived in Khartoum. It seemed to be someone who worked for the CIA and, like Francisco, did not have great sympathy for what the Americans were doing. "These notes seem to indicate that there was a network of double agents in the 1970s who worked within the CIA but filtered information for the Soviets. They also show that Arpad was somehow involved with them." She added, worried, "It happened more than thirty years ago, but maybe there are people who, for reasons that we do not know, are still interested in them."

As she spoke, she opened the envelope with the notes inside Virgil's book, which seemed to refer to someone called Valerie. Her expression entirely changed.

"What other notes do you have?" she asked, looking frightened.

Pirilo answered her with another question. "Why do you want to know?" The Lady did not answer, and Pirilo insisted, "What did you read that is so worrisome?"

"I have to be honest," she answered. "I cannot say anything now. Let me take these notes to show them to a friend of mine, and then, I promise, I'll tell you. Trust me, I will come back to you, but there's something here that might be ..." and she paused, choosing her words, "very significant."

Pirilo and Bebéi had no reasons to distrust her; although she worked for the CIA, she was a friend who loved Santa Clara and had always honored her commitments. Anyway, the lieutenant just let her take Valerie's notes and did not show her anything else.

When she left, Bebéi commented. "The Lady's expression was the same as Ludmila's when she read Natasha's notes."

27

The Russian notes scared Ludmila. "You must take these notes out of Bebéi's hands; they are dangerous. This woman Natasha was blackmailing the KGB." That was the first thing Ludmila said when Pirilo walked into her house. It took him a long time — and two doses of rum — to understand what exactly she was talking about.

"In one of the folders, there is a clear reference that this Natasha had secret information that would be handed over to leading international newspapers and the United Nations if the KGB did not pay what she was asking for. There are also records of a series of payments she received from someone called Yuri and a list of organizations to which the money was transferred."

Ludmila kept talking, not giving Pirilo a chance to interrupt her. "Inside the folder of Yeats's book, there are notes from this Yuri, and they mention several kidnappings, murders, and disappearances of African leaders, registering that they were all coordinated by Moscow. And it was not just in Congo; there are cases in Angola and Mozambique where opponents of Agostinho Neto and Samora Machel were murdered, and notes discussing the support Soviets gave to Hutus to massacre Tutsis, and even others talking about a coup in Brazzaville to bring Major Ngouabi to power where I don't know how many people were killed. They also mention Siad Barre in Somalia, another guy called Amílcar Cabral in Guinea-Bissau, and all the work the Soviets did to execute their opponents. They also mention other things that only with Princess's help would we be able to understand. They even describe an attempt to kill

Sellassie to put Mengistu Haile Mariam as president of Ethiopia. When I mentioned it to Rasta Bong, he went awry and had to smoke two big joints to calm down. He is now in his room saying his prayers. He told me that he wants to talk to you and that you must immediately open an investigation to find out who tried to kill the Lion of Judah."

Pirilo took an additional shot of rum while listening to everything Ludmila told him and left the house before Rasta had finished his prayers. Nobody, and not even all the marijuana in the world, would soothe his brother that night after learning that someone planned to kill Negus Selassie, Emperor of Ethiopia, Ras Tafari Makonnen, and God of all Blacks, as Rasta Bong used to call him, a direct descendant of King Solomon. It would be a waste of time to try to explain to him that it had all happened forty years ago.

Pirilo went to his friend's tavern to vent his anger and stepped into it shouting. "Now I have this Natasha blackmailing the KGB and the Lady on my back after reading about Valerie. Was this Valerie blackmailing the CIA? And tell me: what do the Miami lawyers have to do with all that?"

The Asturian listened silently while cutting some slices of a moistened *jamón serrano*. Pirilo continued: "What the fuck do I have to do with all this? No one here knew who this Hungarian was; no one cares if a bunch of hoodlums stole his stuff and who in the hell bothers about what is hidden in those damned books." He added, angrily filling his glass with an Albariño wine his Asturian friend had just opened, "Does anyone have any idea what that key is for? And can you explain why I skipped our dominoes this afternoon to wait for the Lady and show her those stupid papers?"

The Asturian remained speechless and Pirilo continued in a more normal tone. "As if this was not enough, now I have to put up with my brother, who will not stop until he finds out who tried to kill Sallasie."

Pirilo concluded, looking into his friend's eyes as if asking for support, "That is why I will no longer follow Bebéi's madness. From now on, I will only deal with issues relevant to City Hall."

The Asturian let him vent completely and calmly replied. "First, I do not need to remind you that Laurence is a very pretty woman." Looking at his friend, he continued, "Do not even try to deny that you didn't notice it. Secondly, the Hungarian hid all those papers for a reason. Maybe because he had some interest in the blackmailing." Finally, the Asturian stressed in a friendly way, "You will have an excuse to meet Laurence, and why bother? All this happened so long ago that there is nothing to worry about."

Pirilo did not reply but seemed calmer. He had even sat down to share the serrano ham with his friend when his telephone rang. It was Ilona.

"Our friend Theo Cavafys just called me saying he's coming to Santa Clara. He said that the Cossack called him asking for a favor. He wants Theo to come to Santa Clara to help some of his friends. And I hope that you are seated. He said that a couple of Russians, probably ex-KGB like the Cossack, are coming to Santa Clara to talk to Bebéi," and she added, "Does it make any sense? Two ex-KGB coming to talk to him." Pirilo kept a dazzled expression, looking, appalled, to his Asturian friend. Ilona continued. "Theo has no idea what they want, but he asked me to warn you; it seems that it is something important, and Theo believes that you should be with Bebéi when he meets these KGB guys."

Pirilo hung up the telephone with the same expression he always had after losing a dominoes game. He did not want to get involved with all the craziness anymore, but what could he do? Angry or not, he would have to help Bebéi handle these Russians who had probably discovered that the Hungarian was involved with Natasha.

Both the lieutenant and the Asturian knew that the Cossack mentioned by Ilona was an ex-KGB who became a drug lord after the Soviet Union was dissolved. He had also helped Theo Cavafys with some "very lucrative shipments" when the Greek captain was short of money. The Cossack was someone that Pirilo wanted to ignore — a not-so-easy task considering that the Cossack was also the father of Ludmila, his brother's wife.

That same evening, Pirilo reached Cavafys by phone, and confirmed his worst concerns. The Greek captain said that Bebéi had sent a letter to a certain Natasha — the one written by Mrs. Dusanka. The letter triggered the attention of ex-KGB members. According to Cavafys, the Russians were curious about what Bebéi knew about Natasha. The only good news was that Cavafys, who was also worried, was approaching Trinidad with his boat *Ithaca* and would land there to take a plane and meet with the Russians in Santa Clara the following week. At least the lieutenant would have time to sort out his doubts before he met them.

Luckily, not everything was stressful in the city. That morning Laurence, who did not know anything about blackmail or Russians arriving, was cheerful; she was going to the airport to meet a friend of her mother who had learned that she was in Santa Clara and had traveled to meet her there. Bebéi went along with her and had to rent a large van since Mr. Baumgarten was bringing a motorized wheelchair.

He arrived in an excellent mood. He could walk, but with some difficulty, and used a wheelchair, which could represent problems on the cobblestone streets and narrow sidewalks of Santa Clara. "Please do not worry," Mr. Baumgarten reassured Laurence at the airport, "I live in Óbidos, a small town in Portugal very similar to Santa Clara, and that is why I brought this light wheelchair, which is very easy to handle. I can go with it wherever I want. Even if there are problems, you don't need to worry; I can easily overcome them." He added, joking, "The only thing that drives me crazy is to stay locked inside a house; I get so cranky that nobody in this world can stand me."

He was a pleasant and talkative man. In the van, he told them he was ninety years old, born to an Austrian family — a father who had lived in Germany and married a Portuguese woman. He also mentioned that he had met Morgen and had helped her with the Banyamulenge Foundation.

Bebéi took Mr. Baumgarten to the hotel and Ilona's Café. He was a storyteller, just what Ilona liked, but was very picky about choosing wines "Only the best; I do not have much time left to waste with crappy plonk."

In a couple of days, Mr. Baumgarten made many friends. He arrived on the eve of an annual dominoes tournament jointly sponsored by the Spanish embassy and City Hall. The tournament always started on a Friday and ended with final matches on Sunday afternoon, traditionally decided between Moses and Habib's duo, playing against Pirilo and the Asturian. Three years before, the first tournament had been won by Pirilo and the Asturian. The Jewish-Lebanese duo won the following two.

Mr. Baumgarten was a dominoes player, but he only arrived after all players were already enrolled, and he had no one with whom to pair. Diocles rescued him, mentioning a Gypsy girl who was a great domino player but only played with her cousins and uncles.

Mr. Baumgarten met her, played a few games, and the two were the last to sign up — just a few minutes before the deadline.

In the early games on Friday, no one paid attention to them; a thirteen-year-old Gypsy and an old man in a wheelchair did not seem to intimidate their opponents, but they won all their games on Friday and Saturday.

On Sunday, they were a great attraction, beating tough opponents, including the Pirilo duo, to make the final game against the Jew and the Lebanese. The park was crowded, and everybody was rooting for them. When the girl hit the table with her last piece, and they won, the evening became a party, with the Gypsy band playing from the bandstand until dawn.

Pirilo, beaten but impressed, resignedly explained to Bebéi and Laurence that it was not just luck. "Both Mr. Baumgarten and the young Gypsy had an incredible ability to memorize everything. They know precisely the pieces each player has. I'm sure they have a code for communicating through glances, but I could not decode it. They are unbeatable."

The victory in the tournament made the old man popular, which was greatly appreciated by Laurence, who could take care of her own affairs and leave the old man in the park all day long playing chess and dominoes and chatting with Diocles.

Mr. Baumgarten's meals were at Ilona's Café, and like Ilona, he knew how to make anyone relaxed and chatty. He even surprised everyone when he met Frida, and, by some magic, he took her for dinner, spending the evening with her, drinking numerous bottles of wine, and listening to Frida's stories of her radical leftist youth in Germany.

He made such a good impression that he had the supreme honor of being invited to that unique table in the café's kitchen, where Doña Cecy used to eat every night with Diocles.

The only thing that Mr. Baumgarten was not good at was sleeping. He explained that he did not need to, and as Diocles also slept very little, they often stayed in the park until late at night but did not talk. They preferred the silence, both listening to the accordion of the Gypsy.

The arrival of the old man and the dominoes tournament served to calm the lieutenant. He even thought about discreetly inviting Laurence for dinner, but he realized that she was focused on investigating her grandfather's life and not on distractions. Better. He had his own problems to solve: not only were the Russians about to arrive, but the Lady from the American embassy was driving him nuts. She kept calling him daily, reminding him that she was interested in knowing everything Bebéi had found in the Hungarian's books.

He managed to gain some time with lame excuses, but her insistence was firm, and she warned him: "The documents include important information that does not interest either you or Bebéi but will create a huge mess if they fall into the wrong hands."

Despite her pressure, the lieutenant decided not to give her anything else. He respected the Lady and also the Cossack, who, despite his shady businesses, had always been kind to everyone in the city. His decision had nothing to do with eventual preferences between Russians and Americans, Communists or not. The real reason was that he wanted to protect Laurence. He did not know precisely why, but the Hungarian's notes belonged to his heir, Laurence, and until he understood what and why the Hungarian had hidden them, neither Russians nor Americans would touch those papers.

He moved the documents to a safe place where no one could find them and informed the Lady that he would not deliver her the notes.

The reaction was immediate; that same afternoon, the American ambassador, joined by the Mayor, came into his office and asked for him to open his safe.

Pirilo opened it, showed it was empty, and told them the documents were no longer with him. He explained that he had returned them to Laurence and that she had burned them. The Lady didn't believe it, but there was not much that she could do. After that, Pirilo was finally ready to face the Russians, who were coming to question Bebéi.

28

Everybody was eating pizza. The Russians were scheduled to arrive on Saturday, but Friday was hectic. In the early morning hours, the second issue of *The Santa Clara Barrel Organ* circulated with a detailed description of the Mayor's plans for the new city. Jordi wrote and published the newspaper in complete secrecy. The Mayor shouted so loudly when he read it that his wife thought someone had broken into her house and called Pirilo.

"How did he get these documents?" the Mayor was yelling on the telephone to his brother when Pirilo arrived. Only a few people knew the details of the project, and the Mayor ordered a thorough investigation.

Pirilo put all his assistants to work, and they started by questioning everyone who had access to the plans, including City Hall secretaries, drivers, and even the women who served coffee at the Mayor's office. As they all denied it, Pirilo expanded the investigation into the firm of architects and checked the professionals who had participated in developing the new city plans. He was surprised to see that they were all foreigners, and the explanation was that the Mayor's brother, who was already increasingly concerned with security, had instructed the firm to hire only foreigners precisely to avoid leaks.

The only people the lieutenant and his assistants did not question were the cleaning crew of the architecture firm, and it was there that Nadia was working. She had studied in the same school as Jordi. She dreamed of being an architect, and to finance her studies she worked at night on one of the crews that cleaned the firm's office. It was Nadia who had found the plans, taken notes, made copies — everything during the night shifts — and handed them to Jordi.

The Barrel Organ also published some drawings by Nadia that gave an idea of how Santa Clara by the Sea would look after the renewal. With them, everybody finally understood that the Mayor's project represented the end of the city as they knew it. One of the drawings revealed how the ruins of the fort at the end of the boardwalk would join the new shopping mall with the office towers and, worse, it showed that additional towers would be built in an area that included the riverbed and the whole community across the river, where Nadia lived.

The Mayor continued furiously yelling at everyone while not so far from City Hall, in Cathedral Park, Jordi was proudly distributing newspapers next to Arcadio's barrel organ. With the money donated by the Mayor, Jordi had hired two assistants and printed not two but five thousand copies spread throughout the city.

One of the happiest citizens that morning was Cholo, the shoe shiner; the second issue of *The Barrel Organ* had his picture on the front page.

For thirty-six years, Cholo had shined shoes in Plaza del Libertador Bolívar, a few steps from the Mayor's house. He had not attended any school and, though people never suspected, he did not even know how to read. Every morning, he made the daily newspapers available to his clients and, while polishing shoes, Cholo learned the news by listening to their comments. Just as Grená's umbrella was the hub of gossip, his shoeshine chair was the focal point of political discussions, and Cholo, one of the most respected pundits in town. And this without ever reading a single headline.

All that day, the city discussed the Mayor's plans, and friends and curious surrounded Cholo to congratulate him and take selfies in his chair. Still, when the night came, the central meeting point in town was the Friar's pizzeria opening. All local personalities were there, joining tourists and even some illustrious international visitors such as Mr. Baumgarten, who greeted everybody on the sidewalk in his motorized wheelchair. Princess, who had to get ready for the Friday night presentation of Lola Marlene at the drag queen cabaret, also quickly passed by for a pizza slice.

The main subject of all conversations was obviously the plans for the new city. The Mayor had publicly committed himself to attend Friar's restaurant inauguration and could not escape. He went with his wife and spent the night trying to justify why he wanted to change the city.

"The city is so lovely now, Mr. Mayor, why do you want to change it?" It was everyone's question.

The complaints were diverse. Grená said that the sixty-story towers would block the sea breeze, and Carmela added that the streets full of cars would no longer be safe for the children to walk to the parks.

The biggest complaints came from those living on the other side of the river. They had finally realized that everyone living there would have to move away to make room for the new towers.

"Those who own their homes will receive some money, but those who rent houses will leave empty-handed," Jordi warned.

The angriest were the young people like Nadia. There, they were at least close to the city. All they had to do was to cross the bridge to be in the old town. But everything would change. The new houses that the City Hall would offer them were beyond the airport. They already felt excluded as they did not have money to do things they wanted. Now, they would be banished to a distant place.

Even those living within the city feared they would have to leave; their town would be invaded by shops and restaurants for tourists, and new residents who would come to work in the offices and live in the towers.

Bebéi brought Zoubir to the opening. The poor dog was restless among all these guests walking around him, until a pizza slice fell on the floor, and he ate it. After that, he concealed himself under the table, lurking anxiously for other accidents. Bebéi sat at the table of honor with Doña Cecy, Ilona, and Laurence. Every man who attended the inauguration passed there at least once to look at Laurence.

"It's you that they are looking at," said Bebéi, respectfully teasing Doña Cecy. "They all know your risotto."

The Lady was also at the pizzeria, but her concern was not the Mayor's plans; she had been told by Pirilo that the Hungarian papers were burned but insisted, "There may still be documents inside the apartment that you haven't found. I can send my team to search, and let's check if there's anything else hidden there." The idea seemed harmless, but Pirilo's current focus was on the Russians, and he preferred to wait.

Gigi and Friar Bernard were thrilled and wanted to thank everyone, which was impossible; there were so many people inside and outside the pizzeria that they could not greet them all. According to the comments, which included a very critical evaluation by Juanita, Doña Cecy, and Lais, the three great chefs of Santa Clara, the Friar Pizza was "divine."

The Mayor kept his dignity as much as possible but started losing patience with everyone questioning his plans. The Serbian prudently suggested he leave; he was not ready for an open discussion with the villagers, and she had already warned him.

The pizzeria had to close at ten-thirty since it was in a residential area, but the guests went to Ilona's Café to continue the celebration. Pirilo went with them, which caught Ilona's attention. "It's the first time he's come to our café for a late-night drink," she whispered in Doña Cecy's ear. But Pirilo did not stay long; Laurence happily sang, talked, and danced, ignoring him. He decided to go to Paris Street and meet his friends. Why do I need further problems, he thought.

That same night, the Mayor met his friends at his home. They were all concerned, and the Romanian insisted they had to start immediately with a promotional effort: "The Arabs must give us money to finance it," he said. "If we don't counterattack, the opposition will grow, and we will not be able to stop them."

Everyone agreed that their main problem was public relations. The Mayor then asked the Egyptian if all the properties were already purchased and registered. To his surprise, the Egyptian shared unwelcome news.

"There's only one property that is not under our control, and from what the lawyers told me, we might have some problems."

The Mayor choked on his whiskey and almost tripped over the rug; even the headache he had begun to feel with all the questioning inside the pizzeria disappeared.

"You said everything was fine; why are you telling us we might have problems?"

The Egyptian answered, embarrassed: "There is a parcel right at the end of the boardwalk, beside the ruins of the old fort. This property belongs to a foreigner who lived in Santa Clara and moved away a few years ago. We have already negotiated with a law firm in Miami that manages his assets. We were going to trade his plot for another property of the same size near the city. According to the lawyers, it will be a secure exchange; they would continue to have a registered property of twenty-six thousand square feet among the assets of the foreigner, and we would have the lot we need for our project. As I explained to you, everything was going fine, and we had advanced half of the money to the lawyers, but from what they just told me, a granddaughter of the owner has emerged, and we will have to negotiate with her."

"What the fuck!" blasted the Mayor. "This will delay our project."

The Mayor's brother intervened, worried. "And what happens if she refuses to sell?"

"The problem can always be solved," said the Mayor, trying to regroup and show leadership. "We can always confiscate the lot for social interest, but the process will take time and could expose us to political pressures." He continued, staring at the Egyptian with an enraged expression, "Tell your Arab bosses that it is better to pay whatever this woman asks," he explained, looking towards his brother. "To negotiate expropriation in the poor neighborhood is not a problem, but confiscating oceanfront properties of foreign people can represent a serious and unpleasant challenge."

When the meeting had ended and he was alone with his brother, he vented his anger. "Call that Arab who is your friend and tell him that the Egyptian they sent us is useless. He knows how to find nice whores, but at work, he's totally incompetent. How is it possible that he reassured us that everything was fine when there was still a property pending, and worse, right in the middle of the project."

29

The Russians were looking for Natasha. Captain Cavafys arrived Monday morning. He did not come in one of those taxis that usually brought him from the port to Ilona's Café. This time, he landed near the pier in a new helicopter but walked to the boardwalk complaining. "This is for the birds. Men should keep their feet on the ground or the deck of a safe vessel." Despite the modernity of the flying equipment, he was the old and grumpy Cavafys, wearing the same navy blue jacket, a *Caban Breton* that he had worn for over two decades, and a bouzouki bag hanging from the back of his right shoulder. Beside him were the two Russians visiting Santa Clara for the first time with the sole purpose of asking Bebéi a few questions.

From the boardwalk, they walked to Ilona's Café, where Bebéi and Pirilo were waiting for them. Even though Natasha's secret was the subject of the conversation, Pirilo had chosen not to bring Laurence with them to the meeting. "It's better to wait and be sure we know what they want," he said.

Mr. Baumgarten, who was acting as some sort of adviser for Laurence, agreed with him.

Ilona took them to the last table on the terrace to give them privacy. While walking, Cavafys whispered to alert Pirilo: "It must be something important. The Cossack told me that if it's true that Bebéi knows something about Natasha, he will personally come to Santa Clara. The good news is that he reassured me that those guys are his friends and will not harm Bebéi in any way."

The Russians seemed to be relaxed. As soon as they were seated, they respectfully praised the beauty of Ilona and started to tell jokes, giving the impression that all they wanted was to enjoy that morning of sun, breeze, and a privileged view of the bay.

Ilona opened a bottle of vodka though it wasn't yet noon, and one of the Russians, the older one, bluntly mentioned that Bebéi had written to Natasha. They were curious to know what he knew since it had been a long time since they had had news about her.

Bebéi leaned back in his chair, getting ready to answer, when Pirilo stepped forward. He started by saying that a few days after discovering the Hungarian's apartment was still furnished, some professionals from abroad broke in and stole almost everything there. He also told them that among the few papers they left was Natasha's address in Prague, which was the reason for Bebéi's letter. Pirilo even added, "When we realized that the Hungarian's papers could cause problems, we decided to burn them."

The Russians asked what the papers were about, and Pirilo let Bebéi respond; he knew Bebéi had no idea what Ludmila had discovered about Natasha.

Bebéi told the Russians in detail the whole story of Arpad, from the streets of Budapest to the dispute with his daughter Morgen and the suspicion they had that the Hungarian was a double agent working for the Americans and the Communists, with direct contacts in Havana and Berlin. He did not mention the list of books since Pirilo had explicitly and repeatedly insisted that the list with keywords should not be shown to anyone, especially to the Lady or the Russians.

Pirilo reached three personal conclusions at that meeting: The first was the Russians were friendly since they kept chatting until late afternoon. The second was that they liked to drink — the first bottle of vodka was empty by lunch, and the two Russians had drunk it alone since Cavafys never drank anything but his Greek ouzo; the second bottle was emptied by early afternoon, thanks to the help of Ilona who had lunch with them; and the third was already half empty when Pirilo had to leave for his daily meeting with the Mayor. The third conclusion was that the Russians, though playful, were not at all foolish. Although Bebéi had not mentioned the list of books, the Russians had grasped with their questions that the Hungarian's papers concealed some elements that might interest them.

After Pirilo left, they continued to tell past stories of the Cossack. Cavafys then took the bouzouki out of the bag and played. Bebéi realized the conversation was over and thought about passing by the bed and breakfast to tell Laurence what they had discussed, but he felt lightheaded and went to his apartment to sleep. He had not drunk, but the scent of vodka and the little sip he had every time the Russians proposed a new toast had made him dizzy. Bebéi could barely walk straight, and it was only thanks to Zoubir that he managed to get to his apartment.

When Bebéi returned to the park, it was already dark, and the first familiar face he saw was Mr. Baumgarten. The old man had taught the Gypsy girl to play chess, and she was such a fast learner that he was explaining some classic chess openings to her. The two were playing at one of the tables under Diocles's attentive gaze and Bebéi, who didn't know the game, stayed beside them just out of friendship.

That night, Pirilo also joined them at the park. Unusual, Bebéi thought; Pirilo was never in the park at night. But he was there, walking and talking with Laurence. When the two of them approached, discussing the meeting with the Russians, Mr. Baumgarten, still focused on El Chess game, asked Pirilo a question without moving his head: "The embassy Lady knows that the Russians are here?"

"Yes," answered the lieutenant, "I told her when we met at the pizzeria."

Baumgarten moved his bishop to protect his queen and asked a follow-up question: "Are the Russians aware that the Lady is also interested in the Hungarian's papers?"

Pirilo thought momentarily: "We didn't talk specifically about that, but from what they mentioned at lunch, I have the impression they are suspicious that the Americans also have interest in the Hungarian's papers."

"How nice," Mr. Baumgarten replied.

Pirilo disagreed. "I do not think it's nice. If the Russians and the Americans know that both are interested in the papers, they might try to do something drastic to get them."

"I don't think so," replied Mr. Baumgarten, indicating with his finger a movement for the Gypsy girl. "From what I learned in mystery books I like to read, the more people know, the more protected Laurence and Bebéi should feel. None of us, not even your police, can protect them if the Americans or the Russians decide to do something. But if both parties know that their enemy is interested in what they know, they might be the ones who will care to protect them."

Pirilo kept pondering, and Mr. Baumgarten continued: "Laurence and Bebéi don't know where the papers are, and it should stay that way. Nobody will be interested in harming them."

Pirilo understood; he was the only one who knew where the papers were and, therefore, the only one at risk. He did not mention the key. Bebéi was the only one who knew where it was hidden.

They were still observing the chess game when Laurence surprised them with more news. "So much talk about the Russians — I almost forgot to tell you I got a phone call from the Miami firm saying they have a buyer for Arpad's property in Santa Clara and want to talk about it."

"Be careful" was Pirilo's immediate reaction. "If you want to meet them, it's okay, but it's better to have Mr. Baumgarten or me with you."

Laurence was visibly upset by his comment. "Why," she replied with a sarcastic look, "Don't you think that I'm capable of discussing selling a property by myself?"

Pirilo stuttered for a second. "Of course you can, but these guys in Miami do not seem reliable."

His answer was not enough to appease Laurence, and she decided to return to the inn. Mr. Baumgarten smiled without taking his eyes from the chessboard.

Bebéi accompanied her and then returned to his apartment. The next day promised to be very busy, and the reason was not the papers or the Mayor's plans, but Madam Ambassador of France, his boss.

She was in a terrible mood, and from what Carmela confirmed, the problem was the same. The young women of Santa Clara were queueing up to take private lessons with Chombo Zen, and he had no time to dedicate to Madam Ambassador. A big problem for everyone in the embassy since without Chombo Zen's attention and care, Madam Ambassador would be unbearable!

30

*A **property in the center of the project.*** The Arabs provided the money, and Santa Clara by the Sea woke up filled with billboards announcing the city's giant leap into the future. The date of the joyous transition was precisely defined: August 11th, the day the city celebrates her patron saint. Everything was already settled. At the traditional bands' parade, the Mayor would authorize the initial works and celebrate a groundbreaking ceremony at the boardwalk in front of the old fort.

The drawings on the billboards scattered all over town were impressive: huge tower buildings with bold architecture like wealthy Arab cities and new marinas with yachts as big as those seen in Monaco on a Grand Prix day. The people who appeared in the illustrations seemed to be coming out of those European magazines that Priscilla, the hairdresser, liked to read featuring the latest gossip about royal families.

From the historic town everyone knew, the only recognizable place was Cathedral Park, which in the drawing looked like the great Piazza de San Marco in Venice, full of tables, chairs, and tourists.

There was not a single corner in the whole city without a poster. "Not even in elections we have as many," according to Grená. And if some billboards were impressive, even more striking was the ad that appeared on television, a two-and-a-half-minute video repeated until weariness. It began with images of the old city where new, modern, and colorful constructions seemed to blossom, transforming the old town into the Santa Clara of the future.

The river that divided the city from the more impoverished neighborhood disappeared entirely, as in a magician's trick. In its place, new megatowers bloomed, each one more beautiful and daring than the other. On the city's north side, a new, large, modern Miami-looking avenue connected the old town to the capital, with casinos, hotels, and megatowers. Everyone shown in the video was elegantly dressed, and the cars were fantastic.

The Mayor, wearing an elegant suit, appeared in a national TV interview, and was praised as a champion in attracting foreign investment. Or, as one reporter introduced him, "a politician who has finally understood the benefits of globalization and launches Santa Clara by the Sea toward a promising future."

The figures that were mentioned also caused astonishment. The number of new jobs to be created by the construction was higher than the current inhabitants; the amount of cement to be used would be enough to build a bridge connecting the Caribbean to Miami, and the income to be generated was measured in figures that outweighed anyone's capacity of understanding; particularly those who lived around the narrow cobblestone streets of the historic town.

In the staff meeting they had at the end of the afternoon, the Mayor asked Pirilo about people's initial reactions, and the only response that occurred to him was to say that there was no initial reaction since everyone was still paralyzed in shock.

In front of the barbershop, one of the posters showed the new avenue connecting Santa Clara with the capital, and Rasta Bong was swearing that by the drawing on the billboard, the avenue was going to pass right over his house, and where the room of his mother was, the illustration showed a colossal traffic light.

"How are you going to live on a traffic light?" he asked Grená.

In another poster showing the new Cathedral Park, there was a restaurant serving Arabic food where Princess had his bookstore. The small shed where Diocles slept with his cats was replaced by elegant public bathrooms for tourists, which led Null-and-void to comment to the philosopher: "You'll wake up soaking in pee every morning."

Reacting rationally was impossible. "The river would disappear," noticed Gigi, "How can a river disappear? Where will they send all the water that now flows into the sea?"

According to the drawings, the manors facing the boardwalk would remain, but compared to the massive towers that stretched north and south, they were barely visible.

"Your house and your restaurant are going to be a trace and a dot in the drawing of the new town," was Gigi's comment that made Ilona so angry that she immediately instructed the waiters, "From now on, the Mayor is strictly forbidden from dining at the café."

Even the young at Lucia's fitness academy, enthusiastic supporters of modernization, were outraged. The old warehouse where Lucia had set up the gym was replaced in the drawings by a modern walking bridge connecting the new shopping center to Cathedral Park.

"Do not worry," said Lucia's father, "you'll have a new gym in one of the towers. I already set it up with the Mayor."

But the problem was not the location. To leave the gym inside one of the towers and get into a car parked underground was not what they fancied. The fun was to get off the workout wearing a still-sweaty outfit, cross the park showcasing their well-shaped bodies and have coffee-with-books in Princess's bookstore.

"Like it or not, there's nothing we can do," Null-and-void explained to his drunken friends at the church's stairs. "An enormous amount of money is involved in these projects, and it's not us, a bunch of drifters, who will be able to stop it."

The debate lasted through the evening in every house, corner, bar, and restaurant of the city, but at Ilona's Café, Laurence did not want to talk about it. Her day had been hectic: first a meeting with the lawyers and then with the Mayor. It was those encounters that she wanted to talk about.

"The lawyers found a buyer with an excellent proposal for my grandfather's property." They had offered much more than they had been expecting. "Apparently, they need it for the new city project," she explained.

"Let me understand what you are saying," intervened Jordi, who was still serving tables at the restaurant to round off his meager salary as a teacher. "Does this mean that if you do not sell the land, they cannot build the new city?"

"It's not that simple," Laurence explained. "In the meeting with the Mayor, he was very considerate and explained that the project was important for the city and that he could not stop it. He also recommended that I accept the offer and said that those who did not agree to sell their properties, unfortunately, would be expropriated since the new city is a project of social interest. He even told me he would personally talk to the Arabs and do everything possible to persuade them to increase their offer even more." Laurence continued, "Everyone I spoke to after that confirmed that the Mayor was right. City Hall is expropriating those who refuse to sell their properties, and from what a lawyer who is Ilona's friend explained to me, it's far better to accept the price they are offering and sell it, for the payment to be made faster."

"But what do you want?" Ilona asked. "Do you really want to sell it?"

"I asked the lawyers for a few days to think about it."

"After thinking for a few days," Mr. Baumgarten interrupted, "the next thing you're going to do is to tell them that, at the price they offered, the deal is off. I'm sure they're ready to pay more."

Laurence smiled. She was curious about the property, and Ilona mentioned she knew it well: "When I bought my house, I also considered that lot. It's a beautiful parcel right near the fort." Ilona went on explaining, "The waterfront is about the same size as my property, and it's close to the military training camp."

"Right in the center of the shopping mall of the new city," interrupted Jordi.

"Right in the middle," Ilona confirmed. "It's a big plot. For me, it was too distant from the café. That's why I bought the house that I have now. I also remember trying to contact the owner at that time. I didn't know it was Arpad, but I was told that the owner did not want to sell it."

Ilona interrupted the conversation when Pirilo crashed into the café and approached their table. He was pleased. He had just received a phone call from the Lady of the American Embassy. She would also join them at Ilona's Café, and he explained, "She told me that she had interesting news to tell us."

They remained on the terrace waiting for the Lady, and Mr. Baumgarten commented, "Santa Clara is a lot more fun than any city I've lived in." Bebéi, by his side, nodded, agreeing.

31

The mysterious Agent Z. In Santa Clara by the Sea, the unexpected seems part of the routine, but what the Lady told them that night surprised everyone. She was elegant as always with an understated dress and a scarf of beige and orange design. The simplicity of her elegance contrasted, as always, with the exuberance of Lola Marlene, who arrived with a red glittering dress: "Sorry, but I didn't have time to change," and looking at the Lady, she continued. "It's your fault. You told me to come running, that you had thrilling news to tell us, and I did. This is a design that I will use in my performance at the nightclub, and now, changing subjects: won't you introduce me to your friends?" The reason for that comment was that the Lady was not alone. Beside her were the two Russians, eyes wide open, staring at Lola. The Lady introduced them without hesitation: "These two gentlemen are ex-KGB, now working for SVR, which you probably know is the foreign intelligence service of the Russians."

They all sat around a table at the end of the terrace; even Captain Cavafys was there. Ilona had the nearby space blocked so they could talk privately. It was the Lady who, after asking for a mojito for her and a bottle of vodka for the Russians, began to share what she knew about Agent Z.

"As you found out, Mr. Arpad Corvinus was not just an official who helped the CIA in Congo. He was also an informant of Barbarroja."

Everyone there listened attentively, but unquestionably, the one having more fun out of all those Cold War stories was Mr. Baumgarten. "I've never had such a great vacation," he commented, whispering to Ilona.

"Thanks to the contact with the Stasi," continued the Lady, "Arpad approached the KGB and, for many years, worked as a double agent. That's what you discovered, and we thank you very much for that." After pausing to increase the suspense, she continued, "But what you don't know is what Arpad did after he left Congo in 1976, and I confess that neither the Russians nor we knew it."

She paused again to take a long sip of her mojito. She also wanted to slow down her excitement since she was surprised by all she had discovered in the last few days.

"The documents Bebéi found indicate that Arpad had contacts with someone named Francisco in Angola and an Agent K in Khartoum. One worked with the CIA, and the other with the KGB. Both seemed frustrated with their work and had some relationship with the German Stasi."

No one moved while listening. An elephant could have entered the restaurant's terrace at that moment and they would neither have blinked nor stopped listening to the Lady.

"The two names were investigated years ago by both the Russians and us, for we suspected that one of them could be the man or woman who was blackmailing us."

Bebéi's eyes sparkled, and while listening, he thought it had all started with the seagull that helped him discover the Hungarian's apartment.

The Lady went on. "What I'm going to tell you is a story that many of us thought was a legend, but we now know it was real. At the end of the seventies, we began to receive threats from a Canadian woman who claimed to have evidence that the CIA had been involved in a series of politically motivated attempts in Africa. And they were not small peanuts. There were some very significant events, such as the death of United Nations Secretary-General Dag Hammarskjöld in a plane crash. The CIA preferred to pay what she asked, to avoid the unflattering information being made public." The Lady then stopped for another sip of mojito. "As you can imagine, we did our best to find out who Valerie was. We knew that she lived in Quebec, and we traced all the ransom we paid, which was transferred to non-governmental organizations supporting African populations, such as the Banyamulenge Foundation created by Laurence's mother. The blackmailing continued until the eighties when we learned that if we had our Valerie, the Russians had their Natasha. She lived in Prague and was blackmailing the KGB and, after its dissolution, the SVR in the same way that Valerie was blackmailing us."

The eyes and ears of the lieutenant could not have been more attentive; he only stopped to look at Laurence, who did not return his glance. The Lady continued: "It was then that we decided to join efforts," and she said that looking at the Russians. "We realized that Valerie and Natasha were probably the same person since much information related to Hutus and the Tutsis appeared in both blackmailing operations. We investigated various agents, including Francisco, who was actually a Portuguese woman, and Agent K, a Hindu, but we never checked Arpad."

When the Lady said that, Cavafys, who was by Ilona's side, murmured to himself, "I knew that I'd seen him before," but Ilona only listened. She didn't want to get distracted.

The Lady continued. "As I explained, he was a bureaucratic employee who only did minor jobs, and it was just now, thanks to your investigations and the list that Bebéi prepared —" She stopped to look at Bebéi before continuing. "— That you tried to hide but that I got a hold of a copy, that we finally discovered the identity of Agent Z."

The Lady then showed the list filled with all the information:

A - Auden - French - Algeria
B - Böll- Spanish - Barbarroja
C - Conrad - French - Congo
D - Durrell - Spanish - Dominican Republic

E - Eliot - German - Eszter
F - France - - Portuguese - Francisco
G - Grass - Spanish - Guevara
H - Hesse - Hungarian - Horthy
I - Ibsen - English - Indonesia
J - Joyce - Hungarian - Janus
K - Kafka - English - Agent K
L - Lawrence - Hungarian - Lali
M - Márai - English - Morgen
N- Neruda - Russian - Natasha
O- Orwell - German - Otto
P- Pasternak - Czech - Prague
Q- Quasimodo - French - Quebec
R - Rilke - Russian - Russia
S- Szabó - Spanish - Santa Clara
T - Tolstoy - German - Tamara
U - Unamuno - English - USA
V - Virgil - English - Valerie
W - Whitman - English- Walden
X - Xingjian - The last book
Y- Yeats - Russian — Yuri
Z - Zola — Agent Z

"And since you still don't know some of the things there, I'll explain. The CIA's contact with Valerie was through an agent named Walden and the KGB's contact with Natasha was made by Agent Yuri. The U and the R are for the USA and Russia. The person who has been blackmailing us for all these years became known in both countries as Agent Z. And now we know Agent Z, this astonishing person, was Bebéi's neighbor," looking at Laurence, she added, "Your grandfather, Arpad Corvinus. That is the reason we all want to know where the documents are that Valerie and Natasha used to threaten our intelligence agencies?"

Bebéi and the lieutenant examined the list, and the Lady continued: "Apparently, Arpad decided to take revenge on both the

Americans and the Soviets for everything he had seen in Africa, and he did it brilliantly. We never managed to find out who he was, and what was intriguing; we knew he did not do it for the money since most of the ransom was transferred to organizations that supported the victims of the political war between our countries. He stopped blackmailing us when he realized that the Russians and the Americans were working together, and we would probably find out his identity. Still, he never handed over the papers he had. Agent Z disappeared without a trace. Never again did Walden receive a message from Valerie or Yuri from Natasha. We knew their addresses, and our agencies kept surveilling them. For more than ten years, there was no movement until Natasha received Bebéi's letter and until Lieutenant Pirilo handed me the notes inside the book of Virgil."

Pirilo explained that he only had the documents found inside the books. He immediately called one of his assistants to fetch all the folders he had hidden in a place nobody would find: the little shed behind the Cathedral where Diocles slept with his cats. Pirilo wanted to be cautious, and while they waited, he repeated that he only had what was inside the books.

The Lady realized that Pirilo was trying to prevent Bebéi from speaking, and as she already knew them well, she did not confront them. That was not the place to do it.

When the folders arrived, she and the Russias read them. Notably, the notes inside Walden and Yuri's folders, and the Lady commented. "Here are the descriptions of what he was doing, but now we are looking for the documents he possessed."

The Lady and the Russians insisted on knowing what was inside the two last books, the X and Z of the list. Pirilo showed the Xingjian book, which had a handwritten line on the last page: *My final book ... what's the use to keep reading?*

"And what about Zola's book," the Lady asked. "What was there?"

Pirilo chose not to respond. First, he wanted to talk to Laurence. The only person who knew where the key was hidden was Bebéi, who kept staring motionless at Pirilo.

The Lady realized it would be useless to insist and proposed: "Neither you nor those who invaded the apartment found anything. Let us look for it. If there is anything inside, we will find it with our equipment."

Pirilo did not object, but Mr. Baumgarten, who had been silent, intervened: "I imagine that to do this detailed search, you will probably damage a few things inside the apartment. I think it would be fair that, after you are finished, the governments of your countries entirely refurbish the apartment and leave it in perfect order for Miss Laurence to live there, including new furniture, carpets, and curtains." He added, looking affably at the Lady and the Russians, "Don't you agree?"

The Lady and the Russians smiled and nodded, accepting. Mr. Baumgarten then looked at Laurence: "With that, you'll have your apartment ready to live in, and you will not have to spend another penny on the bed and breakfast."

32

Preparing a Portuguese soup. The following day, Pirilo did something he had not done in a long time: he accompanied Mr. Baumgarten to the Food Market following an unusual request the old man had made the night before: "I am craving to eat the soup of chickpeas and sausage that my wife makes me."

"You can ask Doña Cecy or Lais; they will certainly prepare it for you," was Pirilo's suggestion.

"I know, and they're both excellent cooks. So good that they will make it in their own way. What I want is the soup prepared exactly as my wife does. It's a Portuguese soup, and Portuguese women have a special way of doing it."

Pirilo, who was no friend of a stove, had to offer his house kitchen, — barely used since he only ate in the Asturian Tavern or at his brother's house on Sundays, when Grená prepared the lunch.

Mr. Baumgarten explained: "If I try to make my soup in the kitchen of Ilona's Café, there will be so many opinions that I will end up in a bad mood. I want a kitchen where I can cook without any woman advising at my back."

Bebéi did not offer his kitchen since his apartment was on the third floor, and it would be challenging to take the wheelchair there. The simplest solution was Pirilo's house, and as the lieutenant had already contributed with the kitchen, he joined Bebéi and Mr. Baumgarten on their tour of the market, which unexpectedly turned out to be an excellent opportunity to chat.

"First of all, it is crucial that we find a good sausage. We've had the chickpeas soaking in water since yesterday, and I asked Mr. Bebéi to cook them for an hour and a half so that we did not have to wait too long for them to cook today. But now we must find an excellent sausage."

Finding it took them an extremely long time; Mr. Baumgarten was very demanding and knowledgeable about what he was looking for; he asked for details about the sausage preparation and even how the pigs were fed.

While they were circulating from one stand to the other, they kept talking, and Mr. Baumgarten mentioned, "At least now we know what the Hungarian was hiding, and we have Russians and Americans looking together for the lost documents, but there is still something I don't understand," he said. "Who tried to steal from Mr. Bebéi's apartment?"

Every time he chatted with Mr. Baumgarten, Pirilo felt important. The old man always gave him the impression of being genuinely interested in learning from his opinions, and the truth was that Mr. Baumgarten's questions always helped Pirilo think.

"I believe it was the Miami lawyers, but not for the reasons the Lady told us. The Miami lawyers didn't have the slightest clue about who the Hungarian was and much less about the documents he had hidden. The lawyers intended to sell Arpad's property to Arab investors, and they broke into the apartment to prevent us from finding out he owned the lot near the fort."

"Very interesting and, as always, very wise," said Mr. Baumgarten. "Now that we have found a good sausage, we must buy the vegetables. We need onion, garlic, carrot, celery, and sweet potatoes, but Lieutenant Pirilo, what is your opinion? Do you believe that the lawyers will not bother Mr. Bebéi again? Remember that they tried for a second time to break into his apartment."

"I don't think so," said Pirilo with an almost arrogant expression. "At that time, they were worried about an heir's claim, but now that they know Laurence, the only way to get the property is by buying it."

"That's ingenious thinking, but there is one aspect that is not yet clear to me: the property still belongs to Mr. Arpad, and as they have not concluded the process of settling the estate, I wonder what would happen if something like an accident occurs to Miss Laurence or, God forbid, that she dies. In this case, the property would remain in Mr. Arpad's estate, and the lawyers would be able to sell it to investors, don't you think?"

Pirilo kept thinking, and Mr. Baumgarten added, "What worries me is that we have made Miss Laurence a target; if they want the property at any cost, a good alternative could simply be to eliminate the heiress."

For Pirilo, the idea of murders in Santa Clara by the Sea seemed like paranoia, and he tried to shorten the discussion. "You're probably right, but you can be sure that nothing will happen to her."

"I'm sure it won't," insisted Baumgarten, "but let us not forget that we are talking about a project of millions and millions of dollars, and they already hired professionals to break into the Hungarian's apartment and gag Mr. Bebéi in the bathroom. Can you imagine what they might do if Miss Laurence refuses to sell the property? But before we move on, let's look at that stand. I believe the sweet potatoes there seem inviting."

Bebéi listened and became concerned. Could anyone want to harm Laurence? But Pirilo reassured them. "We'll give her special protection. I'll put an escort by her side twenty-four-seven."

"A smart decision, Mr. Lieutenant. Better safe than sorry. Now, just for fun while we look for some bay leaves and cumin, tell me, Mr. Lieutenant, what could our enemies do? Let's not forget that they are willing to pay more than a million dollars to have their land and certainly would not hesitate to use this million to hire a hit man to kill her. Tell me, Mr. Lieutenant, you, who are good at these investigations, what do you think they would do in the hypothetical case they want to hire a professional to kill someone like her?"

Pirilo liked these challenges. It reminded him of the questions that his assistant Cristine asked him. "If I wanted to kill someone, the first thing would be to hire a killer who could do the job, which would not be difficult as there are many in this market."

"So it's easy to find a killer? I didn't know," replied Mr. Baumgarten. "And tell me now, how could we know if someone was trying to hire a contract killer?"

That question was not easy, but while he waited for Mr. Baumgarten to finish his shopping, Pirilo kept pondering.

When they had left the market and made their way back to the house, Pirilo finally replied. "To ask would not help us; in this world of professional killers, no one answers questions. The best alternative, in my humble opinion," and he said this without any humbleness, "would be to pass the information on the market that we are looking for a murderer to kill Laurence and that we are willing to pay an absurd amount of money. This news would spread quickly and confuse the hired killer, who would probably be interested in whether we can pay more than the others."

"What a great idea, Mr. Lieutenant! Can you see, Mr. Bebéi, the difference between a professional like Lieutenant Pirilo and two curious joes like us? An idea like this would never cross my mind, and I do not think yours, either, do you?"

As it took a good fifteen minutes for them to get to Pirilo's house, Mr. Baumgarten went on asking questions, slowing down the speed of his wheelchair to allow his companions to walk beside him. "How can we protect our Laurence while waiting for the professional murderers to contact us? The idea of an escort seems reasonable to me. Still, I imagine that if the killer is a good professional, the protection of a single policeman would certainly not be enough, don't you agree, Mr. Lieutenant?"

Pirilo was feeling proud of the old man's respect for his answers, and took advantage to show off his knowledge. "Our killer, surely, would not be someone from Santa Clara and would have to move around the city to find the best place to attack her. Since our town is small, what we could do is to ask Miss Laurence not to wander so much. Secondly, we can pass a word of caution to those always walking the streets. Besides Mr. Bebéi, who will certainly be very attentive while walking his dog, we can ask for additional help from the Useless Brethren, who, in a limited way, can watch since they are always attentive to foreigners. Also to Diocles, who spends all day in Cathedral Park, to the Gypsies of the band, who have many contacts in the underground, and to the friends of Jordi who live on the other side of the river and hang frequently around town. I'm sure that with all of them attentive, we will immediately identify someone with suspicious behavior."

Bebéi then interrupted to contribute to Laurence's protection plan. "I'll propose that she keeps my dog. He is an excellent guardian. Whenever someone tries to approach me from behind, he barks." The idea seemed appealing, and they all agreed.

Inside Pirilo's kitchen, after braising the vegetables with a little bit of bacon and adding the sausage, the chickpeas, and some spices from former Portuguese colonies that Mr. Baumgarten had in a small plastic bag, he covered everything with boiling water and followed with his questions. "Your idea of passing on the information that we're willing to pay a lot to anyone who helps us eliminate Laurence sounds wise to me, but tell me, how would we do it?"

And while they were drinking a Porto wine, Bebéi's favorite drink, and waiting for the soup to cook, Pirilo continued to display his knowledge: "We have a good network of informants that allows us to reach Latin gangs in Mexico and Central and South America, and we also have valuable contacts in Kingston and Port of Spain for the Caribbean. To reach Miami and the United States, we can ask the Lady's help; her network of informants allowed us to find out who broke into Bebéi's apartment in less than twenty-four hours. Finally, for the Europeans and the whole drug traffickers network, we can count on the Cossack, Ludmila's father — and we don't need to bother her, she hates her father. I will ask Cavafys to help us contacting him."

"Excellent; I believe that with all this help, we can reach the killer before he or she comes to town." Then Mr. Baumgarten confessed with a worried expression, "I suspect that Miss Laurence will not sell the property. She is delighted with Santa Clara, and this worries me." Mr. Baumgarten felt he needed to clarify. "I am not worried about the Mayor, who is your boss and who I know is a respectable person." Pirilo thought it wiser not to comment about the Mayor's integrity, and Mr. Baumgarten continued, "There are many interests and a lot of money involved in the project. I do not understand how those things work, but I imagine that for those people engaged in the project, eliminating our Laurence might be an attractive option."

While they patiently waited for the soup to cook, eating a few slices of *jamón serrano*, Pirilo made some phone calls to put the whole plan in motion. He was not entirely convinced that Laurence was in danger, but he agreed with Mr. Baumgarten: "Better safe than sorry."

"We never know," added the old man after tasting the soup with the wooden spoon.

Bebéi followed their conversation silently. He wondered if Pirilo was displaying his knowledge or if it was Mr. Baumgarten, with his smile and sweet way of saying things, who was driving Pirilo to put together the scheme he envisaged to protect Laurence.

33

A wheelchair gang invades the city. Laurence arrived for lunch, and they sat around the table to enjoy the soup. According to Bebéi, it was as good as the one prepared by Doña Cecy.

The lunch turned out to be stimulating. Along with the soup, they chatted. First, they talked about Arpad. It was Bebéi who brought up the issue. "He did so many things in his past and he lived here for ten years without a friend and not a single person to share his adventures,"

Mr. Baumgarten surprisingly intervened, toasting solemnly with a bit of nostalgia and respect in his words. "Arpad was a music teacher who rarely left his apartment and had a few memory lapses while teaching, a virtuoso violinist who would probably be one of the greatest in Europe if he had not lost his fingers, a deportee in a Siberian prison camp rescued by a woman who died at the barricades of Budapest, a spy who worked in Africa for the CIA, the Stasi, the Cubans, and the Russians, and who knew the dirty side of the Cold War when newly liberated African nations were devastated by the world superpowers trying to make their selfish geopolitical interests prevail. He was a solitary avenger who took justice into his own hands and made Americans and Soviets pay, at least in part, for the damage they had caused. Maybe a bureaucratic employee of little expression, as the Lady said, but one who, for ten years, fooled the most powerful secret services in the world. A Hungarian half-Gypsy who fancied playing his violin for people in the streets of Budapest but who lived in bitterness and ended up in the solitude of his apartment."

How could it be that nobody in Santa Clara knew who he was? And that was not the only question puzzling Bebéi. They had already figured out the Hungarian's life, but no one had explained why one day he left his apartment, leaving the cutlery in the kitchen sink and vanishing without a word.

That same day, even before they went to the market, Bebéi had passed by Ilona's Café to get the key hidden in the keyholder of her office; it was time to give it to Laurence. It was a frantic morning. Later, when Bebéi passed by the hotel to pick up Mr. Baumgarten, they crossed paths with the Lady, escorting an American who had just arrived in Santa Clara. He must undoubtedly be someone important since she had waited for him at the airport, and what had caught their attention was that the old man also had a motorized wheelchair.

"How about if we invite him to a wheelchair race on the board-walk?" Mr. Baumgarten had suggested, smiling.

At lunch, while eating the soup, Bebéi handed the key to Laurence. He also explained to her that there was nothing written and no notes inside Zola's book.

Pirilo reiterated that only Laurence could decide whether or not to hand the key over to the Lady and the Russians. Still, he favored delivering it. "Otherwise, they will not stop pressing."

Laurence did not answer. She wanted to think a little more, and the only one to ask any question was Mr. Baumgarten: "Was there any indication together with the key?"

"None," replied Bebéi, "It was attached with tape to a page in the middle of the book."

"What page?" asked Mr. Baumgarten.

"Page 256," replied Bebéi.

"As you know," said Mr. Baumgarten, "I like mystery books, and I wonder if there was no mark in the envelope, key, or book indicating what kind of safe or drawer this key opens."

"I suppose there must be some secret safe inside the apartment," Pirilo intervened. "Knowing how the Lady's staff works, I have no doubt they will find it. I imagine this is the key we will need to open it …"

"I would not be so sure, Mr. Lieutenant," interrupted Mr. Baumgarten. "This key does not appear to be from an apartment safe. It is a solid key that reminds me of these European postal boxes that must withstand time and endless openings and closings."

They examined the key, but since none of them was a locksmith or a specialist in vaults, Laurence proposed, "Let's wait and see if they find any safe in the apartment. Then we'll decide if we give them the key or not."

After lunch, Laurence wanted to visit Arpad's lot, and Bebéi volunteered to take Mr. Baumgarten and her there. Pirilo declined to go. He returned to his office disappointed; Laurence hadn't looked into his eyes at all over the lunch. But he was not upset; Cristine, his assistant, was finally coming back to Santa Clara.

Jordi was euphoric. The day before she had called: "I've finished all work, talked to teachers, and they authorized me to advance my return. I miss you and want to kiss you even more than last time."

The euphoria was such that Jordi thought of all possible ways to kidnap Cristine at the airport and take her to a deserted island, but he had to accept that her mother and her friends were also entitled to see her.

Pirilo had agreed with Jordi that on the afternoon Cristine would drop into his office, but what he did not know was that his ex-assistant had reserved for him a not-so-pleasant surprise.

Cristine entered Pirilo's office with large round glasses framing her eyes and hugged everyone. Pirilo was proud; he was her mentor and had hired her when she was still a college student. Cristine embraced him affectionately but shocked him by saying she would not keep working at City Hall. "The commitment the Mayor made me sign was that when I returned from Boston, I would work in Santa Clara. He privately explained to me that he had altered the scholarship contract, and where it was written that I should work in City Hall, he changed it to "work in Santa Clara." The reason was that he and his brother wanted me to work in some private businesses where the two were partners. Well, he acted smartly, and now I'm going to be even smarter: I will fulfill my commitment and work in Santa Clara, but not for him or his partners; I will work with Jordi on *The Santa Clara Barrel Organ*. We will dedicate ourselves to investigative journalism," and she even provoked Pirilo, "Who knows, maybe one day you'll decide to tell the Mayor to go to hell and come to work with us."

Pirilo gave her a half smile; the truth was that working in City Hall without her was only half of the fun.

Cristine was happy to be back but was surprised and mentioned to Jordi when they left City Hall: "I thought I'd meet everyone in barricades defending the city, but no one mentioned the New Santa Clara since I arrived."

"It's amazing," Jordi replied. "It's as if everyone believes that it will never happen. I fear the day they find out, it will be too late to stop it."

They did not discuss it further. Ilona, who was very fond of Jordi and knew he was short of money, had given them a night in a small boutique hotel in the mountains, near the city, where they could give each other as many kisses as they wanted.

Meanwhile, at the end of the boardwalk, Bebéi and Zoubir were guiding Laurence and Baumgarten on a wild field trip. The topography around the old fort was not the most appropriate for a wheelchair, which did not seem to bother Mr. Baumgarten, who was grinning and jostling all over the place.

Right after crossing the fort ruins, they reached a small beach surrounded by large rocks where the river meets the sea. From there, they could see the whole bay and, to the right, the mangroves and the distant cliffs.

"This is Arpad's plot, and I understand they wish to build the shopping center here," said Laurence. "In this whole area, where we see the mangroves and the community, those bastards plan to build the new towers with plenty of offices and apartments."

It was hard to believe what Laurence was saying. At that moment, the only sounds they could hear were the waves crashing on the rocks and the purring and squawking of the seagulls. Between them and the horizon, only the sea.

One of the seagulls flew next to them. Bebéi even joked to Zoubir, "I think it's your friend who misses the balcony."

The seagull flew over the fort, climbed high in the sky, and then lowered toward them, hovering within reach of their hands to attract their attention. It flew then high over the city and along the coastline, following the mangrove and disappearing above the cliffs.

"It seems she's telling us something," said Laurence.

As she followed the seagull with her eyes, she thought her grandfather had bought that property and never wanted to sell it because he hoped Morgen's daughter might want to live there.

When they returned to the city at sunset, they saw a helicopter arriving; it seemed to be the same helicopter in which Cavafys had arrived with the Russians. Bebéi accompanied Laurence and Baumgarten to the hotel and saw the Greek captain and the two Russians walking toward the heliport on the pier. Bebéi followed them.

They were there to receive another man, an older one who, coincidentally, also had a motorized wheelchair. "I think the wheelchair race will be very competitive," commented Bebéi to Cavafys, who did not understand.

Cavafys explained that the Russian was the former boss of the Cossack in the KGB and was in Santa Clara to follow up on the search for the Hungarian's papers.

The first thing the old Russian did was cuddle Zoubir and thank Bebéi in a perfect French for honoring Arpad's memory and keeping the papers safe, assuring him that everything that belonged to Arpad would be transferred to his heiress.

"You are an admirable man," said the old Russian to Bebéi, who went home wondering if there was something about a motorized wheelchair that made its owners seem so kind.

34

Wheelchairs gathered at the park. Colonel Viera was still at the peak of his paranoia. He insisted that everyone was being watched. "They have cameras and microphones everywhere. They know everything you say and even what you think," the Colonel explained to Mr. Baumgarten, who was enjoying the morning sun in his wheelchair in front of the hotel. The plan to protect Laurence had already been implemented, and everyone was alert, but as of that morning there was no news.

Inside the hotel lobby, the Russian in his motorized wheelchair watched them. He was at the hotel for the same reason as Mr. Baumgarten: the hotel had good access ramps for wheelchairs. From there, they could access the park without disturbing anyone.

As one wheelchair drew the other, the Russian approached Mr. Baumgarten to join him in listening to the Colonel's complaints. "Even in the confessionary of the Church, there are microphones. The same is true in each of the love nests of Paris Street; everything that happens there is recorded. You can't even scratch your balls in peace anymore."

When Colonel Viera paused, struggling to focus his thoughts, the Russian took the opportunity to introduce himself. He said he had just arrived, and Mr. Baumgarten, who knew he was ex-KGB, introduced himself as Laurence's friend.

They continued to listen to the Colonel's harangue, warning that government, businesspeople, communists, priests, and even his ex-wife were watching him twenty-four hours a day. The two old men listened attentively as if they were impressed.

From the hotel terrace, another old foreigner, the American Lady's friend, saw the two wheelchairs and approached them. He came to the park, introduced himself, and, along with the other two, continued to listen to the Colonel's speech about the invasion of privacy in the modern world. A very timely assertion, since if the Russian was the former KGB supreme chief, the old American was responsible for all CIA operations in Africa during the Cold War.

The Russian and the American knew each other but had never met. In their spy world, the only thing they knew about each other was their code names: Ivanov for the KGB and Smith for the CIA.

Both were in Santa Clara for the same reason: to find and destroy Arpad's papers.

When the Colonel got tired of repeating his arguments and went away, the three men began an engaging conversation comparing their wheelchairs. The Russian's wheelchair was made in Pakistan, the American's in China, and Mr. Baumgarten's in Turkey.

They were all aware that on that same morning, experts from both countries were looking with a magnifying lens at every corner of Arpad's apartment. If anything was there, it would indeed be found. The only one with fresh news was the American, and what he said confirmed Mr. Baumgarten's suspicions.

"We found out that the Miami law firm hired professionals to clean out the Hungarian's apartment and prevent any heirs from being identified. The lawyers had no idea who Arpad was and could not imagine what he had hidden there. Luckily, they had not destroyed everything they took, and we managed to retrieve at least the photos." He also explained: "According to the elegant Lady who works in our embassy, Mr. Bebéi has a privileged memory, and she assured me that with his help, it would be possible to place all photos in their original places and check if they give us some clue of where the documents might be."

Mr. Baumgarten was thrilled with his holidays in the tropics. Mysterious notes hidden inside books and secret agents from the

CIA and KGB were much more than he had experienced in Portugal, but he did not mention the key to his new friends. Laurence had yet to decide what to do with it. Actually, the Russian and the American did everything they could to find out if he knew anything else, but he bravely resisted their cross-examination.

The only thing that worried him was when the American said that the Miami lawyers were in contact with an Egyptian named El Waun, someone known to the secret services for his total lack of scruples. The American even commented, "When necessary, he resorts to violence, and my guys have serious suspicions that he would not hesitate to kill those who cross his path."

While they were chatting, the Gypsy girl arrived, and Mr. Baumgarten proposed a game of dominoes. His two new friends agreed. They played in the park, waiting for the Lady, and nobody who walked by bothered to pay attention to them — only Diocles, who sat behind the girl with his fat yellow cat in his lap.

The Lady only arrived later, escorted by Bebéi, who had taken a few days off from the embassy to help Laurence. Along with them were Pirilo and Cristine who, after a night of kisses with Jordi, had been summoned by Pirilo to help him understand the mystery of the Hungarian.

The Lady explained that they had checked the apartment using the most modern equipment and had not found anything. It was not there that the Hungarian had hidden his papers. She confirmed what the old American said; they had recovered the photos and a few musical instruments. The Lady explained that, unfortunately, the papers in the drawers had been destroyed, emphasizing that they were probably scores and musical notes as Arpad, Agent Z, would never leave secret documents inside unlocked drawers.

Bebéi took advantage of the gathering to ask if anyone knew why the Hungarian had left the apartment without washing the dishes and never returned. No one answered him.

Cristine was the only one who dared say something and mentioned that it was essential to know what the Hungarian had done in the last weeks before disappearing. "You are so obsessed with understanding what he did ten, twenty, or forty years ago that you don't seem to understand that the reason for his disappearance is probably something that happened ten, twenty, or forty days before he left."

No one commented — an indication that Cristine was right. Pirilo insisted that Cristine help him with the investigation. She accepted but with one condition: City Hall would pay for a whole week in the hotel where she had spent the previous night with Jordi.

However, her main concern was not the Hungarian's papers but Santa Clara's future. As soon as the gathering was over, she went to the barbershop, where Jordi was working on the new issue of *The Barrel Organ*.

Cristine arrived, sharing the good news about the hotel, and immediately began to push him: "We have to do something. It's useless to prepare a newspaper if we do not have a city where we can sell it. I'm shocked by everyone's passivity." Along with them was Nadia, now responsible for the illustrations and layout. She had even brought a cousin to help her, a younger woman, about sixteen years old, who had been involved in drugs, but Nadia reassured them. "She is trying to rehabilitate, and has been completely clean for a few weeks."

"It's not that the people are passive," Nadia explained. "What happens is that everyone is stuck; nobody knows what to do. Even worse, people think nothing can be done to stop the Mayor's plans."

Cristine decided to walk around the city but kidded with Jordi before leaving: "Santa Clara has changed in my absence. We might not have motorcycle gangs, but I realize we have our wheelchair gang strolling through the park." She then visited Grená, who updated her with recent rumors, greeted Null-and-void and the members of the Useless Brethren, and ate empanadas at Lais's window. After that quick tour, she felt at home again.

Inside the Hungarian's apartment, Bebéi and Laurence helped put the photos back on the wall. One hundred and nine, to be precise. Laurence was happy with the pictures and also with some African masks that had been recovered with them. As agreed, the Lady was going to return to a refurbished apartment, and while they hung the photos on the wall, contractors were installing new kitchen cabinets, carpets, and curtains in the rooms.

The photo hanging was an easier task. They followed Bebéi's recollection and hung them all on the dining room wall. It was clear that they followed a chronological order: from the oldest at the right bottom to the latest in the upper left.

Some photos did not follow the order and were placed more prominently on other walls. An old photo of Lali dancing in the streets of Budapest, a picture of Eszter smiling in Berlin, and a photo of Morgen wearing a safari jacket that Laurence said she always used when traveling in the mountains. In Morgen's picture, one could see a lake that, according to Laurence, was Lake Kivu on the Congo border with Burundi and Rwanda.

"The three great women of Arpad's life," said Bebéi, "and now you have to put up a picture of yourself since you are the fourth woman around Arpad."

On the wall, there were pictures of Arpad next to someone who seemed to be very important, probably Horthy. A photo of a child in gala dress that looked like Arpad, playing violin on an elegant stage that, according to Mr. Baumgarten, who was brought to the apartment thanks to the help of the Lady's bodyguards, was from the Budapest National Theater. There were photos of Nazi soldiers in the streets of Budapest and pictures of the Soviets when they invaded the city; a picture of Eszter with Arpad in front of a small hut in the snow that by the clothes and the sick expression of Arpad was probably taken upon his release from Kolyma. Photos of Berlin destroyed by the war and the Binder family with Eszter and an older lady, probably her mother. There were images of friends in Berlin and a teenage girl that seemed to be Tamara. Photos of Algiers, the city of Bebéi's father, and a picture of Arpad with several government officials. Bebéi insisted that the man who appeared in the center and could not be recognized was his father. Pictures of Congo that Laurence explained were from Kinshasa, Kisangani, and the Congo mountains. In one of them, Arpad was next to a bald man with a tie and a suit that Mr. Baumgarten swore was Che Guevara.

"You are only missing a picture of this Otto guy who can get tickets for soccer games and get you into college," Bebéi teased.

"Of course, there is none," Mr. Baumgarten replied. "If he was a secret agent of the Stasi, he could not let himself be photographed."

They set up the apartment and looked at every detail of each photo. There was nothing there that could lead him to the documents.

At least Arpad's memories were restored, and the books and the masks were returning to the apartment that was now Laurence's.

"We should also hang a photo of the seagull here," Laurence told Bebéi. "She is the one who brought us all here."

35

Why did the Hungarian leave with no warning? Cristine was Pirilo's favorite assistant, and the first thing she did to discover why the Hungarian had vanished was talk with Carmela, the school headmaster from when Arpad was still a teacher. From what Carmela recalled, Arpad only warned her at the end of the school year that he would no longer be teaching. Cristine also remembered that around mid-year, he suspended the orchestra's rehearsals, and it was with this information that Cristine began to build a timeline of Arpad's last days: *June: he interrupted the orchestra's rehearsals. November: he informed Carmela that he would leave school.*

From the law firm — which, now that Lady and her friends had applied pressure, was replying to everything they requested — she discovered that Arpad's last visit to their office was Thursday, December 12, 1996. Lastly, according to the power company's records, the final energy consumption in his apartment happened in December, and she noted: *He visited the law office on December 12 and disappeared between December 12 and December 31.*

Something Cristine also recalled while talking with Jordi was that a few times in class Arpad had seemed to forget what he was doing. Was he sick?

The physician who had attended the teachers had passed away. His son, who had followed up with the clinic, inherited his father's patient records. Finding them was a little tricky since the son kept the older ones in a dusty storage room. Still, with Jordi's help, Cristine found Arpad's medical record, which indicated that in July of that same year, the doctor had initiated a series of tests, suspecting Arpad had Alzheimer's Disease. At the beginning of November, he visited the doctor, who confirmed the diagnosis: *The recurrence of memory loss is increasing, indicating rapid progression of the disease. Signs of mood swings are visible, which seems consistent with early symptoms of dementia.* With this information, it was not difficult to understand what had happened.

"The most precious things your grandfather had were the memories of the moments he lived," Cristine explained to Laurence at the park. The two were sitting on a bench under the shade of a guayacan; at Laurence's feet lay, Zoubir, her guardian dog, watchful of the surroundings. Next to them, Mr. Baumgarten, in his wheelchair, and Bebéi, standing up, listened to their conversation. "Probably when he realized that his memory was failing, he placed the pictures on the wall in an organized manner and kept his notes filed in the twenty-six books to facilitate his recollection. He might have been trying to fight his memory loss or preserving all information in case Morgen's daughter showed up. Who knows? But the hypothesis of Alzheimer's is confirmed by what he wrote in Xingjian's book: "*My final book ... what's the use to keep reading?*"

So much time had passed, it was impossible to know, but what Cristine said seemed to be close to the truth, and she continued: "He visited the law firm and left everything settled, which shows that he hoped that one day you might come to Santa Clara. He even bought a property for you. Your grandfather did everything to avoid anyone knowing about his death, and it's understandable: he wanted to give you as much time as possible to find him. He left everything handy," Cristine added. "When he finally got the necessary courage, he left the apartment, turned off the electricity, and went somewhere to die. Probably in the sea, maybe carrying stones to take him deep to the bottom. It was important to his plan that his body would never float; he didn't want anyone else to find it since all he did was for you."

Mr. Baumgarten held Laurence's hands and spoke. "He definitely knew you existed. Among the Congo photos I saw on the wall is one of your father, and you told me that Arpad never met him. But the picture proves he knew Morgen was married and even if he didn't know for sure, Arpad hoped she had a child. Why did he never get the courage to go to Kisangani? We will never know. Maybe he feared that Morgen would never forgive him for what he did."

After a pause to give Laurence time to deal with her grief, Mr. Baumgarten continued. "According to what the Lady told us, the money he got from KGB and CIA was sent to the foundation that your mother created, and from what you told us, those donations allowed the foundation to carry on its work. He bought that plot for you but never dared to return to Africa, and he died alone. It's a shame he left before he received your letter. He would undoubtedly have returned to Kisangani to see you, but that doesn't matter anymore. Thanks to Bebéi and the seagull, you got to know him better."

Laurence just listened. She could not speak or think and wanted to walk alone on the boardwalk. She wanted to watch the seagulls flying, and only Zoubir followed her.

From the park, after talking with Laurence, Cristine went straight to meet Jordi to help him with the third edition of *The Santa Clara Barrel Organ*. The main article was ready; it was written by Jordi and Gigi and had a provocative title: "They are Stealing Your Water." It described the supposedly confidential plans of the new dam that would be built upstream to hold the river's waters.

Gigi discovered the whole scheme. "How is it possible that the river disappears in the city's new plans?" That was the question she asked Jordi, and from that starting point, they dug until they discovered what the Mayor and his partners were plotting.

The apartments, offices, and shops of the new Santa Clara would need plenty of additional water, and the Mayor had granted a French company — of which he and his brother were also partners — a concession to build a giant dam that would sell water to the new Santa Clara. The article described, with illustrations by Nadia, where the dam would be and explained how the water would be channeled and distributed into the city.

Their article pointed out that the new buildings would use all cleanly flowing water and throw it into the sea as sewage without any treatment. The Mayor's plan of retaining the water upstream would allow Arab investors to build the commercial center where the current river flowed, secure the water needed for the new towers, and, more importantly, provide an absurd amount of money for the Mayor and his partners, who would have a monopoly over the distribution of drinking water in Santa Clara by the Sea.

The newspaper had also chosen a selected citizen to feature: Diocles, who, after Lais and Cholo, was chosen for an exceptional reason. Besides being known and respected by all, the philosopher had just received a notice commanding him to leave the shed where he slept with his cats, in order to allow for the construction of new public toilets.

They worked the whole evening and only stopped because Jordi was desperately hungry. They went to the Friar's pizzeria which, on that night, looked like a town hall meeting of angry citizens.

Everybody was complaining, all enraged. On the sidewalk, wholly wasted, Robespierre proposed resorting to arms, supported by Frida and Colonel Viera. Moriarty, the Canadian hippie and eternal pacifist, suggested that a delegation try to convince the Mayor to give up, and Null-and-void was silent since he did not know what to say.

Inside the pizzeria, Grená was the leading voice. She had discovered they would close part of the boardwalk to start the works for the new marina, and La Pajerita would have nowhere to sleep. Everyone there was frustrated. They could oppose the project, but they could not stop it. Investors had already bought most of the land, and City Hall was expropriating those who resisted. The plans and drawings were ready, and the investors had assured all the construction funding.

Sitting around one of the tables, Bebéi asked Ilona, "Would I be able to walk Zoubir on the streets?" And it was Gigi who answered, saying there would be so many vehicles that they would probably restrict dog-walking hours.

Suddenly, Priscilla, the hairdresser who had worked until late, crashed inside the pizzeria. "Something happened in the park. I heard dogs loudly barking and people yelling. When I got there, I saw Pirilo chasing and handcuffing a young guy who was running. Oh my goodness. Our nightmare is starting!"

Most of the people there ran to the park, and when Bebéi got there, he realized that Laurence was involved. The handcuffed man had been taken to City Hall, and a crowd, including Pirilo, surrounded her.

"It seems that someone tried to attack Laurence, and Zoubir started to bark," explained Pirilo. Zoubir was still shivering, and Bebéi tried to calm him.

"I didn't see him coming," said Laurence. "I was walking when Zoubir started to bark. I turned back and saw a man close to me, but, I don't know, he continued running. Thank goodness the lieutenant was near and caught him."

"But did he attack you?" Ilona asked.

"No, it seems he didn't have time," Laurence replied.

Bebéi followed Pirilo to City Hall, where, after questioning the young man, Pirilo explained embarrassingly, "False alarm. The kid was just jogging. He is seventeen years old, lives across the river, and had no weapons with him. Probably he got too close to Laurence and scared Zoubir."

"Difficult to believe," replied Bebéi, defensively. "He never barks for no reason. If he was barking, as Laurence said, it's because he felt she was in danger."

But nothing else happened that night. The kid was released, and everybody retired to their homes. Only Bebéi, Mr. Baumgarten, and Diocles remained on a park bench until very late.

Mr. Baumgarten was worried. "For them, eliminating Laurence is the easiest path." Bebe kept repeating next to him, "If he barked, there was a reason." Diocles was listening, thinking they should be even more alert to protect Laurence.

36

They put the Mayor up against the wall. The truth is that the protection system was working; not even the jogger could get close to Laurence. But after the incident, the tension rose and was the source of some confusion.

Those who watched the streets were alert to any unusual behavior, but sometimes they overdid it. On Sunday, when the Archbishop arrived for Mass, the ice cream seller grew suspicious of a man in dark clothes who seemed to be stalking Laurence and warned Diocles, who informed the others. The suspect looked at her three times, which should not be noticeable as every man would look three times at Laurence, but what caught the ice cream seller's attention was that after Laurence entered the bed and breakfast, he still stood there as if waiting.

Later, when the mass was over, the Archbishop walked to the Mayor's house, where every Sunday, the Mayor's wife served refreshments and cookies for her Catholic friends. The man in a dark suit followed the Archbishop for no apparent reason and returned to the park, sitting on a bench near the bed and breakfast.

At noon, Laurence left, and the suspect stared at her again. Diocles saw, sat beside him, and tried to initiate a conversation. The suspect avoided talking. Priscilla, the hairdresser, passed by on her way to the bookshop and recognized him. "He's a weirdo, a sadomasochist, and violent. Once, we had a date, but never again. Some gay friends also complained, and we put a chill on him. Now he's in the park in a black suit and a dark tie. Very strange." Diocles notified Pirilo, who immediately sent a police officer to watch him.

Their suspicion rose when the police officer saw the suspect entering a house belonging to the vicar through a half-hidden entrance in the alley. The house was adjoined to Laurence's bed and breakfast.

The police officer quickly warned Pirilo, who went there immediately. The vicar, a very religious man, was surprised by his arrival and tried to prevent Pirilo from entering. The confusion was immense and never clearly explained. The only thing known for sure was that Pirilo caught the suspect inside the bedroom where the Archbishop was resting. The explanations about who the suspect was and what he was doing there were never clear. The official version from the church was that the Archbishop was indisposed, and the suspect was a nurse medicating him; a story that nobody believed, but as the suspect was not there to kill Laurence, Pirilo thought it best to let him go and forget what he had seen.

"I'd rather have the Archbishop in bed with a sadomasochist than running behind first communion boys" was Grená's opinion when she heard what happened. She even added, outraged: "Can you believe that this is the Archbishop who expelled Friar Bernard from the church because he was in love with Gigi?"

Another problem with even more profound consequences was caused by the team monitoring the cameras. The system with all new equipment allowed Pirilo's assistants to follow anyone in the streets, and what seemed to be a woman dressed in men's clothes with sunglasses and a hat attracted the attention of one of them.

"How can you be sure it's a woman?" Pirilo asked, and the assistant's answer was fast. "I might not understand how these modern cameras work, but I know what an ass looks like, and that ass is not a man's ass," which was confirmed later when a better-placed camera allowed for complete identification. The ass belonged to Minda, the Venezuelan public relations official and new lover of the Mayor, who, aware of the cameras, was walking in disguise to join Chombo Zen in his apartment. For Pirilo, it was irrelevant with whom Minda was sleeping, and the case was closed, but the story of the ass became a joke that reached the Mayor, who was not happy at all to know that his favorite ass was in Chombo Zen's hands.

The good news was that the surveillance system was working, and many eyes were protecting Laurence. Even Frida was part of it. For some reason that nobody understood, she spent the whole weekend over the river, where Nadia and her cousin lived.

Mr. Baumgarten was still worried, "The killer would come from where we're not expecting." He was waiting for Laurence to decide whether she would sell the property, but time passed and she was still hesitating. He thought the time had arrived for a private conversation. "You're the only one who can decide your future," said Mr. Baumgarten. They talked inside his hotel room; he did not want to have this conversation with her in the streets. "Now, you know who your grandfather was and his whole effort to have everything settled for you. If you want to stay, you have an apartment, a beautiful oceanfront property to build a new house, and a bank account with all you need. But if you want to leave, you can go wherever you want with your pockets full of money. For sure, the investors will pay whatever you ask for the land. It's up to you. Arpad's actions empowered you to choose. But the sooner you decide, the better it is."

Laurence knew what she wanted; she felt comfortable in Santa Clara. Back in Africa, in Kisangani, her grandmother had passed away, and her father knew she no longer wanted to stay there. She was considering living in Santa Clara, a cozy little town, and she had confided this to Bebéi, but now the city would change ... or maybe not. Perhaps she could do something to preserve it.

"I knew your grandfather and how his mind worked," Mr. Baumgarten insisted. Before continuing, he took her to the bathroom, where he turned on the shower and kept flushing the toilet while speaking. Laurence was not surprised; she was getting used to Mr. Baumgarten's concern with hidden microphones.

"This key is not from a safe. I know it," he said, whispering in her ears. "It's the key to one of the mailboxes at the post office near the Ferenc Puskás soccer stadium in Budapest. Please don't ask me how I know it; it doesn't matter. It was there that your grandfather Arpad and your grandmother Eszter had a mailbox, and it was also there that Lali kept her valuables while dancing in the streets. Your grandfather left you the mailbox number. The envelope with the key was in the sixth part of Germinal's fourth chapter on page 256. I knew him enough to assure you that the documents are inside mailbox 6-4-256. No one from Santa Clara can stop the Mayor's project, but you have the key both the Russians and the Americans want, and you can use it. If you prefer to leave with the money, you can. Nobody will ever know about our conversation, but if you want, you can use the key and the papers to stop the project."

Laurence was stunned, and Mr. Baungarteem continued whispering and flushing the toilet. "The Mayor and the investors will not be able to move on with their project if you have the Russians and the Americans on your side."

Laurence wanted to live in Santa Clara. She believed that the seagull who had brought her from Kisangani was carrying the spirit of her grandfather, and the seagull's flight while she walked on the property confirmed her instincts. She loved the city the way it was, with its parks, trees, and its people, and she did not want a new town with towers, shopping centers, cars, and hurried people crossing everywhere. Mr. Baumgarten had shown her how, and now it was up to her.

The following morning, she went to the park, determined to present her conditions to the two old spies in their wheelchairs. "You help me to convince the Mayor to abandon the New Santa Clara project, and I'll give you the key and tell you where Arpad hid the documents."

It did not take too long for the Americans and the Russians to answer. They briefly consulted their government authorities and confirmed that same evening that they accepted her conditions.

"Some things are better left forgotten in the past," said the American, and the Russian wholeheartedly agreed.

The Lady was chosen to talk to the Mayor, but he resisted; too much money was involved, including a massive profit for him. The Lady threatened to make his secret accounts in Grand Cayman public and reminded him that she could even block them as part of a money laundering investigation. "But I will completely ignore those accounts if the new Santa Clara project is suspended."

The Mayor knew he was cornered but did not want to give up. He needed time; he and his Serbian adviser knew that the Lady could not endure the pressure for a long time. "Deep down, they are bureaucrats, and as much as they want to do things their way, they will have to deal with all sorts of pressures from their governments. Time plays in our favor," said the Serbian. "If we can withstand for a few weeks, their strength will wane, and they will back down."

The tension increased even more when one of the Lady's assistants working with the lieutenant explained what he had found. "Pirilo's strategy worked, and those hired to eliminate Laurence have made contact, wondering if we can pay more. The bad news is that the agreement was not made with a single professional killer but with a whole group, a Honduran gang from San Pedro Sula, mostly of young drug addicts. They received a substantial advance for the bounty and passed the order to the gang; now, it will be difficult to reverse. Their members act independently and are experts in this type of work. Their modus operandi is usually the same: they attack with two guys on a motorcycle; while one drives, the other on the back shoots the target. Even if we agree with them to pay and abort the killing, it might take a few days or even weeks for the instructions to reach all members. We will increase surveillance, but I warn you, it would be challenging to prevent gang members from getting close to Laurence. She must stop walking on the streets!"

That information caused great concern. The Lady gathered Laurence's friends for an emergency meeting at the park in front of the hotel. There, it would be easy for the three older men in wheelchairs to attend.

"Investors are not murderers," she started. "For them, it's irrelevant where they earn their money. If they can't do this project, they will invest elsewhere, but from what we know, they have an Egyptian involved, El Waun, who is fully committed to delivering the Santa Clara project to the Arabs. If the project fails, he is the one who will take responsibility. And that means losing money and reputation. He is probably the one who advanced the money to the killers, and with him around Laurence is in permanent danger."

Everyone agreed that it was a must to take Laurence elsewhere, but she adamantly refused: "Here I feel safe," she said, "Zoubir and the seagull protect me twenty-four hours a day," an argument that did not convince anyone. But she was determined. "I will stay in Santa Clara until everything is fully settled." And she added, looking defiantly at the Lady, "It's up to you to convince the Mayor. He must stop the project."

The Lady didn't know what else she could do. Her government wanted the documents back, but the Mayor was resisting.

Mr. Baumgarten proposed an alternative: "We must eliminate this pressure on Laurence," and explained how this could be done. "We could transfer ten square feet of the property to the US government and another ten to the Russians. Both countries will become co-owners, and the Mayor will not be able to confiscate the land."

The Lady immediately rejected the proposal: "It's craziness; this would entail an absurd bureaucracy, and it would take us months, perhaps years, to get all necessary authorizations from our governments to do it." Both the Russian and the American in their wheelchairs nodded, agreeing.

"What a pity," said Mr. Baumgarten, winking at Laurence. "If in forty-eight hours we do not have these twenty square feet transferred to your governments, we will hand over the key to a large international newspaper, probably *The Guardian*." He then turned his wheelchair to leave. "I apologize, but I must go now since I have a chess game with my young Gypsy friend." Laurence liked his challenge and followed him with Zoubir on the leash. Coincidentally or not, Zoubir peed on a trashcan, lifting his leg as if endorsing their decision.

It took hours for the Russians and the Americans to go back and forth with their authorities. Later, when Mr. Baumgarten struggled to break the Alekhine's Defense of the young Gypsy, the Lady reached him with a tired but elegant expression: "Okay, do not worry and don't do anything. We will all do our best to complete the transfers in time."

Laurence smiled proudly, but Mr. Baumgarten did not beam; the young Gypsy was putting pressure on his pawns. Unbelievable. She was trying to counterattack his towers. The two old spies on wheelchairs who had arrived with the Lady approached to help Mr. Baumgarten confront the girl and, as everything seemed to be back to normal, the Gypsy with the accordion, who was on a nearby bench, began to play a nostalgic song.

Bebéi seized the peaceful moment to pet Zoubir and remind him that his mission had not yet been accomplished. Bebéi whispered to him not to leave Laurence alone for a single minute and pay particular attention to motorcycles — which was not a problem since Zoubir deeply hated them.

Pirilo was immediately informed of the deal, but his thought was the same as Bebéi's: Laurence was still under threat. She was stubborn, opinionated, bullheaded, and was constantly questioning him. Even pushier than his assistant, Cristine. But she was somehow different from the women he knew. "Protected by a seagull," an absurdity! How could a seagull and a dog defend her from a real killer? He designated two additional bodyguards by Laurence's side and instructed his staff to check the documents of all the motorcycles circulating throughout the town. "Every motorcycle with someone on the back should be stopped."

"Is that enough to protect her?" Bebéi asked Diocles when he heard about Pirilo's instructions.

"We better keep our eyes open," Diocles replied. "They might come on a motorcycle, but they may also come innocently jogging with a concealed weapon. How can we be sure? That runner they caught might have been preparing his attack, checking how close he could get to our Laurence."

37

Santa Clara will always face the sea. After the two embassies had officially informed the Mayor about the transfer of twenty square feet of Laurence's land to both countries, he was forced to give up and suspend the project. Advised by the Serbian, as always, he did it in a neo-revolutionary way with a live broadcast from Cathedral Park where he announced, in tears and surrounded by children, that he had decided to postpone the project.

"I know that this project would bring progress and wealth to some, but I also know that the primary beneficiaries would be the investors and bankers. I now realize that the people of our city, with whom I grew up, would not benefit from the New Santa Clara. The towers and a new shopping center would be for others. My wife, working daily with those in need, reminded me that our leading obligation should be securing our children's future. We have to hand over to them a city where they can live as well as we live, which is why I will suspend the works. The resources we have, although they are limited, will be invested exclusively to benefit those living in our town."

As the Mayor was a great speaker, the polls conducted by his team in the following days showed ninety percent approval, which would ensure his reelection, whoever the opposition candidate might be.

"Be careful," said Ilona. "He said to postpone and not to abandon. He will keep trying."

"And we will keep resisting," replied Gigi, feeling self-confident as a pizzeria manager and conscious citizen.

In a private meeting with his close partners organized by the Italian, the Mayor tried to be positive. He used biblical words: "We were struck down but not destroyed." He added with a mischievous smile, "Maybe on another day."

Meanwhile, even if they had not pocketed the full proceeds of the new project, the Mayor and his friends would continue to profit from the existing schemes. What bothered him the most was that, no matter how hard he tried, he could not get an invitation to the farewell party for the Castle. According to the new edition of *The Santa Clara Barrel Organ*, the event would be the New Santa Clara burial celebration.

Jordi's newspaper, now highly awaited every Wednesday, published an article about "Good and Bad Changes" in the third issue. The Mayor's project exemplified the wrong changes, changes that came from outside and did not respond to the people's needs. The good ones, according to the newspaper, were those stemming from new aspirations, such as the transformation of the Castle from an ancient bordello to a new boutique hotel for modern women.

The article included a whole history of Paris Street from the first brothels at the beginning of the last century, which later evolved into cabarets and nightclubs, notably the Castle, set up many years earlier as the first independent women's house in Paris Street. Inside that place, no man was in control; all decisions were made by the women who worked there. They were the only ones to make decisions about, control, and profit from the money collected. The article mentioned the founders: Ilona, who was also the Santa Clara citizen honored in the third issue; Frida — a picture showed her, young and pretty, arriving from Germany — and a third woman, a Cuban, who left Santa Clara to marry a European count and was now returning as a wealthy widow to transform the old property into a boutique hotel.

The building would be fully renewed, and the idea was to establish a woman-friendly hotel, but as the Cuban honestly recognized, "Nobody knows what a women-friendly hotel is, and even if they think they know it, we don't trust them. We will discover it by ourselves, working together with female clients and friends."

The party happened a few days after the Mayor publicly announced his surrender, and they had some special rules. It was a women's party and only for them. Men would only attend by invitation from one of the women who had worked at the house, and few had this honor. Bebéi and Cavafys went with Ilona, and Diocles was invited by Doña Cecy, who, before becoming the cook at Ilona's Café, had been responsible for cleaning the Castle. The members of the Useless Brethren, Null-and-void, Robespierre, Colonel Viera, and Moriarty, all entered as guests of Frida, and Rasta Bong and Pirilo were guests of Ludmila, who was forced to leave early to go to the hospital; the baby was coming.

The three older men with their motorized wheelchairs were special guests of the Cuban since everyone in town was charmed by their cheerfulness. Friar Bernard joined Gigi, who also brought an unexpected guest: the Mayor's wife. They had become friends thanks to the social work the Mayor's wife did with the Friar. Princess attended as Lola Marlene's guest wearing a colorful dress as daring as that of the Lady from the American embassy, who was with him. Cristine and Jordi proudly joined Cristine's mother, who had worked at the Castle.

Everyone important was there except the Mayor. The irony was that even the Serbian was there, as a special guest of the Cuban, and also the Mayor's non-exclusive lover Minda. All his women were there, but not the Mayor, whom no woman wanted there despite all money he had spent in the house.

Drink and dance were the main rules, and everybody abided by them. Curiously, Frida was sober. Pirilo was the only one who knew the reason. Frida was suspicious. She had taken the mission of protecting Laurence seriously and had a suspect in mind. "But I have no evidence," she said to Pirilo, "It's only a suspicion, and until I can prove it, I will not give you the name."

With the party's enthusiasm, no one paid attention to Frida until she surprisingly rewarded the young cousin of Nadia with a punch on the chin. The young woman, rehabilitated or not, ended up under the table and remained unconscious until she was hand-cuffed.

Nadia's mother had worked in the house and had brought Nadia's cousin, who spent most of the time at her side. "Rehabilitating, a cow's ass," Frida explained, with all the diplomacy and elegance she had. "I saw Nadia's cousin buying white powder near the river's bridge two days ago. Initially, I thought she was staring at Laurence because she liked women, but I discovered she had a boyfriend, and guess who he is?" Frida asked and answered herself, "The kid caught jogging near Laurence. I was suspicious, but I was not sure. Tonight, I saw her carrying a bag. What did she need a bag for? I grabbed it and saw the gun inside it. The punch was just a friendly perk to make Pirilo's life easier."

In the bag, there was a pistol with an ultra-modern silencer, and inside the room where she had been staying in Nadia's house, they found fifty thousand dollars, which forced her to confess that she and her boyfriend were part of the Honduran Mara of San Pedro Sula and that Laurence was not her first murder assignment.

"While everyone was looking for a man to be the killer, only Frida would be suspicious of a sixteen-year-old girl." Ilona added, "A sixteen-year-old professional killer who kills to buy cocaine ... sad times!"

What happened at the party, only those who were there could tell. The only story that reached Grená's umbrella the next day was that the women chose Captain Cavafys as the most pleasant man who had ever visited the Castle, leaving envy in the hearts of Pirilo and other young men much more handsome than the grumpy Greek. The Cuban who handed Cavafys the prize, a bottle of French Champagne, explained: "In addition to being a great lover who understands the needs of a woman like few, he dances, he plays the bouzouki, and he can recite beautiful poems while resting after love."

Bebéi still does not remember when he left or how he got home. When he woke up the next day, he was in the hall of his apartment in his tank top, underwear, shoes, and a sock only on his left foot. He even had to buy a new hat since the one he always carried disappeared that night and was never found again.

At dawn, a few women remained around the Castle's pool. The men were already sleeping or wasted, and Ilona was chatting with Laurence. "Cavafys told me something interesting. He said that he had met Mr. Baumgarten before. He told me the story of a Portuguese woman who lived in Maputo, Mozambique. Apparently, she had a bar well known to all sailors navigating the Indian Ocean. Cavafys told me he met her again a few years ago in Tenerife and that she was with her German husband, who, Cavafys swore, was Mr. Baumgarten. He told me that the story he heard in Maputo was that she was a spy."

After a sip of tequila, Ilona continued, "I remember that Mr. Baumgarten told me that his wife was a Portuguese woman. Do you think he could have been married to a spy and didn't tell us?"

"He didn't tell us anything about himself," replied Laurence. "I asked, but I believe he wants to keep his past in secrecy."

Gigi, who was also at the swimming pool with the Lady of the Embassy, approached them. She was wasted but still lucid. "Do you know what amazes me in the whole story of your grandfather?" And, looking into Laurence's eyes, she answered. "The women of his life: Lali, Eszter, Morgen, and you. Arpad had an amazing life because he had the privilege of having these strong women beside him."

"The same can be said about Santa Clara," replied Laurence promptly. "What would this city be without you, Ilona, Grená, Doña Cecy, and the young Cristine? Men in Santa Clara are no more than useful accessories."

"Fully agree," replied Ilona and the Lady together.

"Perhaps my Friar is an exception," said Gigi, managing to sit on a chair that, according to her after a whole night drinking, didn't stop shaking.

"Maybe," said Ilona, "There are some nice men here like the Friar, Bebéi, Diocles, and even Pirilo, but they are only nice when they don't behave like men."

"In vino veritas," added the Lady.

"You know what I think?" said Gigi, who was full of energy despite all drinks. "The Mayor is hopeless, but he will try again. He believes that money can make him attractive. His wife, however, is an interesting woman. Conservative, of course, but she is doing a hell of a job with the Friar. And she was great at the party. She danced, and she even sang. The Serbian also is not ..."

"Better not to say anything about her," interrupted Ilona. "She is now in bed with our Cuban host."

"But I thought that she liked men," said the Lady.

"Maybe," replied Ilona, "but tonight, I can assure you she was converted and is now in bed with our Cuban friend."

Their conversation kept flowing with the rising sun, illuminating a new morning.

On Monday, Bebéi and Laurence accompanied Mr. Baumgarten to the airport. It was time for him to go back to Portugal.

Bebéi was still intrigued; he wanted to confirm a suspicion he had, so he wrote a note thanking Mr. Baumgarten for his visit.

He only delivered it personally when they got into the van.

Mr. Baumgarten read it carefully, and when he finished reading, he handed the letter back to Bebéi. "Thank you for your letter, and I want you to know that I feel the same admiration and affection for you."

"Why are you returning the letter?" asked Bebéi.

"It's an old habit," explained Mr. Baumgarten, "I could never keep the letters I received. They carried secrets, and it would be a lack of respect to throw away something written affectionately; I have always preferred to return the letters to the person who wrote them."

Bebéi smiled, looking at Laurence. Now they knew who Mr. Baumgarten was.

Mr. Baumgarten noticed the expression on their faces and confessed: "Now you know that I am Otto, a friend of your grandparents, and I invite you both to visit my house in Portugal and try the sausage soup with chickpeas prepared by my wife. I assure you it's even better than the one we made. I think you'll both enjoy meeting her. Until now, you have only known her code name, which doesn't look like a woman's name. She is Francisco, a charming and sweet Portuguese woman who lives with me in Óbidos and was also Arpad's friend."

No more secrets to hide. Diocles went back to his shed at the park. There had been so many demonstrations of support for him and his cats that the Mayor abandoned the idea of building public baths there. Cristine started to work with Jordi in *The Santa Clara Barrel Organ* and was hired as a part-time consultant to help Pirilo. The Useless continued to drink and curse, and Colonel Viera kept insisting that cameras were filming everywhere, which was true. The only ones that surprised Pirilo were two very modern tiny microphones found at Cholo's shoeshine chair and under Grená's umbrella. Who put them there was a mystery. Pirilo prudently avoided further investigations, since he believed they were part of the Mayor's brother's plan to monitor political opponents and learn if anyone else was robbing in the city, since he and his brother had a monopoly in this area.

Laurence remained in Santa Clara and continued to be friends with Pirilo, each one in their place. According to what Bebéi told Grená, the seagull often visited Laurence's terrace at night as if protecting her sleep.

Grená was also happy since she had a granddaughter as beautiful as Laurence, a combination of her son Rasta's African exuberance and Ludmila's sparkling green eyes and strong personality.

Bebéi continued walking the cobblestone streets, peacefully following Zoubir. He liked to enjoy the serenity of the city and the sound of the barrel organ that would keep enchanting tourists in Santa Clara by the Sea.

www.ingramcontent.com/pod-product-compliance
Lightning Source LLC
Chambersburg PA
CBHW032035310726
48972CB00002B/678